TALES FROM PLANET EARTH
ARTHUR C. CLARKE

TALES FROM PLANET EARTH
ARTHUR C. CLARKE

ILLUSTRATED BY MICHAEL WHELAN

A
BYRON
PREISS
BOOK

BANTAM BOOKS
NEW YORK · TORONTO · LONDON · SYDNEY · AUCKLAND

*Special thanks to Russ Galen, Lou Aronica, Robert
Simpson, David M. Harris, and Alice Alfonsi.*

TALES FROM PLANET EARTH

A Bantam Spectra Book / June 1990

Library of Congress Cataloging-in-Publication Data

Clarke, Arthur Charles, 1917–
Tales from the planet earth / Arthur C. Clarke.
p. cm.
ISBN 0-553-34883-3
1. Science fiction, English. I. Title.
PR6005.L36T28 1990
823'.914—dc20   89–18347
                                                        CIP

Published simultaneously in the United States and Canada

CONTENTS

PREFACE

Arthur Charles Clarke (b. 1917) is, of all science fiction writers, the one who is most like me.

He would, of course, deny this hotly. He would point out—quite correctly—that he is more than two years older that I am, that he is much balder than I am, and that he is much less handsome than I am. But what of that? It is no disgrace to be ancient, bald and ugly.

Where the similarity comes in is that Arthur has had (like myself) a thoroughgoing scientific education, and he makes use of it to write what is called "hard science fiction." His style is something like mine, and we are often confused—at least our books are.

The first science fiction book that my dear wife, Janet, ever read was Arthur's *Childhood's End;* the second was my *Foundation and Empire.* Unable to remember which was which in very clear fashion, she ended up marrying me when I think she was after Arthur.

Here, however, is a collection of Arthur's science fiction stories, science fiction dealing with science, extrapolated intelligently. How you will enjoy it!

I must tell you something about Arthur. We have known each other for some forty years and in all that time we have never stopped heaving loving insults at each other. (This is also true of Harlan Ellison and myself, and of Lester del Rey and myself.) It's a form of male bonding. Women, I'm afraid, don't understand this.

When two gentlemen of the lower-class persuasion meet each other (two cowboys, two truckdrivers) one is liable to hit the other a thwack on the shoulder and say, "How are you, you consarned varmint, you double-dealing son of a bitch." That is roughly the equivalent of saying, "Greetings, my friend, and how are you getting along?"

Well, Arthur and I do the same but, of course, in formal English to which we endeavor to introduce a soupçon of wit. Thus, last year a plane crashed in Iowa and roughly half the passengers were killed while half survived. It turned out that one of the survivors had kept calm during the perilous attempts to land by reading an Arthur C. Clarke novel and this was reported in a news article.

Arthur, as is his wont, promptly Xeroxed five million copies of the article and sent one to everyone he knew or ever heard of. I got one of them and at the bottom of the copy he sent to me, he wrote in his handwriting, "What a pity he didn't read one of your novels. He would have slept through the whole wretched ordeal."

It was the work of a moment to send Arthur a letter which said, "On the contrary, the reason he was reading your novel was that if the plane did crash, death would come as a blessed release."

I recited this exchange of loving commentary at the World Science Fiction Convention held in Boston over the Labor Day weekend in 1989. One woman who reported on the convention heard the tale with shocked disapproval. I don't know her, but I imagine her to be chemically free of any sense of humor and to know nothing of any form of male bonding—*any* form. In any case, my remark knocked her right out of her bloomers, and she spoke very disapprovingly of it in *Locus*.

Of course, I wouldn't dream of allowing any ridiculous woman to get in the way of any loving exchanges Arthur and I might have, so I'll end with another one. This time I'll start it.

I am writing this introduction without charge out of sheer love for Arthur. He, of course, would never dream of returning the favor because he is a penny-pincher and doesn't have my loving ability to place artistry and benevolence above sheer pelf.

There! I await, with a certain dread, Arthur's answer.

Isaac Asimov
New York City

I was delighted to read Isaac's introduction to Tales From Planet Earth. *As he says, I'm the writer who most resembles him. To repeat a remark I made before, we're both almost as good as we* think *we are.*

One minor correction: I didn't send out five million copies of the Time *article Isaac refers to. I sent only one—to Isaac himself, knowing full well that he would pass on the news to the rest of the world.*

Finally, here's my reply to his closing challenge in the way that will give him the greatest apprehension.

I hereby volunteer to write the preface for his next book.

Arthur C. Clarke
Colombo, Sri Lanka

THE ROAD
TO THE SEA

CHECKING MY RECORDS, I FIND THAT "THE ROAD TO THE Sea" was completed over forty years ago. There is little that I need to say about it, except that it anticipates or encapsulates all the themes that I developed in more detail in later works, especially *The City and the Stars* and *The Songs of Distant Earth*.

One minor point: I'm amused to see that I predicted not only the invention of ultraportable music players—but the fact that they would quickly become such a public menace that they would have to be banned. The second part of this prophecy, alas, has not yet been fulfilled.

The first leaves of autumn were falling when Durven met his brother on the headland beside the Golden Sphinx. Leaving his flyer among the shrubs by the roadside, he walked to the brow of the hill and looked down upon the sea. A bitter wind was toiling across the moors, bearing the threat of early frost, but down in the valley Shastar the Beautiful was still warm and sheltered in its crescent of hills. Its empty quays lay dreaming in the pale, declining sunlight, the deep blue of the sea washing gently against their marble flanks. As he looked down once more into the hauntingly familiar streets and gardens of his youth, Durven felt his resolution failing. He was glad he was meeting Hannar here, a mile from the city, and not among the sights and sounds that would bring his childhood crowding back upon him.

Hannar was a small dot far down the slope, climbing in his old unhurried, leisurely fashion. Durven could have met him in a moment with the flyer, but he knew he would receive little thanks if he did. So he waited in the lee of the great Sphinx, sometimes walking briskly to and fro to keep warm. Once or twice he went to the head of the monster and stared up at the still face brooding upon the city and the sea. He remembered how as a child in the gardens of Shastar he had seen the crouching shape upon the sky line, and had wondered if it was alive.

Hannar looked no older than he had seemed at their last meeting, twenty years before. His hair was still dark and thick, and his face unwrinkled, for few things ever disturbed the tranquil life of Shastar and its people. It seemed bitterly unfair, and Durven, gray with the years of unrelenting toil, felt a quick spasm of envy stab through his brain.

Their greetings were brief, but not without warmth. Then Hannar walked over to the ship, lying in its bed of heather and crumpled gorse bushes. He rapped his stick upon the curving metal and turned to Durven.

"It's very small. Did it bring you all the way?"

"No: only from the Moon. I came back from the Project in a liner a hundred times the size of this."

"And where is the Project—or don't you want us to know?"

"There's no secret about it. We're building the ships out in space beyond Saturn, where the sun's gravitational gradient is almost flat and it needs little thrust to send them right out of the solar system."

Hannar waved his stick toward the blue waters beneath them, the colored marble of the little towers, and the wide streets with their slowly moving traffic.

"Away from all this, out into the darkness and loneliness—in search of what?"

Durven's lips tightened into a thin, determined line.

"Remember," he said quietly, "I have already spent a lifetime away from Earth."

"And has it brought you happiness?" continued Hannar remorselessly.

Durven was silent for a while.

"It has brought me more than that," he replied at last. "I have used my powers to the utmost, and have tasted triumphs that you can never imagine. The day when the First Expedition returned to the solar system was worth a lifetime in Shastar."

"Do you think," asked Hannar, "that you will build fairer cities than this beneath those strange suns, when you have left our world forever?"

"If we feel that impulse, yes. If not, we will build other things. But build we must; and what have your people created in the last hundred years?"

"Because we have made no machines, because we have turned our backs upon the stars and are content with our own world, don't think we have been completely idle. Here in Shastar we have evolved a way of life that I do not think has ever been surpassed. We have studied the art of living; ours is the first aristocracy in which there are no slaves. That is our achievement, by which history will judge us."

"I grant you this," replied Durven, "but never forget that your paradise was built by scientists who had to fight as we have done to make their dreams come true."

"They have not always succeeded. The planets defeated them once; why should the worlds of other suns be more hospitable?"

It was a fair question. After five hundred years, the memory of the first failure was still bitter. With what hopes and dreams had Man set out for the planets, in the closing years of the twentieth century—only to find them not merely barren and lifeless, but fiercely hostile! From the sullen fires of the Mercurian lava seas to Pluto's creeping glaciers of solid nitrogen, there was nowhere that he could live unprotected beyond his own world; and to his own world, after a century of fruitless struggle, he had returned.

Yet the vision had not wholly died; when the planning had been abandoned, there were still some who dared to dream of the stars. Out of that dream had come at last the Transcendental Drive, the First Expedition—and now the heady wine of long-delayed success.

"There are fifty solar-type stars within ten years' flight of Earth," Durven replied, "and almost all of them have planets. We believe now that the possession of planets is almost as much a characteristic of a G-type star as its spectrum, though we don't know why. So the search for worlds like Earth was bound to be successful in time; I don't think that we were particularly lucky to find Eden so soon."

"Eden? Is that what you've called your new world?"

"Yes; it seemed appropriate."

"What incurable romantics you scientists are! Perhaps the name's too well chosen; all the life in that first Eden wasn't friendly to Man, if you remember."

Durven gave a bleak smile.

"That, again, depends on one's viewpoint," he replied. He pointed toward Shastar, where the first lights had begun to glimmer. "Unless our ancestors had eaten deeply from the Tree of Knowledge, you would never have had this."

"And what do you suppose will happen to it now?" asked Hannar bitterly. "When you have opened the road to the stars, all the strength and vigor of the race will ebb away from Earth as from an open wound."

"I do not deny it. It has happened before, and it will happen again. Shastar will go the way of Babylon and Carthage and New York. The future is built on the rubble of the past; wisdom lies in facing that fact, not in fighting against it. I have loved Shastar as much as you have done—so much so that now, though I shall never see it again, I dare not go down once more into its streets. You ask me what will become of it, and I will tell you. What we are doing will merely hasten the end. Even twenty years ago, when I was last here, I felt my will being sapped by the aimless ritual of your lives. Soon it will be the same in all the cities of Earth, for every one of them apes Shastar. I think the Drive has come none too soon; perhaps even you would believe me if you had spoken to the men who have come back from the stars, and felt the blood stirring in your veins once more after all these centuries of sleep. For your world is dying, Hannar; what you have now you may hold for ages yet, but in the end it will slip from your fingers. The future belongs to us; we will leave you to your dreams. We also have dreamed, and now we go to make our dreams come true."

The last light was catching the brow of the Sphinx as the sun sank into the sea and left Shastar to night but not to darkness. The wide streets were luminous rivers carrying a myriad of moving specks; the towers and pinnacles were jeweled with colored lights, and there came a faint sound of wind-borne music as a pleasure boat put slowly out to sea. Smiling a little, Durven watched it draw away from the curving quay. It had been five hundred years or more since the last merchant ship had unloaded its cargo, but while the sea remained, men would still sail upon it.

There was little more to say; and presently Hannar stood alone upon the hill, his head tilted up toward the stars. He would never see his brother again; the sun, which for a few hours had gone from his sight, would soon have vanished from Durven's forever as it shrank into the abyss of space.

Unheeding, Shastar lay glittering in the darkness along the edge of the sea. To Hannar, heavy with foreboding, its doom seemed already almost upon it. There was truth in Durven's words; the exodus was about to begin.

Ten thousand years ago other explorers had set out from the first cities of mankind to discover new lands. They had found them, and had never returned, and Time had swallowed their deserted homes. So must it be with Shastar the Beautiful.

Leaning heavily on his stick, Hannar walked slowly down the hillside toward the lights of the city. The Sphinx watched him dispassionately as his figure vanished into the distance and the darkness.

It was still watching, five thousand years later.

• • •

Brant was not quite twenty when his people were expelled from their homes and driven westward across two continents and an ocean, filling the ether with piteous cries of injured innocence. They received scant sympathy from the rest of the world, for they had only themselves to blame, and could scarcely pretend that the Supreme Council had acted harshly. It had sent them a dozen preliminary warnings and no fewer than four positively final ultimatums before reluctantly taking action. Then one day a small ship with a very large acoustic radiator had suddenly arrived a thousand feet above the village and started to emit several kilowatts of raw noise. After a few hours of this, the rebels had capitulated and begun to pack their belongings. The transport fleet had called a week later and carried them, still protesting shrilly, to their new homes on the other side of the world.

And so the Law had been enforced, the Law which ruled that no community could remain on the same spot for more than three lifetimes. Obedience meant change, the destruction of traditions, and the uprooting of ancient and well-loved homes. That had been the very purpose of the Law when it was framed, four thousand years ago; but the stagnation it had sought to prevent could not be warded off much longer. One day there would be no central organization to enforce it, and the scattered villages would remain where they were until Time engulfed them as it had the earlier civilizations of which they were the heirs.

It had taken the people of Chaldis the whole of three months to build new homes, remove a square mile of forest, plant some unnecessary crops of exotic and luxurious fruits, re-lay a river, and demolish a hill which offended their aesthetic sensibilities. It was quite an impressive performance, and all was forgiven when the local Supervisor made a tour of inspection a little later. Then Chaldis watched with great satisfaction as the transports, the digging machines, and all the paraphernalia of a mobile and mechanized civilization climbed away into the sky. The sound of their departure had scarcely faded when, as one man, the village relaxed once more into the sloth that it sincerely hoped nothing would disturb for another century at least.

Brant had quite enjoyed the whole adventure. He was sorry, of course, to lose the home that had shaped his childhood; and now he would never climb the proud, lonely mountain that had looked down upon the village of his birth. There were no mountains in this land—only low, rolling hills and fertile valleys in which forests had run rampant for millennia, since agriculture had come to an end. It was warmer, too, than in the old country, for they were nearer the equator and had left behind them the fierce winters of the North. In almost every respect the change was for the good; but for a year or two the people of Chaldis would feel a comfortable glow of martyrdom.

These political matters did not worry Brant in the least. The entire sweep of human history from the dark ages into the unknown future was considerably less important at the moment than the question of Yradne and her feelings toward him. He wondered what Yradne was doing now, and tried to think of an excuse for going to see her. But that would mean meeting her parents, who would embarrass him by their hearty pretense that his call was simply a social one.

He decided to go to the smithy instead, if only to make a check on Jon's movements. It was a pity about Jon; they had been such good friends only a short while ago. But love was friendship's deadliest enemy, and until Yradne had chosen between them they would remain in a state of armed neutrality.

The village sprawled for about a mile along the valley, its neat, new houses arranged in calculated disorder. A few people were moving around in no particular hurry, or gossiping in little groups beneath the trees. To Brant it seemed that everyone was following him with their eyes and talking about him as he passed—an assumption that, as it happened, was perfectly correct. In a closed community of fewer than a thousand highly intelligent people, no one could expect to have any private life.

The smithy was in a clearing at the far end of the village, where its general untidiness would cause as little offense as possible. It was surrounded by broken and half-dismantled machines that Old Johan had not got around to mending. One of the community's three flyers was lying, its bare ribs exposed to the sunlight, where it had been dumped weeks ago with a request for immediate repair. Old Johan would fix it one day, but in his own time.

The wide door of the smithy was open, and from the brilliantly lit interior came the sound of screaming metal as the automatic machines fashioned some new shape to their master's will. Brant threaded his way carefully past the busy slaves and emerged into the relative quiet at the back of the shop.

Old Johan was lying in an excessively comfortable chair, smoking a pipe and looking as if he had never done a day's work in his life. He was a neat little man with a carefully pointed beard, and only his brilliant, ceaselessly roaming eyes showed any signs of animation. He might have been taken for a minor poet—as indeed he fancied himself to be—but never for a village blacksmith.

"Looking for Jon?" he said between puffs. "He's around somewhere, making something for that girl. Beats me what you two see in her."

Brant turned a slight pink and was about to make some sort of reply when one of the machines started calling loudly for attention. In a flash Old Johan was out of the room, and for a minute strange crashings and bangings and much bad language floated through the doorway. Very soon, however, he was back again in his chair, obviously not expecting to be disturbed for quite a while.

"Let me tell you something, Brant," he continued, as if there had been no interruption. "In twenty years she'll be exactly like her mother. Ever thought of that?"

Brant hadn't, and quailed slightly. But twenty years is an

eternity to youth; if he could win Yradne in the present, the future could take care of itself. He told Johan as much.

"Have it your own way," said the smith, not unkindly. "I suppose if we'd all looked that far ahead the human race would have died out a million years ago. Why don't you play a game of chess, like sensible people, to decide who'll have her first?"

"Brant would cheat," answered Jon, suddenly appearing in the entrance and filling most of it. He was a large, well-built youth, in complete contrast to his father, and was carrying a sheet of paper covered with engineering sketches. Brant wondered what sort of present he was making for Yradne.

"What are you doing?" he asked, with a far from disinterested curiosity.

"Why should I tell you?" asked Jon good-naturedly. "Give me one good reason."

Brant shrugged his shoulders.

"I'm sure it's not important—I was only being polite."

"Don't overdo it," said the smith. "The last time you were polite to Jon, you had a black eye for a week. Remember?" He turned to his son, and said brusquely: "Let's see those drawings, so I can tell you why it can't be done."

He examined the sketches critically, while Jon showed increasing signs of embarrassment. Presently Johan snorted disapprovingly and said: "Where are you going to get the components? They're all nonstandard, and most of them are submicro."

Jon looked hopefully around the workshop.

"There aren't very many of them," he said. "It's a simple job, and I was wondering . . ."

". . . if I'd let you mess up the integrators to try to make the pieces? Well, we'll see about that. My talented son, Brant, is trying to prove that he possesses brains as well as brawn, by making a toy that's been obsolete for about fifty centuries. I hope you can do better than that. Now when I was your age . . ."

His voice and his reminiscences trailed off into silence. Yradne had drifted in from the clangorous bustle of the machine shop, and was watching them from the doorway with a faint smile on her lips.

It is probable that if Brant and Jon had been asked to describe Yradne, it would have seemed as if they were speaking of two entirely different people. There would have been superficial points of resemblance, of course. Both would have agreed that her hair was chestnut, her eyes large and blue, and her skin that rarest of colors—an almost pearly white. But to Jon she seemed a fragile little creature, to be cherished and protected; while to Brant her self-confidence and complete assurance were so obvious that he despaired of ever being of any service to her. Part of that difference in outlook was due to Jon's extra six inches of height and nine inches of girth, but most of it came from profounder psychological causes. The person one loves never really exists, but is a projection focused through the lens of the mind onto whatever screen it fits with least distortion. Brant and Jon had quite different ideals, and each believed that Yradne embodied them. This would not have surprised her in the least, for few things ever did.

"I'm going down to the river," she said. "I called for you on the way, Brant, but you were out."

That was a blow at Jon, but she quickly equalized.

"I thought you'd gone off with Lorayne or some other girl, but I knew I'd find Jon at home."

Jon looked very smug at this unsolicited and quite inaccurate testimonial. He rolled up his drawings and dashed off into the house, calling happily over his shoulder: "Wait for me—I won't be long!"

Brant never took his eyes off Yradne as he shifted uncomfortably from one foot to the other. She hadn't actually invited *anyone* to come with her, and until definitely ordered off, he was going to stand his ground. But he remembered that there was a somewhat ancient saying to the effect that if two were company, three were the reverse.

Jon returned, resplendent in a surprising green cloak with diagonal explosions of red down the sides. Only a very young man could have got away with it, and even Jon barely succeeded. Brant wondered if there was time for him to hurry home and change into something still more startling, but that would be too great a risk to take. It would be flying in the face of the enemy; the battle might be over before he could get his reinforcements.

"Quite a crowd," remarked Old Johan unhelpfully as they departed. "Mind if I come along too?" The boys looked embarrassed, but Yradne gave a gay little laugh that made it hard for him to dislike her. He stood in the outer doorway for a while, smiling as they went away through the trees and down the long, grass-covered slope to the river. But presently his eyes ceased to follow them, as he lost himself in dreams as vain as any that can come to man—the dreams of his own departed youth. Very soon he turned his back upon the sunlight and, no longer smiling now, disappeared into the busy tumult of the workshop.

Now the northward-climbing sun was passing the equator, the days would soon be longer than the nights, and the rout of winter was complete. The countless villages throughout the hemisphere were preparing to greet the spring. With the dying of the great cities and the return of Man to the fields and woods, he had returned also to many of the ancient customs that had slumbered through a thousand years of urban civilization. Some of those customs had been deliberately revived by the anthropologists and social engineers of the third millennium, whose genius had sent so many patterns of human culture safely down the ages. So it was that the spring equinox was still welcomed by rituals which, for all their sophistication, would have seemed less strange to primitive man than to the people of the industrial cities whose smoke had once stained the skies of Earth.

The arrangements for the Spring Festival were always the subject of much intrigue and bickering between neighboring villages. Although it involved the disruption of all other activities for at least a month, any village was greatly honored to be chosen as host for the celebrations. A newly settled community, still recovering from transplantation, would not, of course, be expected to take on such a responsibility. Brant's people, however, had thought of an ingenious way of regaining favor and wiping out the stain of their recent disgrace. There were five other villages within a hundred miles, and all had been invited to Chaldis for the Festival.

The invitation had been very carefully worded. It hinted delicately that, for obvious reasons, Chaldis couldn't hope to arrange as elaborate a ceremonial as it might have wished, and thereby implied that if the guests wanted a really good time they had better go elsewhere. Chaldis expected one acceptance at the most, but the inquisitiveness of its neighbors had overcome their sense of moral superiority. They had all said that they would be delighted to come; and there was no possible way in which Chaldis could now evade its responsibilities.

There was no night and little sleep in the valley. High above the trees a row of artificial suns burned with a steady, blue-white brilliance, banishing the stars and the darkness and throwing into chaos the natural routine of all the wild creatures for miles around. Through lengthening days and shortening nights, men and machines were battling to make ready the great amphitheater needed to hold some four thousand people. In one respect at least, they were lucky: there was no need for a roof or any artificial heating in this climate. In the land they had so reluctantly left, the snow would still be thick upon the ground at the end of March.

Brant woke early on the great day to the sound of aircraft

falling down from the skies above him. He stretched himself wearily, wondering when he would get to bed again, and then climbed into his clothes. A kick with his foot at a concealed switch and the rectangle of yielding foam rubber, an inch below floor level, was completely covered by a rigid plastic sheet that had unrolled from within the wall. There was no bed linen to worry about because the room was kept automatically at body temperature. In many such ways Brant's life was simpler than those of his remote ancestors—simpler through the ceaseless and almost forgotten efforts of five thousand years of science.

The room was softly lit by light pouring through one translucent wall, and was quite incredibly untidy. The only clear floor space was that concealing the bed, and probably this would have to be cleared again by nightfall. Brant was a great hoarder and hated to throw anything away. This was a very unusual characteristic in a world where few things were of value because they could be made so easily, but the objects Brant collected were not those that the integrators were used to creating. In one corner a small tree trunk was propped against the wall, partly carved into a vaguely anthropomorphic shape. Large lumps of sandstone and marble were scattered elsewhere over the floor, until such time as Brant decided to work on them. The walls were completely covered with paintings, most of them abstract in character. It would have needed very little intelligence to deduce that Brant was an artist; it was not so easy to decide if he was a good one.

He picked his way through the debris and went in search of food. There was no kitchen; some historians maintained that it had survived until as late as A.D. 2500, but long before then most families made their own meals about as often as they made their own clothes. Brant walked into the main living room and went across to a metal box set in the wall at chest level. At its center was something that would have been quite familiar to every human being for the last fifty centuries—a ten-digit impulse dial. Brant called a four-figure number and waited. Nothing whatsoever happened. Looking a little annoyed, he pressed a concealed button and the front of the apparatus slid open, revealing an interior which should, by all the rules, have contained an appetizing breakfast. It was completely empty.

Brant could call up the central food machine to demand an explanation, but there would probably be no answer. It was quite obvious what had happened—the catering department was so busy preparing for the day's overload that he'd be lucky if he got any breakfast at all. He cleared the circuit, then tried again with a little-used number. This time there was a gentle purr, a dull click, and the doors slid open to reveal a cup of some dark, steaming beverage, a few not-very-exciting-looking sandwiches, and a large slice of melon. Wrinkling up his nose, and wondering how long mankind would take to slip back to barbarism at this rate, Brant started on his substitute meal and very soon polished it off.

His parents were still asleep as he went quietly out of the house into the wide, grass-covered square at the center of the village. It was still very early and there was a slight chill in the air, but the day was clear and fine, with that freshness which seldom lingers after the last dew has gone. Several aircraft were lying on the green, disgorging passengers, who were milling around in circles or wandering off to examine Chaldis with critical eyes. As Brant watched, one of the machines went humming briskly up into the sky, leaving a faint trail of ionization behind it. A moment later the others followed; they could carry only a few-dozen passengers and would have to make many trips before the day was out.

Brant strolled over to the visitors, trying to look self-assured yet not so aloof as to discourage all contacts. Most of the strangers were about his own age—the older people would be arriving at a more reasonable time.

They looked at him with a frank curiosity which he returned with interest. Their skins were much darker than his, he noticed, and their voices were softer and less modulated. Some of them even had a trace of accent, for despite a universal language and instantaneous communication, regional variations still existed. At least, Brant assumed that they were the ones with accents; but once or twice he caught them smiling a little as he spoke.

Throughout the morning the visitors gathered in the square and made their way to the great arena that had been ruthlessly carved out of the forest. There were tents and bright banners here, and much shouting and laughter, for the morning was for the amusement of the young. Though Athens had swept like a dwindling but never-dying beacon for ten thousand years down the river of time, the pattern of sport had scarcely changed since those first Olympic days. Men still ran and jumped and wrestled and swam; but they did all these things a good deal better now than their ancestors. Brant was a fair sprinter over short distances and managed to finish third in the hundred meters. His time was just over eight seconds, which was not very good, because the record was less than seven. Brant would have been much amazed to learn that there was a time when no one in the world could have approached this figure.

Jon enjoyed himself hugely, bouncing youths even larger than himself onto the patient turf, and when the morning's results were added up, Chaldis had scored more points than any of the visitors, although it had been first in relatively few events.

As noon approached, the crowd began to flow amoebalike down to Five Oaks Glade, where the molecular synthesizers had been working since the early hours to cover hundreds of tables with food. Much skill had gone into preparing the prototypes which were being reproduced with absolute fidelity down to the last atom; for though the mechanics of food production had altered completely, the art of the chef had survived, and had even gone forward to victories in which Nature had played no part at all.

The main feature of the afternoon was a long poetic drama—a pastiche put together with considerable skill from the works of poets whose very names had been forgotten ages since. On the whole Brant found it boring, though there were some fine lines here and there that had stuck in his memory:

> For winter's rains and ruins are over,
> And all the season of snows and sins . . .

Brant knew about snow, and was glad to have left it behind. Sin, however, was an archaic word that had dropped out of use three or four thousand years ago; but it had an ominous and exciting ring.

He did not catch up with Yradne until it was almost dusk, and the dancing had begun. High above the valley, floating lights had started to burn, flooding the woods with ever-changing patterns of blue and red and gold. In twos and threes and then in dozens and hundreds, the dancers moved out into the great oval of the amphitheater, until it became a sea of laughing, whirling forms. Here at last was something at which Brant could beat Jon handsomely, and he let himself be swept away on the tide of sheer physical enjoyment.

The music ranged through the whole spectrum of human culture. At one moment the air pulsed to the throb of drums that might have called from some primeval jungle when the world was young, and a little later, intricate tapestries of quarter tones were being woven by subtle electronic skills. The stars peered down wanly as they marched across the sky, but no one saw them and no one gave any thought to the passage of time.

Brant had danced with many girls before he found Yradne. She looked very beautiful, brimming over with the enjoyment of life, and she seemed in no hurry to join him when there were so many others to choose from. But at last they were circling together in the whirlpool, and it gave Brant no small pleasure to think that Jon was probably watching them glumly from afar.

They broke away from the dance during a pause in the music because Yradne announced that she was a little tired. This suited Brant admirably, and presently they were sitting together under one of the great trees, watching the ebb and flow of life around them with that detachment that comes in moments of complete relaxation.

It was Brant who broke the spell. It had to be done, and it might be a long time before such an opportunity came again.

"Yradne," he said, "why have you been avoiding me?"

She looked at him with innocent, open eyes.

"Oh, Brant," she replied, "what an unkind thing to say; you know it isn't true! I wish you weren't so jealous: you can't expect me to be following you around *all* the time."

"Oh, very well!" said Brant weakly, wondering if he was making a fool of himself. But he might as well go on now he had started.

"You know, *some* day you'll have to decide between us. If you keep putting it off, perhaps, you'll be left high and dry like those two aunts of yours."

Yradne gave a tinkling laugh and tossed her head with great amusement at the thought that she could ever be old and ugly.

"Even if you're too impatient," she replied, "I think I can rely on Jon. Have you seen what he's given me?"

"No," said Brant, his heart sinking.

"You *are* observant, aren't you! Haven't you noticed this necklace?"

On her breast Yradne was wearing a large group of jewels, suspended from her neck by a thin golden chain. It was quite a fine pendant, but there was nothing particularly unusual about it, and Brant wasted no time in saying so. Yradne smiled mysteriously and her fingers flickered toward her throat. Instantly the air was suffused with the sound of music, which first mingled with the background of the dance and then drowned it completely.

"You see," she said proudly, "wherever I go now I can have music with me. Jon says there are so many thousands of hours of it stored up that I'll never know when it repeats itself. Isn't it clever?"

"Perhaps it is," said Brant grudgingly, "but it isn't exactly new. Everyone used to carry this sort of thing once, until there was no silence anywhere on Earth and they had to be forbidden. Just think of the chaos if we all had them!"

Yradne broke away from him angrily.

"There you go again—always jealous of something you can't do yourself. What have you ever given me that's half as clever or useful as this? I'm going—and don't try to follow me!"

Brant stared open-mouthed as she went, quite taken aback by the violence of her reaction. Then he called after her, "Hey, Yradne, I didn't mean . . ." But she was gone.

He made his way out of the amphitheater in a very bad temper. It did him no good at all to rationalize the cause of Yradne's outburst. His remarks, though rather spiteful, had been true, and sometimes there is nothing more annoying than the truth. Jon's gift was an ingenious but trivial toy, interesting only because it now happened to be unique.

One thing she had said still rankled in his mind. What *was* there he had ever given Yradne? He had nothing but his paintings, and they weren't really very good. She had shown no interest in them at all when he had offered her some of his best, and it had been very hard to explain that he wasn't a portrait painter and would rather not try to make a picture of her. She had never really understood this, and it had been very difficult not to hurt her feelings. Brant liked taking his inspiration from Nature, but he never copied what he saw. When one of his pictures was finished (which occasionally happened), the title was often the only clue to the original source.

The music of the dance still throbbed around him, but he had lost all interest; the sight of other people enjoying themselves was more than he could stand. He decided to get away from the crowd, and the only peaceful place he could think of was down by the river, at the end of the shining carpet of freshly planted glow-moss that led through the wood.

He sat at the water's edge, throwing twigs into the current and watching them drift downstream. From time to time other idlers strolled by, but they were usually in pairs and took no notice of him. He watched them enviously and brooded over the unsatisfactory state of his affairs.

It would almost be better, he thought, if Yradne did make up her mind to choose Jon, and so put him out of his misery. But she showed not the slightest sign of preferring one to the other. Perhaps she was simply enjoying herself at their expense, as some people—particularly Old Johan—maintained; though it was just as likely that she was genuinely unable to choose. What was wanted, Brant thought morosely, was for one of them to do something really spectacular which the other could not hope to match.

"Hello," said a small voice behind him. He twisted around and looked over his shoulder. A little girl of eight or so was staring at him with her head slightly on one side, like an inquisitive sparrow.

"Hello," he replied without enthusiasm. "Why aren't you watching the dance?"

"Why aren't you in it?" she replied promptly.

"I'm tired," he said, hoping that this was an adequate excuse. "You shouldn't be running around by yourself. You might get lost."

"I am lost," she replied happily, sitting down on the bank beside him. "I like it that way." Brant wondered which of the other villages she had come from; she was quite a pretty little thing, but would look prettier with less chocolate on her face. It seemed that his solitude was at an end.

She stared at him with that disconcerting directness which, perhaps fortunately, seldom survives childhood. "*I* know what's the matter with you," she said suddenly.

"Indeed?" queried Brant with polite skepticism.

"You're in love!"

Brant dropped the twig he was about to throw into the river, and turned to stare at his inquisitor. She was looking at him with such solemn sympathy that in a moment all his morbid self-pity vanished in a gale of laughter. She seemed quite hurt, and he quickly brought himself under control.

"How could you tell?" he asked with profound seriousness.

"I've read all about it," she replied solemnly. "And once I saw a picture play and there was a man in it and he came down to a river and sat there just like you and presently he jumped into it. There was some awful pretty music then."

Brant looked thoughtfully at this precocious child and felt relieved that she didn't belong to his own community.

"I'm sorry I can't arrange the music," he said gravely, "but in any case the river isn't really deep enough."

"It is farther along," came the helpful reply. "This is only a baby river here—it doesn't grow up until it leaves the woods. I saw it from the flyer."

"What happens to it then?" asked Brant, not in the least interested, but thankful that the conversation had taken a more innocuous turn. "I suppose it reaches the sea?"

She gave an unladylike sniff of disgust.

"Of course not, silly. All the rivers this side of the hills go to the Great Lake. I know that's as big as a sea, but the *real* sea is on the other side of the hills."

Brant had learned very little about the geographical details of his new home, but he realized that the child was quite correct.

The ocean was less than twenty miles to the north, but separated from them by a barrier of low hills. A hundred miles inland lay the Great Lake, bringing life to lands that had been desert before the geological engineers had reshaped this continent.

The child genius was making a map out of twigs and patiently explaining these matters to her rather dull pupil.

"Here we are," she said, "and here's the river, and the hills, and the lake's over there by your foot. The sea goes along here—and I'll tell you a secret."

"What's that?"

"You'll never guess!"

"I don't suppose I will."

Her voice dropped to a confidential whisper. "If you go along the coast—it isn't very far from here—you'll come to Shastar."

Brant tried to look impressed, but failed.

"I don't believe you've ever heard of it!" she cried, deeply disappointed.

"I'm sorry," replied Brant. "I suppose it was a city, and I know I've heard of it somewhere. But there were such a lot of them, you know—Carthage and Chicago and Babylon and Berlin—you simply can't remember them all. And they've all gone now, anyway."

"Not Shastar. It's still there."

"Well, some of the later ones are still standing, more or less, and people often visit them. About five hundred miles from my old home there was quite a big city once, called . . ."

"Shastar isn't just *any* old city," interrupted the child mysteriously. "My grandfather told me about it: he's been there. It hasn't been spoiled at all and its still full of wonderful things that no one has anymore."

Brant smiled inwardly. The deserted cities of Earth had been the breeding places of legends for countless centuries. It would be four—no, nearer five—thousand years since Shastar had been abandoned. If its buildings were still standing, which was of course quite possible, they would certainly have been stripped of all valuables ages ago. It seemed that Grandfather had been inventing some pretty fairy stories to entertain the child. He had Brant's sympathy.

Heedless of his skepticism, the girl prattled on. Brant gave only half his mind to her words, interjecting a polite "Yes" or "Fancy that" as occasion demanded. Suddenly, silence fell.

He looked up and found that his companion was staring with much annoyance toward the avenue of trees that overlooked the view.

"Good-by," she said abruptly. "I've got to hide somewhere else—here comes my sister."

She was gone as suddenly as she had arrived. Her family must have a busy time looking after her, Brant decided: but she had done him a good turn by dispelling his melancholy mood. Within a few hours, he realized that she had done very much more than that.

Simon was leaning against his doorpost watching the world go by when Brant came in search of him. The world usually accelerated slightly when it had to pass Simon's door, for he was an interminable talker and once he had trapped a victim there was no escape for an hour or more. It was most unusual for anyone to walk voluntarily into his clutches, as Brant was doing now.

The trouble with Simon was that he had a first-class mind, and was too lazy to use it. Perhaps he might have been luckier had he been born in a more energetic age; all he had ever been able to do in Chaldis was to sharpen his wits at other people's expense, thereby gaining more fame than popularity. But he was quite indispensable, for he was a storehouse of knowledge, the greater part of it perfectly accurate.

"Simon," began Brant without any preamble. "I want to learn something about this country. The maps don't tell me much—they're too new. What was here, back in the old days?"

Simon scratched his wiry beard.

"I don't suppose it was very different. How long ago do you mean?"

"Oh, back in the time of the cities."

"There weren't so many trees, of course. This was probably agricultural land, used for food production. Did you see that farming machine they dug up when the amphitheater was being built? It must have been old; it wasn't even electric."

"Yes," said Brant impatiently. "I saw it. But tell me about the cities around here. According to the map, there was a place called Shastar a few hundred miles west of us along the coast. Do you know anything about it?"

"Ah, Shastar," murmured Simon, stalling for time. "A very interesting place; I think I've even got a picture of it around somewhere. Just a moment while I go and see."

He disappeared into the house and was gone for nearly five minutes. In that time he made a very extensive library search, though a man from the age of books would hardly have guessed this from his actions. All the records Chaldis possessed were in a metal case a meter on a side; it contained, locked perpetually in subatomic patterns, the equivalent of a billion volumes of print. Almost all the knowledge of mankind, and the whole of its surviving literature, lay here concealed.

It was not merely a passive storehouse of wisdom, for it possessed a librarian. As Simon signaled his request to the tireless machine, the search went down, layer by layer, through the almost infinite network of circuits. It took only a fraction of a second to locate the information he needed, for he had given the name and the approximate date. Then he relaxed as the mental images came flooding into his brain, under the lightest of self-hypnosis. The knowledge would remain in his possession for a few hours only—long enough for his purpose—and would then fade away. Simon had no desire to clutter up his well-organized mind with irrelevancies, and to him the whole story of the rise and fall of the great cities was a historical digression of no particular importance. It was an interesting, if a regrettable, episode, and it belonged to a past that had irretrievably vanished.

Brant was still waiting patiently when he emerged, looking very wise.

"I couldn't find any pictures," he said. "My wife has been tidying up again. But I'll tell you what I can remember about Shastar."

Brant settled himself down as comfortably as he could: he was likely to be here for some time.

"Shastar was one of the very last cities that man ever built. You know, of course, that cities arose quite late in human culture—only about twelve thousand years ago. They grew in number and importance for several thousand years, until at last there were some containing millions of people. It is very hard for us to imagine what it must have been like to live in such places—deserts of steel and stone with not even a blade of grass for miles. But they were necessary, before transport and communication had been perfected, and people had to live near each other to carry out all the intricate operations of trade and manufacture upon which their lives depended.

"The really great cities began to disappear when air transport became universal. The threat of attack in those far-off, barbarous days also helped to disperse them. But for a long time . . ."

"I've studied the history of that period," interjected Brant, not very truthfully. "I know all about . . ."

". . . for a long time there were still many small cities which were held together by cultural rather than commercial links. They had populations of a few score thousand and lasted for centuries after the passing of the giants. That's why Oxford and Princeton and Heidelberg still mean something to us, while far larger cities are no more than names. But even these were doomed when the invention of the integrator made it possible for any community, however small, to manufacture without effort everything it needed for civilized living.

"Shastar was built when there was no longer any need, technically, for cities, but before people realized that the culture of cities was coming to its end. It seems to have been a conscious work of art, conceived and designed as a whole, and those who lived there were mostly artists of some kind. But it didn't last very long; what finally killed it was the exodus."

Simon became suddenly quiet, as if brooding on those tumultuous centuries when the road to the stars had been opened up and the world was torn in twain. Along that road the flower of the race had gone, leaving the rest behind; and thereafter it seemed that history had come to an end on Earth. For a thousand years or more the exiles had returned fleetingly to the solar system, wistfully eager to tell of strange suns and far planets and the great empire that would one day span the galaxy. But there are gulfs that even the swiftest ships can never cross; and such a gulf was opening now between Earth and her wandering children. They had less and less in common; the returning ships became ever more infrequent, until at last generations passed between the visits from outside. Simon had not heard of any such for almost three hundred years.

It was unusual when one had to prod Simon into speech, but presently Brant remarked: "Anyway, I'm more interested in the place itself than its history. Do you think it's still standing?"

"I was coming to that," said Simon, emerging from his reverie with a start. "Of course it is; they built well in those days. But why are you so interested, may I ask? Have you suddenly developed an overwhelming passion for archaeology? Oh, I think I understand!"

Brant knew perfectly well the uselessness of trying to conceal anything from a professional busybody like Simon.

"I was hoping," he said defensively, "that there might still be things there worth going to find, even after all this time."

"Perhaps," said Simon doubtfully. "I must visit it one day. It's almost on our doorstep, as it were. But how are *you* going to manage? The village will hardly let you borrow a flyer! And you can't walk. It would take you at least a week to get there."

But that was exactly what Brant intended to do. As, during the next few days, he was careful to point out to almost everyone in the village, a thing wasn't worth doing unless one did it the hard way. There was nothing like making a virtue out of a necessity.

Brant's preparations were carried out in an unprecedented blaze of secrecy. He did not wish to be too specific about his plans, such as they were, in case any of the dozen or so people in Chaldis who had the right to use a flyer decided to look at Shastar first. It was, of course, only a matter of time before this happened, but the feverish activity of the past months had prevented such explorations. Nothing would be more humiliating than to stagger into Shastar after a week's journey, only to be coolly greeted by a neighbor who had made the trip in ten minutes.

On the other hand, it was equally important that the village in general, and Yradne in particular, should realize that he was making some exceptional effort. Only Simon knew the truth, and he had grudgingly agreed to keep quiet for the present. Brant hoped that he had managed to divert attention from his true objective by showing a great interest in the country to the *east* of Chaldis, which also contained several archaeological relics of some importance.

The amount of food and equipment one needed for a two- or three-weeks' absence was really astonishing, and his first calculations had thrown Brant into a state of considerable gloom. For a while he had even thought of trying to beg or borrow a flyer, but the request would certainly not be granted—and would indeed defeat the whole object of his enterprise. Yet it was quite impossible for him to carry everything he needed for the journey.

The solution would have been perfectly obvious to anyone from a less-mechanized age, but it took Brant some little time to think of it. The flying machine had killed all forms of land transport save one, the oldest and most versatile of all—the only one that was self-perpetuating and could manage very well, as it had done before, with no assistance at all from man.

Chaldis possessed six horses, rather a small number for a community of its size. In some villages the horses outnumbered the humans, but Brant's people, living in a wild and mountainous region, had so far had little opportunity for equitation. Brant himself had ridden a horse only two or three times in his life, and then for exceedingly short periods.

The stallion and five mares were in the charge of Treggor, a gnarled little man who had no discernible interest in life except animals. His was not one of the outstanding intellects of Chaldis, but he seemed perfectly happy running his private menagerie, which included dogs of many shapes and sizes, a couple of beavers, several monkeys, a lion cub, two bears, a young crocodile, and other beasts more usually admired from a distance. The only sorrow that had ever clouded his placid life arose from the fact that he had so far failed to obtain an elephant.

Brant found Treggor, as he expected, leaning on the gate of the paddock. There was a stranger with him, who was introduced to Brant as a horse fancier from a neighboring village. The curious similarity between the two men, extending from the way they dressed even to their facial expressions, made this explanation quite unnecessary.

One always feels a certain nervousness in the presence of un-doubted experts, and Brant outlined his problem with some diffidence. Treggor listened gravely and paused for a long time before replying.

"Yes," he said slowly, jerking his thumb toward the mares, "any of them would do—if you knew how to handle 'em." He looked rather doubtfully at Brant.

"They're like human beings, you know; if they don't like you, you can't do a thing with them."

"Not a thing," echoed the stranger, with evident relish.

"But surely you could teach me how to handle them?"

"Maybe yes, maybe no. I remember a young fellow just like you, wanted to learn to ride. Horses just wouldn't let him get near them. Took a dislike to him—and that was that."

"Horses can *tell,*" interjected the other darkly.

"That's right," agreed Treggor. "You've got to be sympa-thetic. Then you've nothing to worry about."

There was, Brant decided, quite a lot to be said for the less-temperamental machine after all.

"I don't want to ride," he answered with some feeling. "I only want a horse to carry my gear. Or would it be likely to object to that?"

His mild sarcasm was quite wasted. Treggor nodded solemnly.

"That wouldn't be any trouble," he said. "They'll all let you lead them with a halter—all except Daisy, that is. You'd never catch *her.*"

"Then do you think I could borrow one of the—er, more amenable ones—for a while?"

Treggor shuffled around uncertainly, torn between two con-flicting desires. He was pleased that someone wanted to use his beloved beasts, but nervous lest they come to harm. Any dam-age that might befall Brant was of secondary importance.

"Well," he began doubtfully, "it's a bit awkward at the mo-ment. . . ."

Brant looked at the mares more closely, and realized why. Only one of them was accompanied by a foal, but it was obvious that this deficiency would soon be rectified. Here was another complication he had overlooked.

"How long will you be away?" asked Treggor.

"Three weeks, at the most; perhaps only two."

Treggor did some rapid gynaecological calculations.

"Then you can have Sunbeam," he concluded. "She won't give you any trouble at all—best-natured animal I've ever had."

"Thank you very much," said Brant. "I promise I'll look after her. Now would you mind introducing us?"

"I don't see why I should do this," grumbled Jon good-naturedly, as he adjusted the panniers on Sunbeam's sleek sides, "especially since you won't even tell me where you're going or what you expect to find."

Brant couldn't have answered the last question even had he wished. In his more rational moments he knew that he would find nothing of value in Shastar. Indeed, it was hard to think of anything that his people did not already possess, or could not obtain instantly if they wished. But the journey itself would be the proof—the most convincing he could imagine—of his love for Yradne.

There was no doubt that she was quite impressed by his preparations, and he had been careful to underline the dangers he was about to face. It would be very uncomfortable sleeping in the open, and he would have a most monotonous diet. He might even get lost and never be seen again. Suppose there were still wild beasts—dangerous ones—up in the hills or the forests?

Old Johan, who had no feeling for historical traditions, had protested at the indignity of a blacksmith having anything to do with such a primitive survival as a horse. Sunbeam had nipped him delicately for this, with great skill and precision, while he was bending to examine her hoofs. But he had rapidly manufactured a set of panniers in which Brant could put everything he needed for the journey—even his drawing materials, from which he refused to be separated. Treggor had advised on the technical details of the harness, producing ancient prototypes consisting largely of string.

It was still early morning when the last adjustments had been completed; Brant had intended making his departure as unobtrusively as possible, and his complete success was slightly mortifying. Only Jon and Yradne came to see him off.

They walked in thoughtful silence to the end of the village and crossed the slim metal bridge over the river. Then Jon said gruffly: "Well, don't go and break your silly neck," shook hands, and departed, leaving him alone with Yradne. It was a very nice gesture, and Brant appreciated it.

Taking advantage of her master's preoccupation, Sunbeam began to browse among the long grass by the river's edge. Brant shifted awkwardly from foot to foot for a moment, then said halfheartedly:

"I suppose I'd better be going."

"How long will you be away?" asked Yradne. She wasn't wearing Jon's present: perhaps she had grown tired of it already. Brant hoped so—then realized she might lose interest equally quickly in anything he brought back for her.

"Oh, about a fortnight—if all goes well," he added darkly.

"Do be careful," said Yradne, in tones of vague urgency, "and don't do anything rash."

"I'll do my best," answered Brant, still making no move to go, "but one has to take risks sometimes."

This disjointed conversation might have lasted a good deal longer had Sunbeam not taken charge. Brant's arm received a sudden jerk and he was dragged away at a brisk walk. He had regained his balance and was about to wave farewell when Yradne came flying up to him, gave him a large kiss, and disappeared toward the village before he could recover.

She slowed down to a walk when Brant could no longer see her. Jon was still a good way ahead, but she made no attempt to overtake him. A curiously solemn feeling, out of place on this bright spring morning, had overcome her. It was very pleasant to be loved, but it had its disadvantages if one stopped to look beyond the immediate moment. For a fleeting instant Yradne wondered if she had been fair to Jon, to Brant—even to herself. One day the decision would have to be made; it could not be postponed forever. Yet she could not for the life of her decide which of the boys she liked the better; and she did not know if she loved either.

No one had ever told her, and she had not yet discovered, that when one has to ask "Am I really in love?" the answer is always "No."

Beyond Chaldis the forest stretched for five miles to the east, then faded out into the great plain which spanned the remainder of the continent. Six thousand years ago this land had been one of the mightiest deserts in the world, and its reclamation had been among the first achievements of the Atomic Age.

Brant intended to go east until he was clear of the forest, and then to turn toward the high land of the North. According to the maps, there had once been a road along the spine of the hills, linking together all the cities on the coast in a chain that ended at Shastar. It should be easy to follow its track, though Brant did not expect that much of the road itself would have survived the centuries.

He kept close to the river, hoping that it had not changed its path since the maps were made. It was both his guide and his highway through the forest; when the trees were too thick, he and Sunbeam could always wade in the shallow water. Sunbeam was quite cooperative; there was no grass here to distract her, so she plodded methodically along with little prompting.

Soon after midday the trees began to thin out. Brant had

reached the frontier that, century by century, had been on the march across the lands that Man no longer wished to hold. A little later the forest was behind him and he was out in the open plain.

He checked his position from the map, and noted that the trees had advanced an appreciable distance eastward since it was drawn. But there was a clear route north to the low hills along which the ancient road had run, and he should be able to reach them before evening.

At this point certain unforeseen difficulties of a technical nature arose. Sunbeam, finding herself surrounded by the most appetizing grass she had seen for a long time, was unable to resist pausing every three or four steps to collect a mouthful. As Brant was attached to her bridle by a rather short rope, the resulting jerk almost dislocated his arm. Lengthening the rope made matters even worse, because he then had no control at all.

Now Brant was quite fond of animals, but it soon became apparent to him that Sunbeam was simply imposing on his good nature. He put up with it for half a mile, and then steered a course toward a tree which seemed to have particularly slender and lissom branches. Sunbeam watched him warily out of the corners of her limpid brown eyes as he cut a fine, resilient switch and attached it ostentatiously to his belt. Then she set off so briskly that he could scarcely keep pace with her.

She was undoubtedly, as Treggor had claimed, a singularly intelligent beast.

The range of hills that was Brant's first objective was less than two thousand feet high, and the slope was very gentle. But there were numerous annoying foothills and minor valleys to be surmounted on the way to the crest, and it was well toward evening before they had reached the highest point. To the south Brant could see the forest through which he had come, and which could now hinder him no more. Chaldis was somewhere in the midst, though he had only a rough idea of its location; he was surprised to find that he could see no signs of the great clearings that his people had made. To the southeast the plain stretched endlessly away, a level sea of grass dotted with little clumps of trees. Near the horizon Brant could see tiny creeping specks, and guessed that some great herd of wild animals was on the move.

Northward lay the sea, only a dozen miles away down the long slope and across the lowlands. It seemed almost black in the falling sunlight, except where tiny breakers dotted it with flecks of foam.

Before nightfall Brant found a hollow out of the wind, anchored Sunbeam to a stout bush, and pitched the little tent that Old Johan had contrived for him. This was, in theory, a very simple operation, but, as a good many people had found before, it was one that could tax skill and temper to the utmost. At last everything was finished, and he settled down for the night.

There are some things that no amount of pure intelligence can anticipate, but which can only be learned by bitter experience. Who would have guessed that the human body was so sensitive to the almost imperceptible slope on which the tent had been pitched? More uncomfortable still were the minute thermal differences between one point and another, presumably caused by the draughts that seemed to wander through the tent at will. Brant could have endured a uniform temperature gradient, but the unpredictable variations were maddening.

He woke from his fitful sleep a dozen times, or so it seemed, and toward dawn his morale had reached its lowest ebb. He felt cold and miserable and stiff, as if he had not slept properly for days, and it would have needed very little persuasion to have made him abandon the whole enterprise. He was prepared— even willing—to face danger in the cause of love; but lumbago was a different matter.

The discomforts of the night were soon forgotten in the

glory of the new day. Here on the hills the air was fresh with the tang of salt, borne by the wind that came climbing up from the sea. The dew was everywhere, hanging thickly on each bent blade of grass—but so soon to be destroyed beyond all trace by the steepening sun. It was good to be alive; it was better to be young; it was best of all to be in love.

They came upon the road very soon after they had started the day's journey. Brant had missed it before because it had been farther down the seaward slope, and he had expected to find it on the crest of the hill. It had been superbly built, and the millennia had touched it lightly. Nature had tried in vain to obliterate it; here and there she had succeeded in burying a few meters with a light blanket of earth, but then her servants had turned against her and the wind and the rain had scoured it clean once more. In a great jointless band, skirting the edge of the sea for more than a thousand miles, the road still linked the cities that Man had loved in his childhood.

It was one of the great roads of the world. Once it had been no more than a footpath along which savage tribes had come down to the sea, to barter with wily, bright-eyed merchants from distant lands. Then it had known new and more exacting masters; the soldiers of a mighty empire had shaped and hewn the road so skillfully along the hills that the path they gave it had remained unchanged down all the ages. They had paved it with stone so that their armies could move more swiftly than any that the world had known; and along the road their legions had been hurled like thunderbolts at the bidding of the city whose name they bore. Centuries later, that city had called them home in its last extremity; and the road had rested then for five hundred years.

But other wars were still to come; beneath crescent banners the armies of the Prophet were yet to storm westward into Christendom. Later still—centuries later—the tide of the last and greatest of conflicts was to turn here, as steel monsters clashed together in the desert, and the sky itself rained death.

The centurions, the paladins, the armored divisions—even the desert—all were gone. But the road remained, of all man's creations the most enduring. For ages enough it had borne his burdens; and now along its whole thousand miles it carried no more traffic than one boy and a horse.

Brant followed the road for three days, keeping always in sight of the sea. He had grown used to the minor discomforts of a nomadic existence, and even the nights were no longer intolerable. The weather had been perfect—long, warm days and mild nights—but the fine spell was coming to an end.

He estimated that he was less than five miles from Shastar on the evening of the fourth day. The road was now turning away from the coast to avoid a great headland jutting out to sea. Beyond this was the sheltered bay along whose shores the city had been built; when it had bypassed the high ground, the road would sweep northward in a great curve and come down upon Shastar from the hills.

Toward dusk it was clear that Brant could not hope to see his goal that day. The weather was breaking, and thick, angry clouds had been gathering swiftly from the west. He was climbing now—for the road was rising slowly as it crossed the last ridge—in the teeth of a gale. He would have pitched camp for the night if he could have found a sheltered spot, but the hill was bare for miles behind him and there was nothing to do but to struggle onward.

Far ahead, at the very crest of the ridge, something low and dark was silhouetted against the threatening sky. The hope that it might provide shelter drove Brant onward: Sunbeam, head well down against the wind, plodded steadily beside him with equal determination.

They were still a mile from the summit when the rain began to fall, first in single, angry drops and then in blinding sheets. It was impossible to see more than a few paces ahead, even when one could open one's eyes against the stinging rain. Brant was already so wet that any additional moisture could add nothing to his discomfort; indeed, he had reached that sodden state when the continuing downpour almost gave him a masochistic pleasure. But the sheer physical effort of fighting against the gale was rapidly exhausting him.

It seemed ages before the road leveled out and he knew he had reached the summit. He strained his eyes into the gloom and could see, not far ahead, a great dark shape, which for a moment he thought might be a building. Even if it was in ruins, it would give him shelter from the storm.

The rain began to slacken as he approached the object; overhead, the clouds were thinning to let through the last fading light of the western sky. It was just sufficient to show Brant that what lay ahead of him was no building at all, but a great stone beast, crouching upon the hilltop and staring out to sea. He had no time to examine it more closely, but hurriedly pitched his tent in its shelter, out of reach of the wind that still raved angrily overhead.

It was completely dark when he had dried himself and prepared a meal. For a while he rested in his warm little oasis, in that state of blissful exhaustion that comes after hard and successful effort. Then he roused himself, took a hand-torch, and went out into the night.

The storm had blown away the clouds and the night was brilliant with stars. In the west a thin crescent moon was sinking, following hard upon the footsteps of the sun. To the north Brant was aware—though how, he could not have said—of the sleepless presence of the sea. Down there in the darkness Shastar was lying, the waves marching forever against it; but strain his eyes as he might, he could see nothing at all.

He walked along the flanks of the great statue, examining the stonework by the light of his torch. It was smooth and unbroken by any joints or seams, and although time had stained and discolored it, there was no sign of wear. It was impossible to guess its age; it might be older than Shastar or it might have been made only a few centuries ago. There was no way of telling.

The hard, blue-white beam of the torch flickered along the monster's wetly gleaming sides and came to rest upon the great, calm face and the empty eyes. One might have called it a human face, but thereafter words faltered and failed. Neither male nor female, it seemed at first sight utterly indifferent to all the passions of mankind; then Brant saw that the storms of ages had left their mark behind them. Countless raindrops had coursed down those adamantine cheeks, until they bore the stains of Olympian tears—tears, perhaps, for the city whose birth and death now seemed almost equally remote.

Brant was so tired that when he awoke the sun was already high. He lay for a moment in the filtered half-light of the tent, recovering his senses and remembering where he was. Then he rose to his feet and went blinking into the daylight, shielding his eyes from the dazzling glare.

The Sphinx seemed smaller than by night, though it was impressive enough. It was colored, Brant saw for the first time, a rich, autumnal gold, the color of no natural rock. He knew from this that it did not belong, as he had half suspected, to any prehistoric culture. It had been built by science from some inconceivably stubborn, synthetic substance, and Brant guessed that its creation must lie almost midway in time between him and the fabulous original which had inspired it.

Slowly, half afraid of what he might discover, he turned his back upon the Sphinx and looked to the north. The hill fell away at his feet and the road went sweeping down the long slope as if impatient to greet the sea; and there at its end lay Shastar.

It caught the sunlight and tossed it back to him, tinted with all the colors of its makers' dreams. The spacious buildings lining the wide streets seemed unravished by time; the great band of marble that held the sea at bay was still unbreached; the parks and gardens, though long overgrown with weeds, were not yet jungles. The city followed the curve of the bay for perhaps two miles, and stretched half that distance inland; by the standards of the past, it was very small indeed. But to Brant it seemed enormous, a maze of streets and squares intricate beyond unraveling. Then he began to discern the underlying symmetry of its design, to pick out the main thoroughfares, and to see the skill with which its makers had avoided both monotony and discord.

For a long time Brant stood motionless on the hilltop, conscious only of the wonder spread beneath his eyes. He was alone in all that landscape, a tiny figure lost and humble before the achievements of greater men. The sense of history, the vision of the long slope up which Man had been toiling for a million years or more, was almost overwhelming. In that moment it seemed to Brant that from his hilltop he was looking over Time rather than Space; and in his ears there whispered the soughing of the winds of eternity as they sweep into the past.

Sunbeam seemed very nervous as they approached the outskirts of the city. She had never seen anything like this before in her life, and Brant could not help sharing her disquiet. However unimaginative one may be, there is something ominous about buildings that have been deserted for centuries—and those of Shastar had been empty for the better part of five thousand years.

The road ran straight as an arrow between two tall pillars of white metal; like the Sphinx, they were tarnished but unworn. Brant and Sunbeam passed beneath these silent guardians and found themselves before a long, low building which must have served as some kind of reception point for visitors to the city.

From a distance it had seemed that Shastar might have been abandoned only yesterday, but now Brant could see a thousand signs of desolation and neglect. The colored stone of the buildings was stained with the patina of age; the windows were gaping, skull-blank eyes, with here and there a miraculously preserved fragment of glass.

Brant tethered Sunbeam outside the first building and made his way to the entrance across the rubble and thickly piled dirt. There was no door, if indeed there had ever been one, and he passed through the high, vaulted archway into a hall which seemed to run the full length of the structure. At regular intervals there were openings into further chambers, and immediately ahead of him a wide flight of stairs rose to the single floor above.

It took him almost an hour to explore the building, and when he left he was infinitely depressed. His careful search had revealed absolutely nothing. All the rooms, great and small, were completely empty; he had felt like an ant crawling through the bones of a clean-picked skeleton.

Out in the sunlight, however, his spirits revived a little. This building was probably only some sort of administrative office and would never have contained anything but records and information machines; elsewhere in the city, things might be different. Even so, the magnitude of the search appalled him.

Slowly he made his way toward the sea front, moving awestruck through the wide avenues and admiring the towering façades on either side. Near the center of the city he came upon one of its many parks. It was largely overgrown with weeds and shrubs, but there were still considerable areas of grass, and he decided to leave Sunbeam here while he continued his explorations. She was not likely to move very far away while there was plenty to eat.

It was so peaceful in the park that for a while Brant was loath to leave it to plunge again into the desolation of the city. There were plants here unlike any that he had ever seen before, the wild descendants of those which the people of Shastar had cherished ages since. As he stood among the high grasses and unknown flowers, Brant heard for the first time, stealing through the calm stillness of the morning, the sound he was always to link with Shastar. It came from the sea, and though he had never heard it before in all his life, it brought a sense of aching recognition into his heart. Where no other voices sounded now, the lonely sea gulls were still calling sadly across the waves.

It was quite clear that many days would be needed to make even the most superficial examination of the city, and the first thing to do would be to find somewhere to live. Brant spent several hours searching for the residential district before it began to dawn on him that there was something very peculiar about Shastar. All the buildings he entered were, without exception, designed for work, entertainment, or similar purposes; but none of them had been designed *to live in*. The solution came to him slowly. As he grew to know the pattern of the city, he noticed that at almost every street intersection there were low, single-storied structures of nearly identical form. They were circular or oval, and had many openings leading into them from all directions. When Brant entered one of them, he found himself facing a line of great metal gates, each with a vertical row of indicator lamps by its side. And so he knew where the people of Shastar had lived.

At first the idea of underground homes was completely repellent to him. Then he overcame his prejudice, and realized how sensible, as well as how inevitable, this was. There was no need to clutter up the surface, and to block the sunlight, with buildings designed for the merely mechanical processes of sleeping and eating. By putting all these things underground, the people of Shastar had been able to build a noble and spacious city—and yet keep it so small that one could walk its whole length within an hour.

The elevators were, of course, useless, but there were emergency stairways winding down into the darkness. Once all this underworld must have been a blaze of light, but Brant hesitated now before he descended the steps. He had his torch, but he had never been underground before and had a horror of losing his way in some subterranean catacombs. Then he shrugged his shoulders and started down the steps; after all, there was no danger if he took the most elementary precautions—and there were hundreds of other exits even if he did lose his way.

He descended to the first level and found himself in a long, wide corridor stretching as far as his beam could penetrate. On either side were rows of numbered doors, and Brant tried nearly a dozen before he found one that opened. Slowly, even reverently, he entered the little home that had been deserted for almost half the span of recorded history.

It was clean and tidy, for there had been no dust or dirt to settle here. The beautifully proportioned rooms were bare of furniture; nothing of value had been left behind in the leisurely, age-long exodus. Some of the semipermanent fittings were still in position; the food distributor, with its familiar selector dial, was so strikingly like the one in Brant's own home that the sight of it almost annihilated the centuries. The dial still turned, though stiffly, and he would scarcely have been surprised to see a meal appear in the materialization chamber.

Brant explored several more homes before he returned to the surface. Though he found nothing of value, he felt a growing sense of kinship toward the people who had lived here. Yet he still thought of them as his inferiors, for to have lived in a city—however beautiful, however brilliantly designed—was to Brant one of the symbols of barbarism.

In the last home he entered he came across a brightly colored room with a fresco of dancing animals around the walls. The pictures were full of a whimsical humor that must have delighted the hearts of the children for whom they had been drawn. Brant examined the paintings with interest, for they were the first works of representative art he had found in Shastar. He was about to leave when he noticed a tiny pile of dust in one corner of the room, and bending down to investigate found himself looking at the still-recognizable fragments of a doll. Nothing solid remained save a few colored buttons, which crumbled to powder in his hand when he picked them up. He wondered why this sad little relic had been left behind by its owner; then he tiptoed away and returned to the surface and the lonely but sunlit streets. He never went to the underground city again.

Toward evening he revisited the park to see that Sunbeam had been up to no mischief, and prepared to spend the night in one of the numerous small buildings scattered through the gardens. Here he was surrounded by flowers and trees, and could almost imagine he was home again. He slept better than he had done since he had left Chaldis, and for the first time for many days, his last waking thoughts were not of Yradne. The magic of Shastar was already working upon his mind; the infinite complexity of the civilization he had affected to despise was changing him more swiftly than he could imagine. The longer he stayed in the city, the more remote he would become from the naïve yet self-confident boy who had entered it only a few hours before.

The second day confirmed the impressions of the first. Shastar had not died in a year, or even in a generation. Slowly its people had drifted away as the new—yet how old!—pattern of society had been evolved and humanity had returned to the hills and the forests. They had left nothing behind them, save these marble monuments to a way of life that was gone forever. Even if anything of value had remained, the thousands of curious explorers who had come here in the fifty centuries since would have taken it long ago. Brant found many traces of his predecessors; their names were carved on walls throughout the city, for this is one kind of immortality that men have never been able to resist.

Tired at last by his fruitless search, he went down to the shore and sat on the wide stonework of the breakwater. The sea lying a few feet beneath him was utterly calm and of a cerulean blue; it was so still and clear that he could watch the fish swimming in its depths, and at one spot could see a wreck lying on its side with the seaweed streaming straight up from it like long, green hair. Yet there must be times, he knew, when the waves came thundering over the massive walls; for behind him the wide parapet was strewn with a thick carpet of stones and shells, tossed there by the gales of centuries.

The enervating peacefulness of the scene, and the unforgettable object lesson in the futility of ambition that surrounded him on every side, took away all sense of disappointment or defeat. Though Shastar had given him nothing of material value, Brant did not regret his journey. Sitting here on the sea wall, with his back to the land and his eyes dazzled by that blinding blue, he already felt remote from his old problems, and could look back with no pain at all, but only a dispassionate curiosity, on all the heartache and the anxiety that had plagued him these last few months.

He went slowly back into the city, after walking a little way along the sea front so that he could return by a new route. Presently he found himself before a large circular building whose roof was a shallow dome of some translucent material. He looked at it with little interest, for he was emotionally exhausted, and decided that it was probably yet another theater or concert hall. He had almost passed the entrance when some obscure impulse diverted him and he went through the open doorway.

Inside, the light filtered through the ceiling with such little hindrance that Brant almost had the impression of being in the open air. The entire building was divided into numerous large halls whose purpose he realized with a sudden stir of excitement. The telltale rectangles of discoloration showed that the walls had once been almost covered with pictures; it was just possible that some had been left behind, and it would be interesting to see what Shastar could offer in the way of serious art. Brant, still secure in his consciousness of superiority, did not expect to be unduly impressed; and so the shock was all the greater when it came.

The blaze of color along the whole length of the great wall smote him like a fanfare of trumpets. For a moment he stood paralyzed in the doorway, unable to grasp the pattern or meaning of what he saw. Then, slowly, he began to unravel the details of the tremendous and intricate mural that had burst suddenly upon his vision.

It was nearly a hundred feet long, and was incomparably the most wonderful thing that Brant had ever seen in his life. Shastar had awed and overwhelmed him, yet its tragedy had left him curiously unmoved. But this struck straight at his heart and spoke in a language he could understand; and as it did so, the last vestiges of his condescension toward the past were scattered like leaves before a gale.

The eye moved naturally from left to right across the painting, to follow the curve of tension to its moment of climax. On the left was the sea, as deep a blue as the water that beat against Shastar; and moving across its face was a fleet of strange ships, driven by tiered banks of oars and by billowing sails that strained toward the distant land. The painting covered not only miles of space but perhaps years of time; for now the ships had reached the shore, and there on the wide plain an army lay encamped, its banners and tents and chariots dwarfed by the walls of the fortress city it was beleaguering. The eye scaled those still inviolate walls and came to rest, as it was meant to do, upon the woman who stood upon them, looking down at the army that had followed her across the ocean.

She was leaning forward to peer over the battlements, and the wind was catching her hair so that it formed a golden mist about her head. Upon her face was written a sadness too deep for words, yet one that did nothing to mar the unbelievable beauty of her face—a beauty that held Brant spellbound, for long unable to tear away his eyes. When at last he could do so, he followed her gaze down those seemingly impregnable walls to the group of soldiers toiling in their shadow. They were gathered around something so foreshortened by perspective that it was some time before Brant realized what it was. Then he saw that it was an enormous image of a horse, mounted on rollers so that it could be easily moved. It roused no echoes in his mind, and he quickly returned to the lonely figure on the wall, around whom, as he now saw, the whole great design was balanced and pivoted. For as the eye moved on across the painting, taking the mind with it into the future, it came upon ruined battlements, the smoke of the burning city staining the sky, and the fleet returning homeward, its mission done.

Brant left only when the light was so poor that he could no longer see. When the first shock had worn off, he had examined the great painting more closely; and for a while he had searched, but in vain, for the signature of the artist. He also looked for some caption or title, but it was clear that there had never been one—perhaps because the story was too well known to need it. In the intervening centuries, however, some other visitor to Shastar had scratched two lines of poetry on the wall:

> Is this the face that launched a thousand ships
> And burned the topless towers of Ilium?

Ilium! It was a strange and magical name; but it meant nothing to Brant. He wondered whether it belonged to history or to fable, not knowing how many before him had wrestled with that same problem.

As he emerged into the luminous twilight, he still carried the vision of that sad, ethereal loveliness before his eyes. Perhaps if Brant had not himself been an artist, and had been in a less susceptible state of mind, the impression would not have been so overwhelming. Yet it was the impression that the unknown master had set out to create, Phoenix-like, from the dying embers of a great legend. He had captured, and held for all future ages to see, that beauty whose service is the purpose of life, and its sole justification.

For a long time Brant sat under the stars, watching the crescent moon sink behind the towers of the city, and haunted by questions to which he could never know the answers. All the other pictures in these galleries had gone, scattered beyond tracing, not merely throughout the world, but throughout the universe. How had they compared with the single work of genius that now must represent forever the art of Shastar?

In the morning Brant returned, after a night of strange dreams. A plan had been forming in his mind; it was so wild and ambitious that at first he tried to laugh it away, but it would give him no peace. Almost reluctantly, he set up his little folding easel and prepared his paints. He had found one thing in Shastar that was both unique and beautiful; perhaps he had the skill to carry some faint echo of it back to Chaldis.

It was impossible, of course, to copy more than a fragment of the vast design, but the problem of selection was easy. Though he had never attempted a portrait of Yradne, he would now paint a woman who, if indeed she had ever existed, had been dust for five thousand years.

Several times he stopped to consider this paradox, and at last thought he had resolved it. He had never painted Yradne because he doubted his own skill, and was afraid of her criticism. That would be no problem here, Brant told himself. He did not stop to ask how Yradne would react when he returned to Chaldis carrying as his only gift the portrait of another woman.

In truth, he was painting for himself, and for no one else. For the first time in his life he had come into direct contact with a great work of classic art, and it had swept him off his feet. Until now he had been a dilettante; he might never be more than this, but at least he would make the effort.

He worked steadily all through the day, and the sheer concentration of his labors brought him a certain peace of mind. By evening he had sketched in the palace walls and battlements, and was about to start on the portrait itself. That night, he slept well.

He lost most of his optimism the next morning. His food supply was running low, and perhaps the thought that he was working against time had unsettled him. Everything seemed to be going wrong; the colors would not match, and the painting, which had shown such promise the day before, was becoming less and less satisfactory every minute.

To make matters worse, the light was failing, though it was barely noon, and Brant guessed that the sky outside had become overcast. He rested for a while in the hope that it might clear again, but since it showed no signs of doing so, he recommenced work. It was now or nothing; unless he could get that hair right he would abandon the whole project. . . .

The afternoon waned rapidly, but in his fury of concentration Brant scarcely noticed the passage of time. Once or twice he thought he noticed distant sounds and wondered if a storm was coming up, for the sky was still very dark.

There is no experience more chilling than the sudden, the utterly unexpected knowledge that one is no longer alone. It would be hard to say what impulse made Brant slowly lay down his brush and turn, even more slowly, toward the great doorway forty feet behind him. The man standing there must have entered almost soundlessly, and how long he had been watching him Brant had no way of guessing. A moment later he was joined by two companions, who also made no attempt to pass the doorway.

Brant rose slowly to his feet, his brain whirling. For a moment he almost imagined that ghosts from Shastar's past had come back to haunt him. Then reason reasserted itself. After all, why should he not meet other visitors here, when he was one himself?

He took a few paces forward, and one of the strangers did likewise. When they were a few yards apart, the other said in a very clear voice, speaking rather slowly: "I hope we haven't disturbed you."

It was not a very dramatic conversational opening, and Brant was somewhat puzzled by the man's accent—or, more accurately, by the exceedingly careful way he was pronouncing his words. It almost seemed that he did not expect Brant to understand him otherwise.

"That's quite all right," Brant replied, speaking equally slowly. "But you gave me a surprise—I hardly expected to meet anyone here."

"Neither did we," said the other with a slight smile. "We had no idea that anyone still lived in Shastar."

"But I don't," explained Brant. "I'm just a visitor like you."

The three exchanged glances, as if sharing some secret joke. Then one of them lifted a small metal object from his belt and spoke a few words into it, too softly for Brant to overhear. He assumed that other members of the party were on the way, and felt annoyed that his solitude was to be so completely shattered.

Two of the strangers had walked over to the great mural and begun to examine it critically. Brant wondered what they were thinking; somehow he resented sharing his treasure with those who would not feel the same reverence toward it—those to whom it would be nothing more than a pretty picture. The third man remained by his side comparing, as unobtrusively as possible, Brant's copy with the original. All three seemed to be deliberately avoiding further conversation. There was a long and embarrassing silence; then the other two men rejoined them.

"Well, Erlyn, what do you think of it?" said one, waving his hand toward the painting. They seemed for the moment to have lost all interest in Brant.

"It's a very fine late third-millennium primitive, as good as anything we have. Don't you agree, Latvar?"

"Not exactly. I wouldn't say it's late third. For one thing, the subject . . ."

"Oh, you and your theories! But perhaps you're right. It's too good for the last period. On second thoughts, I'd date it around 2500. What do you say, Trescon?"

"I agree. Probably Aroon or one of his pupils."

"Rubbish!" said Latvar.

"Nonsense!" snorted Erlyn.

"Oh, very well," replied Trescon good-naturedly. "I've only studied this period for thirty years, while you've just looked it up since we started. So I bow to your superior knowledge."

Brant had followed this conversation with growing surprise and a rapidly mounting sense of bafflement.

"Are all three of you artists?" he blurted out at last.

"Of course," replied Trescon grandly. "Why else would we be here?"

"Don't be a damned liar," said Erlyn, without even raising his voice. "You won't be an artist if you live a thousand years. You're merely an expert, and you know it. Those who can—do; those who can't—criticize."

"Where have you come from?" asked Brant, a little faintly. He had never met anyone quite like these extraordinary men. They were in late middle age, yet seemed to have an almost boyish gusto and enthusiasm. All their movements and gestures were just a little larger than life, and when they were talking to each other they spoke so quickly that Brant found it difficult to follow them.

Before anyone could reply, there was a further interruption. A dozen men appeared in the doorway—and were brought to a momentary halt by their first sight of the great painting. Then they hurried to join the little group around Brant, who now found himself the center of a small crowd.

"Here you are, Kondar," said Trescon, pointing to Brant. "We've found someone who can answer your questions."

The man who had been addressed looked at Brant closely for a moment, glanced at his unfinished painting, and smiled a little. Then he turned to Trescon and lifted his eyebrows in interrogation.

"No," said Trescon succinctly.

Brant was getting annoyed. Something was going on that he didn't understand, and he resented it.

"Would you mind telling me what this is all about?" he said plaintively.

Kondar looked at him with an unfathomable expression. Then he said quietly: "Perhaps I could explain things better if you came outside."

He spoke as if he never had to ask twice for a thing to be done; and Brant followed him without a word, the others crowding close behind him. At the outer entrance Kondar stood aside and waved Brant to pass.

It was still unnaturally dark, as if a thundercloud had blotted out the sun; but the shadow that lay the full length of Shastar was not that of any cloud.

A dozen pairs of eyes were watching Brant as he stood staring at the sky, trying to gauge the true size of the ship floating above the city. It was so close that the sense of perspective was lost; one was conscious only of sweeping metal curves that dwindled away to the horizon. There should have been some sound, some indication of the energies holding that stupendous mass at rest above Shastar; but there was only a silence deeper than any that Brant had ever known. Even the crying of the sea gulls had ceased, as if they, too, were overawed by the intruder who had usurped their skies.

At last Brant turned toward the men gathered behind him. They were waiting, he knew, for his reactions; and the reason for their curiously aloof yet not unfriendly behavior became suddenly clear. To these men, rejoicing in the powers of gods, he was little more than a savage who happened to speak the same language—a survival from their own half-forgotten past, reminding them of the days when their ancestors had shared the Earth with his.

"Do you understand, now, who we are?" asked Kondar.

Brant nodded. "You have been gone a long time," he said. "We had almost forgotten you."

He looked up again at the great metal arch spanning the sky, and thought how strange it was that the first contact after so many centuries should be here, in this lost city of mankind. But it seemed that Shastar was well remembered among the stars, for certainly Trescon and his friends had appeared perfectly familiar with it.

And then, far to the north, Brant's eye was caught by a sudden flash of reflected sunlight. Moving purposefully across the band of sky framed beneath the ship was another metal giant that might have been its twin, dwarfed though it was by distance. It passed swiftly across the horizon and within seconds was gone from sight.

So this was not the only ship; and how many more might there be? Somehow the thought reminded Brant of the great painting he had just left, and of the invading fleet moving with such deadly purpose toward the doomed city. And with that thought there came into his soul, creeping out from the hidden caves of racial memory, the fear of strangers that once had been the curse of all mankind. He turned to Kondar and cried accusingly:

"You're invading Earth!"

For a moment no one spoke. Then Trescon said, with a slight touch of malice in his voice:

"Go ahead, Commander—you've got to explain it sooner or later. Now's a good time to practice."

Commander Kondar gave a worried little smile that first reassured Brant, then filled him with yet deeper forebodings.

"You do us an injustice, young man," he said gravely. "We're not invading Earth. We're evacuating it."

"I hope," said Trescon, who had taken a patronizing interest in Brant, "that *this* time the scientists have learned a lesson—though I doubt it. They just say, 'Accidents will happen,' and when they've cleaned up one mess, they go on to make another. The Sigma Field is certainly their most spectacular failure so far, but progress never ceases."

"And if it does hit Earth—what will happen?"

"The same thing that happened to the control apparatus when the Field got loose—it will be scattered uniformly throughout the cosmos. And so will you be, unless we get you out in time."

"Why?" asked Brant.

"You don't really expect a technical answer, do you? It's something to do with Uncertainty. The Ancient Greeks—or perhaps it was the Egyptians—discovered that you can't define the position of any atom with absolute accuracy; it has a small but finite probability of being anywhere in the universe. The people who set up the Field hoped to use it for propulsion. It would change the atomic odds, as it were, so that a spaceship orbiting Vega would suddenly decide that it really ought to be circling Betelgeuse.

"Well, it seems that the Sigma Field does only half the job. It merely *multiplies* probabilities—it doesn't organize them. And now it's wandering at random through the stars, feeding on interstellar dust and the occasional sun. No one's been able to

devise a way of neutralizing it—though there's a horrible suggestion that a twin should be created and a collision arranged.
If they try that, I know just what will happen."

"I don't see why we should worry," said Brant. "It's still ten
light-years away."

"Ten light-years is much too close for a thing like the Sigma
Field. It's zigzagging at random, in what the mathematicians
call the Drunkard's Walk. If we're unlucky, it'll be here tomorrow. But the chances are twenty to one that the Earth will be
untouched; in a few years, you'll be able to go home again, just
as if nothing had ever happened."

"As if nothing had ever happened!" Whatever the future
brought, the old way of life was gone forever. What was taking
place in Shastar must now be occurring in one form or another,
over all the world. Brant watched wide-eyed as strange machines rolled down the splendid streets, clearing away the rubble of ages and making the city fit for habitation again. As an
almost extinct star may suddenly blaze up in one last hour of
glory, so for a few months Shastar would be one of the capitals
of the world, housing the army of scientists, technicians, and
administrators that had descended upon it from space.

Brant was growing to know the invaders very well. Their
vigor, the lavishness of everything they did, and the almost
childlike delight they took in their superhuman powers never
ceased to astonish him. These, his cousins, were the heirs to all
the universe; and they had not yet begun to exhaust its wonders
or to tire of its mystery. For all their knowledge, there was still a
feeling of experimentation, even of cheerful irresponsibility,
about many of the things they did. The Sigma Field itself was
an example of this; they had made a mistake, they did not seem
to mind in the least, and they were quite sure that sooner or
later they would put things right.

Despite the tumult that had been loosed upon Shastar, as
indeed upon the entire planet, Brant had remained stubbornly

at his task. It gave him something fixed and stable in a world of shifting values, and as such he clung to it desperately. From time to time Trescon or his colleagues would visit him and proffer advice—usually excellent advice, though he did not always take it. And occasionally, when he was tired and wished to rest his eyes or brain, he would leave the great empty galleries and go out into the transformed streets of the city. It was typical of its new inhabitants that, though they would be here for no more than a few months, they had spared no efforts to make Shastar clean and efficient, and to impose upon it a certain stark beauty that would have surprised its first builders.

At the end of four days—the longest time he had ever devoted to a single work—Brant slowed to a halt. He could go on tinkering indefinitely, but if he did he would only make things worse. Not at all displeased with his efforts, he went in search of Trescon.

He found the critic, as usual, arguing with his colleagues over what should be saved from the accumulated art of mankind. Latvar and Erlyn had threatened violence if one more Picasso was taken aboard, or another Fra Angelico thrown out. Not having heard of either, Brant had no compunction in pressing his own claim.

Trescon stood in silence before the painting, glancing at the original from time to time. His first remark was quite unexpected.

"Who's the girl?" he said.

"You told me she was called Helen—" Brant started to answer.

"I mean the one you've *really* painted."

Brant looked at his canvas, then back at the original. It was odd that he hadn't noticed those differences before, but there were undoubtedly traces of Yradne in the woman he had shown on the fortress walls. This was not the straightforward copy he had set out to make. His own mind and heart had spoken through his fingers.

"I see what you mean," he said slowly. "There's a girl back in my village; I really came here to find a present for her—something that would impress her."

"Then you've been wasting your time," Trescon answered bluntly. "If she really loves you, she'll tell you soon enough. If she doesn't, you can't make her. It's as simple as that."

Brant did not consider that at all simple, but decided not to argue the point.

"You haven't told me what you think about it," he complained.

"It shows promise," Trescon answered cautiously. "In another thirty—well, twenty—years you may get somewhere, if you keep at it. Of course the brushwork is pretty crude, and that hand looks like a bunch of bananas. But you have a nice bold line, and I think more of you for not making a carbon copy. Any fool can do that—this shows you've some originality. What you need now is more practice—and above all, more experience. Well, I think we can provide you with that."

"If you mean going away from Earth," said Brant, "that's not the sort of experience I want."

"It will do you good. Doesn't the thought of traveling out to the stars arouse any feelings of excitement in your mind?"

"No; only dismay. But I can't take it seriously because I don't believe you'll be able to make us go."

Trescon smiled, a little grimly.

"You'll move quickly enough when the Sigma Field sucks the starlight from the sky. And it may be a good thing when it comes: I have a feeling we were just in time. Though I've often made fun of the scientists, they've freed us forever from the stagnation that was overtaking your race.

"You have to get away from Earth, Brant; no man who has lived all his life on the surface of a planet has ever seen the stars, only their feeble ghosts. Can you imagine what it means to hang in space amid one of the great multiple systems, with colored suns blazing all around you? I've done that; and I've seen stars floating in rings of crimson fire, like your planet Saturn, but a thousand times greater. And can you imagine night on a world near the heart of the Galaxy, where the whole sky is luminous with star mist that has not yet given birth to suns? Your Milky Way is only a scattered handful of third-rate suns; wait until you see the Central Nebula!

"These are the great things, but the small ones are just as wonderful. Drink your fill of all that the universe can offer; and if you wish, return to Earth with your memories. *Then* you can begin to work; then, and no sooner, you'll know if you are an artist."

Brant was impressed, but not convinced.

"According to *that* argument," he said "real art couldn't have existed before space travel."

"There's a whole school of criticism based on that thesis; certainly space travel was one of the best things that ever happened to art. Travel, exploration, contact with other cultures—that's the great stimulus for all intellectual activity." Trescon waved at the mural blazing on the wall behind them. "The people who created that legend were seafarers, and the traffic of half a world came through their ports. But after a few thousand years, the sea was too small for inspiration or adventure, and it was time to go into space. Well, the time's come for you, whether you like it or not."

"I don't like it. I want to settle down with Yradne."

"The things that people want and the things that are good for them are very different. I wish you luck with your painting; I don't know whether to wish you luck in your other endeavor. Great art and domestic bliss are mutually incompatible. Sooner or later, you'll have to make your choice."

Sooner or later, you'll have to make your choice. Those words still echoed in Brant's mind as he trudged toward the brow of the hill, and the wind came down the great road to meet him. Sunbeam resented the termination of her holiday, so they moved even more slowly than the gradient demanded. But gradually the landscape widened around them, and the horizon moved farther out to sea, and the city began to look more and more like a toy built from colored bricks—a toy dominated by the ship that hung effortlessly, motionlessly above it.

For the first time Brant was able to see it as a whole, for it was now floating almost level with his eyes and he could encompass it at a glance. It was roughly cylindrical in shape, but ended in complex polyhedral structures whose functions were beyond conjecture. The great curving back bristled with equally mysterious bulges, flutings, and cupolas. There was power and purpose here, but nothing of beauty, and Brant looked upon it with distaste.

This brooding monster usurping the sky—if only it would vanish, like the clouds that drifted past its flanks!

But it would not disappear because he willed it; against the forces that were gathering now, Brant knew that he and his problems were of no importance. This was the pause when history held its breath, the hushed moment between the lightning flash and the advent of the first concussion. Soon the thunder would be rolling round the world; and soon there might be no world at all, while he and his people would be homeless exiles among the stars. That was the future he did not care to face— the future he feared more deeply than Trescon and his fellows, to whom the universe had been a plaything for five thousand years, could ever understand.

It seemed unfair that this should have happened in his time, after all these centuries of rest. But men cannot bargain with Fate, and choose peace or adventure as they wish. Adventure and Change had come to the world again, and he must make the best of it—as his ancestors had done when the age of space had opened, and their first frail ships had stormed the stars.

For the last time he saluted Shastar, then turned his back

upon the sea. The sun was shining in his eyes, and the road before him seemed veiled with a bright, shimmering mist, so that it quivered like a mirage, or the track of the Moon upon troubled waters. For a moment Brant wondered if his eyes had been deceiving him; then he saw that it was no illusion.

As far as the eye could see, the road and the land on either side of it were draped with countless strands of gossamer, so frail and fine that only the glancing sunlight revealed their presence. For the last quarter-mile he had been walking through them, and they had resisted his passage no more than coils of smoke.

Throughout the morning, the wind-borne spiders must have been falling in millions from the sky; and as he stared up into the blue, Brant could still catch momentary glimpses of sunlight upon drifting silk as belated voyagers went sailing by. Not knowing whither they would travel, these tiny creatures had ventured forth into an abyss more friendless and more fathomless than any he would face when the time came to say farewell to Earth. It was a lesson he would remember in the weeks and months ahead.

Slowly the Sphinx sank into the sky line as it joined Shastar beyond the eclipsing crescent of the hills. Only once did Brant look back at the crouching monster, whose agelong vigil was now drawing to its close. Then he walked slowly forward into the sun, while ever and again impalpable fingers brushed his face, as the strands of silk came drifting down the wind that blew from home.

HATE

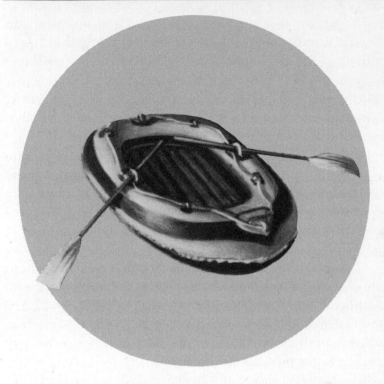

THIS IS GOING TO BE TOO IMPROBABLE FOR FICTION: YOU'LL just have to take my word that I'm not making it up. As I'd completely forgotten the genesis of the story until I dug out my yellowing notebooks, I'm still slightly incredulous.

In February 1960—thirty years before these words will appear in print—the distinguished film producer William Mac-Quitty asked me to write a movie treatment entitled "The Sea and the Stars." This was little more than two years after *Sputnik 1* had opened the space age (October 1957); no human being had then traveled beyond the atmosphere, and despite Liaka and other animal astronauts, there was still doubt in some circles that prolonged survival was possible in weightlessness.

Though we were of course unaware of it at the time, Yuri Gagarin was then in training for the first orbital flight (12 April 1961) and Bill and I were quite certain that the first person in space would be a Russian. We thought it would make a dramatic movie if we had the capsule sinking on the Great Barrier Reef and being discovered, with the trapped occupant still alive, by a diver who—no, I won't spoil the story for you. . . .

Nothing came of the movie treatment, which is what happens to 99 percent of the species. However, I thought it too good an idea to waste, and the next month developed it into a short story. *If* magazine published it in November 1961, retitling it "At the End of the Orbit." I prefer the original: more punch.

Almost simultaneously, I met the first man to go into orbit; one of my most prized possessions is Gagarin's autobiography, inscribed, "This souvenir of our meeting in Ceylon, 11.12.61." Years later, at Star City, I stood in Gagarin's office—exactly as he left it for that fatal training flight, with the clock on the wall stopped at the moment of his death.

When we first met, Bill MacQuitty had just produced the definitive film of the *Titanic* disaster, *A Night to Remember;* he had a special feeling for the subject, because as a boy in Belfast he had watched the ship's launching. Later, he made a determined, but unsuccessful, effort to bring *A Fall of Moondust* to the screen. Failing to film submarine operations on the moon, he returned to Earth with *Above Us the Waves*—the story of the British Navy's attack on the battleship *Turpitz*. He also used Ceylon—where he had worked as a bank official in the thirties—as the background for *The Beachcomber,* a Somerset Maugham tale of colonial days starring that splendid ham, Robert Newton. ("The last film," Bill told me, "in which Bob was—mostly—sober.")

All this may seem a little irrelevant, but it isn't. Because the man who watched the *Titanic* slide down the slipways in 1910, and might have caught me before Stanley Kubrick, has just walked into my office with the first volume of his autobiography. And I'm breaking one of my most ironclad rules, by writing an introduction. . . .

I haven't quite finished. The week after Bill MacQuitty leaves Colombo, the man who *will* (touch wood) finally be filming *A Fall of Moondust* is to arrive, to discuss salvage operations on the moon.

And to make matters even more complicated, I am working on a novel about the *Titanic*'s centennial, in the rapidly approaching year 2012. I raised her once in *Imperial Earth,* but now that Robert Ballard and his team have rediscovered her, it's time to go back to the Grand Banks.

I

Tibor didn't see the thing. He was asleep, and dreaming his inevitable painful dream.

Only Joey was awake on deck, in the cool stillness before dawn, when the meteor came flaming out of the sky above New Guinea. He watched it climb up the heavens until it passed directly overhead, routing the stars and throwing swift-moving shadows across the crowded deck. The harsh light outlined the bare rigging, the coiled ropes and air-hoses, the copper diving-helmets neatly snugged down for the night—even the low, pandanus-clad island half a mile away. As it passed into the southwest, out over the emptiness of the Pacific, it began to disintegrate.

Incandescent globules broke off, burning and guttering in a trail of fire that stretched a quarter of the way across the sky. It was already dying when it raced out of sight. But Joey did not see its end. Still blazing furiously, it sank below the horizon, as if seeking to hurl itself into the face of the hidden sun.

If the sight was spectacular, the utter silence was unnerving. Joey waited and waited and waited, but no sound came from the riven heavens. When, minutes later, there was a sudden splash from the sea, close at hand he gave an involuntary start of surprise—then cursed himself for being frightened by a manta. (A mighty big one, though, to have made so much noise when it jumped.) There was no other sound, and presently he went back to sleep.

In his narrow bunk just aft of the air compressor, Tibor heard nothing. He slept so soundly after his day's work that he had little energy even for dreams. And when they came, they were not the dreams he wanted. In the hours of darkness, as his mind roamed back and forth across the past, it never came to rest amid memories of desire. He had women in Sydney and Brisbane and Darwin and Thursday Island—but none in his dreams. All that he ever remembered when he woke, in the fetid stillness of the cabin, was the dust and fire and blood as the Russian tanks rolled into Budapest. His dreams were not of love, but only of hate.

When Nick shook him back to consciousness, he was dodging the guards on the Austrian border. It took him a few seconds to make the ten-thousand-mile journey to the Great Barrier Reef. Then he yawned, kicked away the cockroaches that had been nibbling at his toes and heaved himself out of his bunk.

Breakfast, of course, was the same as always—rice, turtle eggs and bully-beef, washed down with strong, sweet tea. The best that could be said of Joey's cooking was that there was plenty of it. Tibor was used to the monotonous diet. He made up for it, and for other deprivations, when he was back on the mainland.

The sun had barely cleared the horizon when the dishes were stacked in the tiny galley and the lugger got under way. Nick sounded cheerful as he took the wheel and headed out from the island. The old pearling-master had every right to be, for the patch of shell they were working was the richest that Tibor had ever seen. With any luck, they would fill their hold in another day or two, and sail back to T.I. with half a ton of shell on board. And then, with a little more luck, he could give up this stinking, dangerous job and get back to civilization.

Not that he regretted anything. The Greek had treated him well, and he'd found some good stones when the shells were opened. But he understood now, after nine months on the Reef, why the number of white divers could be counted on the fingers of one hand. Japs and Kanakas and Islanders could take it— but damn few Europeans.

The diesel coughed into silence and the *Arafura* coasted to rest.

They were some two miles from the island, which lay low and green on the water, yet sharply divided from it by its narrow band of dazzling beach. It was no more than a nameless sand bar that a tiny forest had managed to capture. Its only inhabitants were the myriads of stupid muttonbirds that riddled the soft ground with their burrows and made the night hideous with their banshee cries.

There was little talk as the three divers dressed. Each man knew what to do, and wasted no time in doing it. As Tibor buttoned on his thick twill jacket, Blanco, his tender, rinsed out the faceplate with vinegar so that it would not become fogged. Then Tibor clambered down the rope ladder, while the heavy helmet and lead corselet were placed over his head.

Apart from the jacket, whose padding spread the weight evenly over his shoulders, he was wearing his ordinary clothes. In these warm waters there was no need for rubber suits. The helmet simply acted as a tiny diving-bell held in position by its weight alone. In an emergency the wearer could—if he was lucky—duck out of it and swim back to the surface unhampered. Tibor had seen this done. But he had no wish to try the experiment for himself.

Each time he stood on the last rung of the ladder, gripping his shell-bag with one hand and his safety line with the other, the same thought flashed through Tibor's mind. He was leaving the world he knew; but was it for an hour—or was it forever?

Down there on the sea bed was wealth and death, and one could be sure of neither. The chances were that this would be another day of uneventful drudgery, as were most of the days in the pearl-diver's unglamorous life. But Tibor had seen one of his mates die, when his air-hose tangled in the *Arafura*'s prop. And he had watched the agony of another, as his body twisted with the bends. In the sea, nothing was ever safe or certain. You took your chances with open eyes.

And if you lost there was no point in whining.

He stepped back from the ladder, and the world of sun and sky ceased to exist. Top-heavy with the weight of his helmet, he had to back-pedal furiously to keep his body upright. He could see nothing but a featureless blue mist as he sank towards the bottom. He hoped that Blanco would not play out the safety line too quickly. Swallowing and snorting, he tried to clear his ears as the pressure mounted. The right one "popped" quickly enough, but a piercing, intolerable pain grew rapidly in the left, which had bothered him for several days. He forced his hand up under the helmet, gripped his nose and blew with all his might. There was an abrupt, soundless explosion somewhere inside his head, and the pain vanished instantly. He'd have no more trouble on this dive.

Tibor felt the bottom before he saw it.

Unable to bend over lest he risk flooding the open helmet, his vision in the downwards direction was very limited. He could see around, but not immediately below. What he did see was reassuring in its drab monotony—a gently undulating, muddy plain that faded out of sight about ten feet ahead. A yard to his left a tiny fish was nibbling at a piece of coral the size and shape of a lady's fan. That was all. There was no beauty, no underwater fairyland here. But there was money. That was what mattered.

The safety line gave a gentle pull as the lugger started to drift downwind, moving broadside-on across the patch, and Tibor began to walk forward with the springy, slow-motion step forced on him by weightlessness and water resistance. As Number Two diver, he was working from the bow. Amidships was Stephen, still comparatively inexperienced, while at the stern was the head diver, Billy. The three men seldom saw each other while they were working; each had his own lane to search as the *Arafura* drifted silently before the wind. Only at the extremes of their zigzags might they sometimes glimpse one another as dim shapes looming through the mist.

It needed a trained eye to spot the shells beneath their camouflage of algae and weeds, but often the molluscs betrayed themselves. When they felt the vibrations of the approaching diver, they would snap shut—and there would be a momentary, nacreous flicker in the gloom. Yet even then they sometimes escaped, for the moving ship might drag the diver past before he could collect the prize just out of reach. In the early days of his apprenticeship, Tibor had missed quite a few of the big silver-lips, any one of which might have contained some fabulous pearl. Or so he had imagined, before the glamor of the profession had worn off, and he realized that pearls were so rare that you might as well forget them.

The most valuable stone he'd ever brought up had been sold for twenty pounds, and the shell he gathered on a good morning was worth more than that. If the industry had depended on gems instead of mother-of-pearl, it would have gone broke years ago.

There was no sense of time in this world of mist. You walked beneath the invisible, drifting ship, with the throb of the air compressor pounding in your ears, the green haze moving past your eyes. At long intervals you would spot a shell, wrench it from the sea bed and drop it in your bag. If you were lucky, you might gather a couple of dozen on a single drift across the patch. On the other hand, you might not find a single one.

You were alert for danger, but not worried by it. The real risks were simple, unspectacular things like tangled air-hoses or safety lines—not sharks, groupers or octopi. Sharks ran when they saw your air bubbles, and in all his hours of diving Tibor had seen just one octopus, every bit of two feet across. As for groupers—well, *they* were to be taken seriously, for they could swallow a diver at one gulp if they felt hungry enough. But there was little chance of meeting them on this flat and desolate plain. There were none of the coral caves in which they could make their homes.

The shock would not have been so great, therefore, if this uniform, level grayness had not lulled him into a sense of security.

At one moment he was walking steadily towards an unreachable wall of mist, that retreated as fast as he approached. And then, without warning, his private nightmare was looming above him.

II

Tibor hated spiders, and there was a certain creature in the sea that seemed deliberately contrived to take advantage of that phobia. He had never met one, and his mind had always shied away from the thought of such an encounter, but Tibor knew that the Japanese spider crab can span twelve feet across its spindly legs. That it was harmless mattered not in the least. A spider as big as a man simply had no right to exist.

As soon as he saw that cage of slender, jointed limbs emerge from the all-encompassing grayness, Tibor began to scream with uncontrollable terror. He never remembered jerking his safety line, but Blanco reacted with the instantaneous perception of the ideal tender. His helmet still echoing to his screams, Tibor felt himself snatched from the sea bed, lifted towards light and air—and sanity. As he swept upwards, he saw both the strangeness and the absurdity of his mistake, and regained a measure of control. But he was still trembling so violently when Blanco lifted off his helmet that it was some time before he could speak.

"What the hell's going on here?" demanded Nick. "Everyone knocking off work early?"

It was then that Tibor realized that he was not the first to come up. Stephen was sitting amidships, smoking a cigarette and looking completely unconcerned. The stern diver, doubtless wondering what had happened, was being hauled up willy-nilly by his tender, since the *Arafura* had come to rest and all operations had been suspended until the trouble was resolved.

"There's some kind of wreck down there," said Tibor. "I ran right into it. All I could see were a lot of wires and rods."

To his annoyance and self-contempt, the memory set him trembling again.

"Don't see why *that* should give you the shakes," grumbled Nick. Nor could Tibor—here on this sun-drenched deck. It was impossible to explain how a harmless shape glimpsed through the mist could set one's whole mind jangling with terror.

"I nearly got hung up on it," he lied. "Blanco pulled me clear just in time."

"Hmm," said Nick, obviously not convinced. "Anyway, it ain't a ship." He gestured towards the midships diver. "Steve ran into a mess of ropes and cloth—like thick nylon, he says. Sounds like some kind of parachute." The old Greek stared in disgust at the soggy stump of his cigar, then flicked it overboard. "Soon as Billy's up, we'll go back and take a look. Might be worth something—remember what happened to Jo Chambers."

• • •

Tibor remembered; the story was famous the length of the Great Barrier Reef. Jo had been a lone-wolf fisherman who, in the last months of the War, had spotted a DC-3 lying in shallow water a few miles off the Queensland coast. After prodigies of single-handed salvage, he had broken into the fuselage and started unloading boxes of taps and dies, perfectly protected by their greased wrappings. For a while he had run a flourishing import business, but when the police caught up with him he reluctantly revealed his source of supply. Australian cops can be very persuasive.

And it was then, after weeks and weeks of backbreaking underwater work, that Jo discovered what his DC-3 had been carrying besides the miserable few thousand dollars' worth of tools he had been flogging to garages and workshops on the mainland.

The big wooden crates he'd never got round to opening held a week's payroll for the U.S. Pacific Forces.

No such luck here, thought Tibor as he sank over the side again. But the aircraft—or whatever it was—might contain valuable instruments, and there could be a reward for its discovery. Besides, he owed it to himself. He wanted to see exactly what it was that had given him such a fright.

Ten minutes later, he knew it was no aircraft. It was the wrong shape, and it was much too small—only about twenty feet long and half that in width. Here and there on the gently-tapering body were access hatches and tiny ports through which unknown instruments peered at the world. It seemed unharmed, though one end had been fused as if by terrific heat. From the other sprouted a tangle of antennae, all of them broken or bent by the impact with the water. Even now, they bore an incredible resemblance to the legs of a giant insect.

Tibor was no fool. He guessed at once what the thing was. Only one problem remained, and he solved that with little difficulty. Though they had been partly charred away by heat, stenciled words could still be read on some of the hatch-covers. The letters were Cyrillic, and Tibor knew enough Russian to pick out references to electrical supplies and pressurizing systems.

"So they've lost a sputnik," he told himself with satisfaction.

He could imagine what had happened. The thing had come down too fast, and in the wrong place. Around one end were the tattered remnants of flotation bags; they had burst under the impact, and the vehicle had sunk like a stone.

The *Arafura*'s crew would have to apologize to Joey. He hadn't been drinking grog. What he'd seen burning across the stars must have been the rocket carrier, separated from its payload and falling back unchecked into the Earth's atmosphere.

For a long time Tibor hovered on the sea bed, knees bent in the diver's crouch, as he regarded this space creature now trapped in an alien element. His mind was full of half-formed plans, but none had yet come clearly into focus.

He no longer cared about salvage money. Much more important were the prospects of revenge.

Here was one of the proudest creations of Soviet technology—and Szabo Tibor, late of Budapest, was the only man on earth who knew.

There must be some way of exploiting the situation—of doing harm to the country and the cause he now hated with such smoldering intensity. In his waking hours, he was seldom conscious of that hate. Still less did he ever stop to analyze its real cause. Here in this lonely world of sea and sky, of steaming mangrove swamps and dazzling coral strands, there was nothing to recall the past. Yet he could never escape it. And sometimes the demons in his mind would awake, lashing him into a fury of rage or vicious, wanton destructiveness. So far he had been lucky; he had not killed anyone. But some day . . .

An anxious jerk from Blanco interrupted his reveries of vengeance.

He gave a reassuring signal to his tender, and started a closer examination of the capsule. What did it weigh? Could it be hoisted easily? There were many things he had to discover, before he could settle on any definite plans.

He braced himself against the corrugated metal wall and pushed cautiously. There was a definite movement as the capsule rocked on the sea bed. Maybe it could be lifted, even with the few pieces of tackle that the *Arafura* could muster. It was probably lighter than it looked.

Tibor pressed his helmet against a flat section of the hull, and listened intently.

He had half expected to hear some mechanical noise, such as the whirring of electric motors. Instead, there was utter silence. With the hilt of his knife, he rapped sharply on the metal, trying to gauge its thickness and to locate any weak spots. On the third try, he got results: but they were not what he had anticipated.

In a furious, desperate tattoo, the capsule rapped back at him.

Until this moment, Tibor had never dreamed that there might be someone inside. The capsule had seemed far too small.

Then he realized that he had been thinking in terms of conventional aircraft. There was plenty of room here for a little pressure cabin in which a dedicated astronaut could spend a few cramped hours.

As a kaleidoscope can change its pattern completely in a single moment, so the half-formed plans in Tibor's mind dissolved and then crystallized into a new shape. Behind the thick glass of his helmet, he ran his tongue lightly across his lips. If Nick could have seen him now, he would have wondered—as he had sometimes done before—whether his Number Two diver was

wholly sane. Gone were all thoughts of a remote and impersonal vengeance against something as abstract as a nation or a
machine.

Now it would be man to man.

III

"Took your time, didn't you?" said Nick. "What did you
find?"

"It's Russian," said Tibor. "Some kind of sputnik. If we get a
rope around it, I think we can lift it off the bottom. But it's too
heavy to get aboard."

Nick chewed thoughtfully on his eternal cigar.

The pearling master was worried about a point that had not
occurred to Tibor. If there were any salvage operations round
here, everyone would know where the *Arafura* had been drifting. When the news got back to Thursday Island, his private
patch of shell would be cleaned out in no time.

They'd have to keep quiet about the whole affair, or else haul
the damn thing up themselves and not say where they'd found
it. Whatever happened, it looked like being more of a nuisance
than it was worth. Nick, who shared most Australians' profound suspicion of authority, had already decided that all he'd
get for his trouble would be a nice letter of thanks.

"The boys won't go down," he said. "They think it's a bomb.
Want to leave it alone."

"Tell 'em not to worry," replied Tibor. "I'll handle it."

He tried to keep his voice normal and unemotional, but this
was too good to be true. If the other divers heard the tapping
from the capsule, his plans would have been frustrated.

He gestured to the island, green and lovely on the skyline.

"Only one thing we can do. If we can heave it a couple of feet
off the bottom, we can run for the shore. Once we're in shallow
water, it won't be too hard to haul it up on the beach. We can

use the boats, and maybe get a block and tackle on one of those trees."

Nick considered the idea without much enthusiasm. He doubted if they could get the sputnik through the reef, even on the leeward side of the island. But he was all in favor of lugging it away from this patch of shell. They could always dump it somewhere else, buoy the place and still get whatever credit was going.

"Okay," he said. "Down you go. That two-inch rope's the strongest we've got—better take that. Don't be all bloody day; we've lost enough time already."

Tibor had no intention of being all day. Six hours would be quite long enough. That was one of the first things he had learned, from the signals through the wall.

It was a pity that he could not hear the Russian's voice; but the Russian could hear him, and that was what really mattered. When he pressed his helmet against the metal and shouted, most of his words got through. So far, it had been a friendly conversation; Tibor had no intention of showing his hand until the right psychological moment.

The first move had been to establish a code—one knock for "Yes," two for "No." After that, it was merely a matter of framing suitable questions. Given time, there was no fact or idea that could not be communicated by means of these two signals.

It would have been a much tougher job if Tibor had been forced to use his indifferent Russian. He had been pleased, but not surprised, to find that the trapped pilot understood English perfectly.

There was air in the capsule for another five hours; the occupant was uninjured; yes, the Russians knew where it had come down.

That last reply gave Tibor pause. Perhaps the pilot was lying, but it might very well be true. Although something had obviously gone wrong with the planned return to Earth, the tracking ships out in the Pacific must have located the impact point—with what accuracy, he could not guess. Still, did that matter? It might take them days to get here, even if they came racing straight into Australian territorial waters without bothering to get permission from Canberra. He was master of the situation. The entire might of the U.S.S.R. could do nothing to interfere with his plans until it was much too late.

The heavy rope fell in coils on the sea-bed, stirring up a cloud of silt that drifted like smoke down the slow current. Now that the sun was higher in the sky, the underwater world was no longer wrapped in a gray, twilight gloom. The sea-bed was colorless but bright, and the boundary of vision was now almost fifteen feet away.

For the first time, Tibor could see the space-capsule in its entirety. It was such a peculiar-looking object, being designed for conditions beyond all normal experience, that there was an eye-teasing wrongness about it. One searched in vain for a front or a rear. There was no way of telling in what direction it pointed as it sped along its orbit.

Tibor pressed his helmet against the metal and shouted.

"I'm back," he called. "Can you hear me?"

Tap.

"I've got a rope, and I'm going to tie it on to the parachute cables. We're about three kilometers from an island. As soon as we've made you fast we'll head towards it. We can't lift you out of the water with the gear on the lugger, so we'll try to get you up on the beach. You understand?"

Tap.

It took only a few moments to secure the rope; now he had better get clear before the *Arafura* started to lift.

But there was something he had to do first.

"Hello!" he shouted. "I've fixed the rope. We'll lift in a minute. D'you hear me?"

Tap.

"Then you can hear this too. You'll never get there alive. I've fixed *that* as well."

Tap, tap.

"You've got five hours to die. My brother took longer than that, when he ran into your mine field. You understand? I'm from Budapest! I hate you and your country and everything it stands for. You've taken my home, my family, made my people slaves. I wish I could see your face now! I wish I could watch you die, as I had to watch Theo. When you're halfway to the island, this rope is going to break where I cut it. I'll go down and fix another—and that'll break, too. You can sit in there and wait for the bumps."

Tibor stopped abruptly, shaken and exhausted by the violence of his emotion.

There was no room for logic or reason in this orgasm of hate. He did not pause to think, for he dared not. Yet somewhere far down inside his mind the real truth was burning its way up towards the light of consciousness.

It was not the Russians he hated, for all that they had done. It was himself, for he had done more.

The blood of Theo, and of ten thousand countrymen, was upon his own hands. No one could have been a better communist than he was, or have more supinely believed the propaganda from Moscow. At school and college, he had been the first to hunt out and denounce "traitors" (how many had he sent to the labor camps or the AVO torture chambers?). When he had seen the truth, it was far, far too late. And even then he had not fought. He had run.

He had run across the world, trying to escape his guilt; and the two drugs of danger and dissipation had helped him to forget the past. The only pleasures life gave him now were the loveless embraces he sought so feverishly when he was on the mainland, and his present mode of existence was proof that these were not enough.

If he now had the power to deal out death, it was only because he had come here in search of it himself.

There was no sound from the capsule. Its silence seemed contemptuous, mocking. Angrily, Tibor banged against it with the hilt of his knife.

"Did you hear me?" he shouted. "Did you hear me?"

No answer.

"Damn you! I know you're listening! If you don't answer, I'll hole you and let the water in!"

He was sure that he could, with the sharp point of his knife. But that was the last thing he wanted to do; that would be too quick, too easy an ending.

There was still no sound; maybe the Russian had fainted. Tibor hoped not, but there was no point in waiting any longer. He gave a vicious parting bang on the capsule, and signaled to his tender.

Nick had news for him when he broke the surface.

"T.I. radio's been squawking," he said. "The Ruskis are asking everyone to look out for one of their rockets. They say it should be floating somewhere off the Queensland coast. Sounds as if they want it badly."

"Did they say anything else about it?" Tibor asked anxiously.

"Oh, yes. It's been round the Moon a couple of times."

"That all?"

"Nothing else that I remember. There was a lot of science stuff I didn't get."

That figured; it was just like the Russians to keep as quiet as they could about an experiment that had gone wrong.

"You tell T.I. that we'd found it?"

"Are you crazy? Anyway, the radio's crook; couldn't if we wanted to. Fixed that rope properly?"

"Yes—see if you can haul her off the bottom."

The end of the rope had been wound round the mainmast, and in a few seconds it had been drawn taut. Although the sea was calm, there was a slight swell and the lugger was rolling ten or fifteen degrees. With each roll, the gunwales would rise a couple of feet, then drop again. There was a lift here of several tons, but one had to be careful in using it.

The rope twanged, the woodwork groaned and creaked, and for a moment Tibor was afraid that the weakened line would part too soon. But it held, and the load lifted.

They got a further hoist on the second roll—and on the third. Then the capsule was clear of the sea-bed, and the *Arafura* was listing slightly to port.

"Let's go," said Nick, taking the wheel. "Should be able to get her half a mile before she bumps again."

The lugger began to move slowly towards the island, carrying its hidden burden beneath it.

As he leaned on the rails, letting the sun steam the moisture from his sodden clothing, Tibor felt at peace for the first time in—how many months? Even his hate had ceased to burn like fire in his brain. Perhaps, like love, it was a passion that could never be satisfied. But for the moment, at least, it was satiated.

There was no weakening of his resolve. He was implacably set upon the vengeance that had been so strangely—so miraculously—placed within his power. Blood called for blood, and now the ghosts that haunted him might rest at last.

IV

He began to worry when they were two-thirds of the way to the island, and the rope had not parted.

There were still four hours to go. That was much too long. For the first time it occurred to him that his entire plan might miscarry, and might even recoil on his head. Suppose that, despite everything, Nick managed to get the capsule up on the beach before the deadline?

With a deep *twang* that set the whole ship vibrating, the rope came snaking out of the water, scattering spray in all directions.

"Might have guessed," muttered Nick. "She was just starting to bump. You like to go down again, or shall I send one of the boys?"

"I'll take it," Tibor hastily answered. "I can do it quicker than they can."

That was perfectly true, but it took him twenty minutes to locate the capsule. The *Arafura* had drifted well away from it before Nick could stop the engine, and there was a time when Tibor wondered if he would ever find it again.

He quartered the sea-bed in great arcs, and it was not until he had accidentally tangled in the trailing parachute that his search was ended. The shrouds lay pulsating slowly in the current like some weird and hideous marine monster—but there was nothing that Tibor feared now except frustration, and his pulse barely quickened as he saw the whitely looming mass ahead.

The capsule was scratched and stained with mud, but appeared undamaged. It was lying on its side now, looking rather like a giant milk-churn that had been tipped over. The passenger must have been bumped around. But if he'd fallen all the way back from the Moon he must have been well padded and was probably still in good shape. Tibor hoped so. It would be a pity if the remaining three hours were wasted.

Once again he rested the verdigrised copper of his helmet against the no-longer-quite-so-brightly-gleaming metal of the capsule.

"Hello!" he shouted. "Can you hear me?"

Perhaps the Russian would try to balk him by remaining silent—but that surely, was asking too much of any man's self-control. Tibor was right. Almost at once there was the sharp knock of the reply.

"So glad you're there," he called back. "Things are working out just the way I said, though I guess I'll have to cut the rope a little deeper."

The capsule did not answer it. It never answered again, though Tibor banged and banged on the next dive—and on the next.

But he hardly expected it to then, for they'd had to stop for a couple of hours to ride out a squall, and the time-limit had expired long before he made his final descent.

He was a little annoyed about that, for he had planned a farewell message. He shouted it just the same, though he knew he was wasting his breath.

By early afternoon, the *Arafura* had come in as close as she dared. There were only a few feet of water beneath her, and the tide was falling. The capsule broke surface at the bottom of each wave trough, and was now firmly stranded on a sandbank. There was no hope of moving it any further. It was stuck until a high sea disloged it.

Nick regarded the situation with an expert eye.

"There's a six-foot tide tonight," he said. "The way she's lying now, she'll be in only a couple of feet of water at low. We'll be able to get at her with the boats."

They waited off the sandbank while the sun and the tide went down and the radio broadcast intermittent reports of a search that was coming closer but was still far away. Late in the afternoon the capsule was almost clear of the water. The crew rowed the small boat towards it with a reluctance which Tibor found himself sharing, to his annoyance.

"It's got a door in the side," said Nick suddenly. "Jeeze—think there's anyone in it?"

"Could be," answered Tibor, his voice not as steady as he thought.

Nick glanced at him curiously. His diver had been acting strangely all day, but he knew better than to ask him what was wrong. In this part of the world, you soon learned to mind your own business.

The boat, rocking slightly in the choppy sea, had now come alongside the capsule. Nick reached out and grabbed one of the twisted antenna stubs. Then, with catlike agility, he clambered up the curved metal surface. Tibor made no attempt to follow him, but watched silently from the boat as he examined the entrance hatch.

"Unless it's jammed," Nick muttered, "there must be some way of opening it from outside. Just our luck if it needs special tools."

His fears were groundless. The word "Open" had been stencilled in ten languages round the recessed doorcatch, and it took only seconds to deduce its mode of operation. As the air hissed out Nick said "Phew!" and turned suddenly pale. He looked at Tibor as if seeking support, but Tibor avoided his eye.

Then, reluctantly, Nick lowered himself into the capsule.

He was gone for a long time. At first, they could hear muffled bangings and bumpings from the inside, followed by a string of bi-lingual profanity.

And then there was a silence that went on and on and on.

When at last Nick's head appeared above the hatchway, his leathery, wind-tanned face was gray and streaked with tears. As Tibor saw this incredible sight, he felt a sudden ghastly premonition. Something had gone horribly wrong, but his mind was too numb to anticipate the truth. It came soon enough, when

Nick handed down his burden, no larger than an oversized doll.

Blanco took it, as Tibor shrank to the stern of the boat.

As he looked at the calm, waxen face, fingers of ice seemed to close not only upon his heart, but round his loins. In the same moment, both hate and desire died forever within him, as he knew the price of his revenge.

The dead astronaut was perhaps more beautiful in death than she had been in life. Tiny though she was, she must have been tough as well as highly-trained to qualify for this mission. As she lay at Tibor's feet she was neither a Russian, nor the first female human being to have seen the far side of the Moon. She was merely the girl that he had killed.

Nick was talking from a long way off.

"She was carrying this," he said, in an unsteady voice. "Had it tight in her hand. Took me a long time to get it out."

Tibor scarcely heard him, and never even glanced at the tiny spool of tape lying in Nick's palm. He could not guess, in this moment beyond all feeling, that the Furies had yet to close in upon his soul—and that soon the whole world would be listening to an accusing voice from beyond the grave, branding him more irrevocably than any man since Cain.

PUBLICITY
CAMPAIGN

THIS STORY WAS WRITTEN IN MARCH 1953 AND AFTER prompt publication in the London *Evening News* took three years to cross the Atlantic, appearing in *Satellite Science Fiction*'s first issue (October 1956). According to the *Science Fiction Encyclopaedia,* each of the first five issues contained stories of mine; I am ashamed to confess that I'd forgotten the magazine's very existence. . . .

Although the references in the story are somewhat dated, the questions it raises are certainly not. And by a curious coincidence, I reread it the very week the media are ruefully celebrating the fiftieth anniversary of Orson Welles's famous "War of the Worlds" broadcast (CBS's *Mercury Theatre of the Air,* 31 October 1938.)

For the first few decades after the Martians lowered New Jersey real estate values, benevolent aliens were few and far between, perhaps the most notable example being Klatuu in *The Day the Earth Stood Still.* Yet nowadays, largely thanks to *E.T.,* friendly and even cuddly aliens are taken almost for granted. Where does the truth lie?

In recent years, the total absence of any genuine evidence for life elsewhere has prompted a number of scientists to argue that intelligence is very rare in the universe. Some (such as Frank Tipler) have gone so far as to argue that we are completely alone—a proposition that can never be proved, but only disproved. (Wasn't it Pogo who said, "Either way, it's a staggering thought"?)

Of course, hostile and malevolent aliens make for much more exciting stories than benevolent ones. Moreover, the Things You Wouldn't Like to Meet of the 1950s and 60s, as has often been pointed out, were reflections of the paranoia at that time, particularly in the United States. Now that the Cold War has, hopefully, given way to the Tepid Truce, we may look at the skies with less apprehension.

For we have already met Darth Vader—and he is us.

The concussion of the last atom bomb still seemed to linger as the lights came on again. For a long time, no one moved. Then the assistant producer said innocently: "Well, R.B., what do you think of it?"

R.B. heaved himself out of his seat while his acolytes waited to see which way the cat would jump. It was then that they noticed that R.B.'s cigar had gone out. Why, that hadn't happened even at the preview of "G.W.T.W."!

"Boys," he said ecstatically, "we've got something here! How much did you say it cost, Mike?"

"Six and a half million, R.B."

"It was cheap at the price. Let me tell you, I'll eat every foot of it if the gross doesn't beat *Quo Vadis.*" He wheeled, as swiftly as could be expected for one of his bulk, upon a small man still crouched in his seat at the back of the projection room. "Snap out of it, Joe! The Earth's saved! You've seen all these space films. How does this line up with the earlier ones?"

Joe came to with an obvious effort.

"There's no comparison," he said. "It's got all the suspense of *The Thing,* without that awful letdown at the end when you saw the monster was human. The only picture that comes within miles of it is *War of the Worlds*. Some of the effects in that were nearly as good as ours, but of course George Pal didn't have 3D. And that sure makes a difference! When the Golden Gate Bridge went down, I thought that pier was going to hit me!"

"The bit I liked best," put in Tony Auerbach from Publicity, "was when the Empire State Building split right up the middle. You don't suppose the owners might sue us, though?"

"Of course not. No one expects *any* building to stand up to—what did the script call them?—city busters. And, after all, we wiped out the rest of New York as well. Ugh—that scene in the Holland Tunnel when the roof gave way! Next time, I'll take the ferry!"

"Yes, that was very well done—almost *too* well done. But what really got me was those creatures from space. The animation was perfect—how did you do it, Mike?"

"Trade secret," said the proud producer. "Still, I'll let you in on it. A lot of that stuff is genuine."

"What!"

"Oh, don't get me wrong! We haven't been on location to Sirius B. But they've developed a microcamera over at Cal Tech, and we used that to film spiders in action. We cut in the best shots, and I think you'd have a job telling which was micro and which was the full-sized studio stuff. Now you understand why I wanted the Aliens to be insects, and not octopuses, like the script said first."

"There's a good publicity angle here," said Tony. "One thing worries me, though. That scene where the monsters kidnap Gloria. Do you suppose the censor . . . I mean the way we've done it, it almost looks . . ."

"Aw, quit worrying! *That's* what people are supposed to think! Anyway, we make it clear in the next reel that they really want her for dissection, so that's all right."

"It'll be a riot!" gloated R.B., a faraway gleam in his eye as if he was already hearing the avalanche of dollars pouring into the box office. "Look—we'll put another million into publicity! I can just see the posters—get all this down, Tony. WATCH THE SKY! THE SIRIANS ARE COMING! And we'll make thousands of clockwork models—can't you imagine them scuttling around on their hairy legs! People love to be scared, and we'll scare them. By the time we've finished, no one will be able to look at the sky without getting the creeps! I leave it to you, boys—this picture is going to make *history*!"

He was right. *Monsters from Space* hit the public two months later. Within a week of the simultaneous London and New York *premières,* there could have been no one in the western world who had not seen the posters screaming EARTH BEWARE! or had not shuddered at the photographs of the hairy horrors stalking along deserted Fifth Avenue on their thin, many-jointed legs. Blimps cleverly disguised as spaceships cruised across the skies, to the vast confusion of pilots who encountered them, and clockwork models of the Alien invaders were everywhere, scaring old ladies out of their wits.

The publicity campaign was brilliant, and the picture would undoubtedly have run for months had it not been for a coincidence as disastrous as it was unforeseeable. While the number of people fainting at each performance was still news, the skies of Earth filled suddenly with long, lean shadows sliding swiftly through the clouds. . . .

Prince Zervashni was good-natured but inclined to be impetuous—a well-known failing of his race. There was no reason to suppose that his present mission, that of making peaceful contact with the planet Earth, would present any particular problems. The correct technique of approach had been thoroughly worked out over many thousands of years, as the Third Galactic Empire slowly expanded its frontiers, absorbing planet after planet, sun upon sun. There was seldom any trouble: really intelligent races can always cooperate, once they have got over the initial shock of learning that they are not alone in the universe.

It was true that humanity had emerged from its primitive, warlike stage only within the last generation. This, however, did not worry Prince Zervashni's chief adviser, Sigisnin II, Professor of Astropolitics.

"It's a perfectly typical Class E culture," said the professor. "Technically advanced, morally rather backward. However, they are already used to the conception of space flight, and will soon take us for granted. The normal precautions will be sufficient until we have won their confidence."

"Very well," said the prince. "Tell the envoys to leave at once."

It was unfortunate that the "normal precautions" did not allow for Tony Auerbach's publicity campaign, which had now reached new heights of interplanetary xenophobia. The ambassadors landed in New York's Central Park on the very day that a prominent astronomer, unusually hard up and therefore amenable to influence, announced in a widely reported interview that any visitors from space probably would be unfriendly.

The luckless ambassadors, heading for the United Nations Building, had got as far south as 60th Street when they met the mob. The encounter was very one-sided, and the scientists at the Museum of Natural History were most annoyed that there was so little left for them to examine.

Prince Zervashni tried once more, on the other side of the planet, but the news had got there first. This time the ambassadors were armed, and gave a good account of themselves before they were overwhelmed by sheer numbers. Even so, it was not until the rocket bombs started climbing up toward his fleet that the prince finally lost his temper and decided to take drastic action.

It was all over in twenty minutes, and was really quite painless. Then the prince turned to his adviser and said, with considerable understatement: "That appears to be that. And now—can you tell me exactly what went wrong?"

Sigisnin II knitted his dozen flexible fingers together in acute anguish. It was not only the spectacle of the neatly disinfected Earth that distressed him, though to a scientist the destruction of such a beautiful specimen is always a major tragedy. At least equally upsetting was the demolition of his theories and, with them, his reputation.

"I just don't understand it!" he lamented. "Of course, races at this level of culture are often suspicious and nervous when contact is first made. But they'd never had visitors before, so there was no reason for them to be hostile."

"Hostile! They were demons! I think they were all insane." The prince turned to his captain, a tripedal creature who looked rather like a ball of wool balanced on three knitting needles.

"Is the fleet reassembled?"

"Yes, Sire."

"Then we will return to Base at optimum speed. This planet depresses me."

On the dead and silent Earth, the posters still screamed their warnings from a thousand hoardings. The malevolent insectile shapes shown pouring from the skies bore no resemblance at all to Prince Zervashni, who apart from his four eyes might have been mistaken for a panda with purple fur—and who, moreover, had come from Rigel, not Sirius.

But, of course, it was now much too late to point this out.

THE
OTHER TIGER

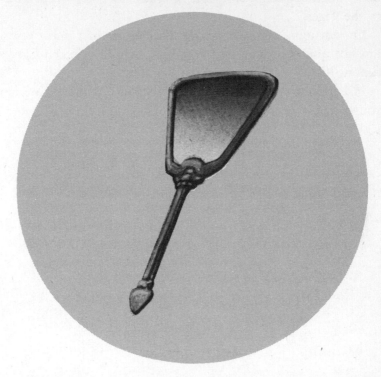

I HAD ALMOST FORGOTTEN THIS STORY UNTIL BYRON PREISS disinterred it—I did not even have a copy and never reprinted it in any of my various collections.

It was written in January 1951 and published in the first issues of *Fantastic Universe,* a magazine that appeared from 1953 to 1960 and that the invaluable *Science Fiction Encyclopaedia* neatly categorizes as "the poor man's *Magazine of Fantasy and Science Fiction.*" My original title was "Refutation" but editor Sam Merwin changed it to "The Other Tiger." This would probably have been meaningless even then to most British readers; for that matter, how many of his own countrymen now remember Frank Stockton's classic short story "The Lady or the Tiger"?

On rereading my own variant after more than thirty years, I'm not quite certain why I failed to include it in the Clarke canon. It may have been because it scared me.

It scares me even more today, for reasons I will explain after you've had a chance of reading it yourself. . . .

"It's an interesting theory," said Arnold, "but I don't see how you can ever prove it." They had come to the steepest part of the hill and for a moment Webb was too breathless to reply.

"I'm not trying to," he said when he had gained his second wind. "I'm only exploring its consequences."

"Such as?"

"Well, let's be perfectly logical and see where it gets us. Our only assumption, remember, is that the universe is infinite."

"Right. Personally I don't see what else it *can* be."

"Very well. That means there must be an infinite number of stars and planets. Therefore, by the laws of chance, every possible event must occur not merely once but an infinite number of times. Correct?"

"I suppose so."

"Then there must be an infinite number of worlds *exactly like Earth,* each with an Arnold and Webb on it, walking up this hill just as we are doing now, saying these same words."

"That's pretty hard to swallow."

"I know it's a staggering thought—but so is infinity. The thing that interests me, though, is the idea of all those other

Earths that aren't exactly the same as this one. The Earths where Hitler won the War and the Swastika flies over Buckingham Palace—the Earths where Columbus never discovered America—the Earths where the Roman Empire has existed to this day. In fact the Earths where all the great *if's* of history had different answers."

"Going right back to the beginning, I suppose, to the one in which the ape-man who would have been the daddy of us all, broke his neck before he could have any children?"

"That's the idea. But let's stick to the worlds we know—the worlds containing *us* climbing this hill on this spring afternoon. Think of all our reflections on those millions of other planets. Some of them are exactly the same but every possible variation that doesn't violate the laws of logic must also exist.

"We could—we *must*—be wearing every conceivable sort of clothes—and no clothes at all. The Sun's shining here but on countless billions of those other Earths it's not. On many it's winter or summer here instead of spring. But let's consider more fundamental changes too.

"We intend to walk up this hill and down the other side. Yet think of all the things that might possibly happen to us in the next few minutes. However improbable they may be, as long as they are *possible,* then somewhere they've got to happen."

"I see," said Arnold slowly, absorbing the idea with obvious reluctance. An expression of mild discomfort crossed his features. "Then somewhere, I suppose, you will fall dead with heart failure when you've taken your next step."

"Not in *this* world." Webb laughed. "I've already refuted it. Perhaps *you're* going to be the unlucky one."

"Or perhaps," said Arnold, "I'll get fed up with the whole conversation, pull out a gun and shoot you."

"Quite possibly," admitted Webb, "except that I'm pretty sure you, on this Earth, haven't got one. Don't forget, though, that in millions of those alternative worlds I'll beat you on the draw."

The path was now winding up a wooded slope, the trees thick on either side. The air was fresh and sweet. It was very quiet as though all Nature's energies were concentrated, with silent intentness, on rebuilding the world after the ruin of winter.

"I wonder," continued Webb, "how improbable a thing can get before it becomes impossible. We've mentioned some unlikely events but they're not completely fantastic. Here we are in an English country lane, walking along a path we know perfectly well.

"Yet in some universe those—what shall I call them?—*twins* of ours will walk around that corner and meet anything, absolutely anything that imagination can conceive. For as I said at the beginning, if the cosmos is infinite, then all possibilities must arise."

"So it's possible," said Arnold, with a laugh that was not quite as light as he had intended, "that we may walk into a tiger or something equally unpleasant."

"Of course," replied Webb cheerfully, warming to his subject. "If it's possible, then it's got to happen to someone, somewhere in the universe. So why not to us?"

Arnold gave a snort of disgust. "This is getting quite futile," he protested. "Let's talk about something sensible. If we don't meet a tiger round this corner I'll regard your theory as refuted and change the subject."

"Don't be silly," said Webb gleefully. "That won't refute anything. There's no way you can—"

They were the last words he ever spoke. On an infinite number of Earths an infinite number of Webbs and Arnolds met tigers friendly, hostile or indifferent. But this was not one of those Earths—it lay far closer to the point where improbability urged on the impossible.

Yet of course it was not totally inconceivable that during the night the rain-sodden hillside had caved inward to reveal an ominous cleft leading down into the subterranean world. As for *what* had laboriously climbed up that cleft, drawn toward the unknown light of day—well, it was really no more unlikely than the giant squid, the boa constrictor or the feral lizards of the Jurassic jungle. It had strained the laws of zoölogical probability but not to the breaking-point.

Webb had spoken the truth. In an infinite cosmos everything must happen somewhere—including their singularly bad luck. For *it* was hungry—very hungry—and a tiger or a man would have been a small yet acceptable morsel to any one of its half dozen gaping mouths.

AFTERWORD

The concept that *every possible* universe may exist is certainly not an original one, but it has recently been revised in a sophisticated form by today's theoretical physicists (insofar as I understand anything that they are talking about). It is also linked with the so-called Anthropic Principle, which now has the cosmologists in a considerable tizzy. (See Tipler and Barrow's *The Anthropic Cosmological Principle*. Even if you have to skip many pages of music, the bits of text between them are fascinating and mind-stretching.)

The anthroposists have pointed out what appear to be some peculiarities of our universe. Many of the fundamental physical constants—which as far as one could see, God could have given any value He liked—are in fact very precisely adjusted, or fine-tuned, to produce the *only* kind of universe that makes our existence possible. A few percentages either way, and we wouldn't be here.

One explanation of this mystery is that in fact all the other possible universes do exist (somewhere!) but, of course, the vast majority are lifeless. Only in an infinitesimally small fraction of the total creation are the parameters such that matter can exist, stars can form—and, ultimately, life can arise. We're here because we couldn't be anywhere else.

But all those elsewhere are *somewhere,* so my story may be uncomfortably close to the truth. Luckily, there's no way that we'll ever be able to prove it.

I think . . .

THE
DEEP RANGE

THE SHORT STORY "THE DEEP RANGE" WAS WRITTEN IN 1954, long before today's almost obsessive interest in the exploration and exploitation of the oceans. A year later, I went to the Great Barrier Reef, as recounted in *The Coast of Coral*. That adventure gave me the impetus—and background—to expand the short story into the novel of the same name, which was completed after I settled down in Ceylon (now Sri Lanka). For this reason, I have never reprinted the original tale in my own collections, and I offer the "compare and contrast" opportunity to hopeful Ph.D. candidates in Eng. Lit.

The concept of whale herding is an idea whose time has not yet come, and I wonder if it ever will. Over the last decade, whales have had such excellent PR that most Europeans and Americans would as soon eat dog- or catburgers. I *did* tackle whale meat once, during World War II: It tasted like rather rough beef.

Yet there is one product from the Deep Range that could be consumed without moral qualms. Whale milk shake, anyone?

There was a killer loose on the range. A copter patrol, five hundred miles off Greenland, had seen the great corpse staining the sea crimson as it wallowed in the waves. Within seconds, the intricate warning system had been alerted: men were plotting circles and moving counters on the North Atlantic chart—and Don Burley was still rubbing the sleep from his eyes as he dropped silently down to the twenty-fathom line.

The pattern of green lights on the tell-tale was a glowing symbol of security. As long as that pattern was unchanged, as long as none of those emerald stars winked to red, all was well with Don and his tiny craft. Air—fuel—power—this was the triumvirate which ruled his life. If any of them failed, he would be sinking in a steel coffin down toward the pelagic ooze, as Johnnie Tyndall had done the season before last. But there was no reason why they should fail; the accidents one foresaw, Don told himself reassuringly, were never the ones that happened.

He leaned across the tiny control board and spoke into the mike. Sub 5 was still close enough to the mother ship for the radio to work, but before long he'd have to switch to the sonics. "Setting course 255, speed 50 knots, depth 20 fathoms, full sonar coverage. . . . Estimated time to target area, 70 minutes. . . . Will report at 10-minute intervals. That is all. . . . Out."

The acknowledgment, already weakening with range, came back at once from the *Herman Melville*.

"Message received and understood. Good hunting. What about the hounds?"

Don chewed his lower lip thoughtfully. This might be a job he'd have to handle alone. He had no idea, to within fifty miles either way, where Benj and Susan were at the moment. They'd certainly follow if he signaled for them, but they couldn't maintain his speed and would soon have to drop behind. Besides, he might be heading for a pack of killers, and the last thing he wanted to do was to lead his carefully trained porpoises into trouble. That was common sense and good business. He was also very fond of Susan and Benj.

"It's too far, and I don't know what I'm running into," he replied. "If they're in the interception area when I get there, I may whistle them up."

The acknowledgment from the mother ship was barely audible, and Don switched off the set. It was time to look around.

He dimmed the cabin lights so that he could see the scanner screen more clearly, pulled the Polaroid glasses down over his eyes, and peered into the depths. This was the moment when Don felt like a god, able to hold within his hands a circle of the Atlantic twenty miles across, and to see clear down to the still-unexplored deeps, three thousand fathoms below. The slowly rotating beam of inaudible sound was searching the world in which he floated, seeking out friend and foe in the eternal darkness where light could never penetrate. The pattern of soundless shrieks, too shrill even for the hearing of the bats who had invented sonar a million years before man, pulsed out into the watery night: the faint echoes came tingling back as floating, blue-green flecks on the screen.

Through long practice, Don could read their message with

effortless ease. A thousand feet below, stretching out to this submerged horizon, was the scattering layer—the blanket of life that covered half the world. The sunken meadow of the sea, it rose and fell with the passage of the sun, hovering always at the edge of darkness. But the ultimate depths were no concern of his. The flocks he guarded, and the enemies who ravaged them, belonged to the upper levels of the sea.

Don flicked the switch of the depth-selector, and his sonar beam concentrated itself into the horizontal plane. The glimmering echoes from the abyss vanished, but he could see more clearly what lay around him here in the ocean's stratospheric heights. That glowing cloud two miles ahead was a school of fish; he wondered if Base knew about it, and made an entry in his log. There were some larger, isolated blips at the edge of the school—the carnivores pursuing the cattle, insuring that the endlessly turning wheel of life and death would never lose momentum. But this conflict was no affair of Don's; he was after bigger game.

Sub 5 drove on toward the west, a steel needle swifter and more deadly than any other creature that roamed the seas. The tiny cabin, lit only by the flicker of lights from the instrument board, pulsed with power as the spinning turbines thrust the water aside. Don glanced at the chart and wondered how the enemy had broken through this time. There were still many weak points, for fencing the oceans of the world had been a gigantic task. The tenuous electric fields, fanning out between generators many miles apart, could not always hold at bay the starving monsters of the deep. They were learning, too. When the fences were opened, they would sometimes slip through with the whales and wreak havoc before they were discovered.

The long-range receiver bleeped plaintively, and Don switched over the TRANSCRIBE. It wasn't practical to send speech any distance over an ultrasonic beam, and code had come back into its own. Don had never learned to read it by ear, but the ribbon of paper emerging from the slot saved him the trouble.

COPTER REPORTS SCHOOL 50–100 WHALES HEADING 95 DEGREES GRID REF X186475 Y438034 STOP. MOVING AT SPEED. STOP. MELVILLE. OUT.

Don started to set the coordinates on the plotting grid, then saw that it was no longer necessary. At the extreme edge of his screen, a flotilla of faint stars had appeared. He altered course slightly, and drove head-on toward the approaching herd.

The copter was right: they were moving fast. Don felt a mounting excitement, for this could mean that they were on the run and luring the killers toward him. At the rate at which they were traveling he would be among them in five minutes. He cut the motors and felt the backward tug of water bringing him swiftly to rest.

Don Burley, a knight in armor, sat in his tiny dim-lit room fifty feet below the bright Atlantic waves, testing his weapons for the conflict that lay ahead. In these moments of poised suspense, before action began, his racing brain often explored such fantasies. He felt a kinship with all shepherds who had guarded their flocks back to the dawn of time. He was David, among ancient Palestinian hills, alert for the mountain lions that would prey upon his father's sheep. But far nearer in time, and far closer in spirit, were the men who had marshaled the great herds of cattle on the American plains, only a few lifetimes ago. They would have understood his work, though his implements would have been magic to them. The pattern was the same; only the scale had altered. It made no fundamental difference that the beasts Don herded weighed almost a hundred tons, and browsed on the endless savannahs of the sea.

The school was now less than two miles away, and Don checked his scanner's continuous circling to concentrate on the sector ahead. The picture on the screen altered to a fan-shaped wedge as the sonar beam started to flick from side to side; now he could count every whale in the school, and even make a good estimate of its size. With a practiced eye, he began to look for stragglers.

Don could never have explained what drew him at once toward those four echoes at the southern fringe of the school. It was true that they were a little apart from the rest, but others had fallen as far behind. There is some sixth sense that a man acquires when he has stared long enough into a sonar screen— some hunch which enables him to extract more from the moving flecks than he has any right to do. Without conscious thought, Don reached for the control which would start the turbines whirling into life. Sub 5 was just getting under way when three leaden thuds reverberated through the hull, as if someone was knocking on the front door and wanted to come in.

"Well I'm damned," said Don. "How did *you* get here?" He did not bother to switch on the TV; he'd know Benj's signal anywhere. The porpoises must have been in the neighborhood and had spotted him before he'd even switched on the hunting call. For the thousandth time, he marveled at their intelligence and loyalty. It was strange that Nature had played the same trick twice—on land with the dog, in the ocean with the porpoise. Why were these graceful sea-beasts so fond of man, to whom they owed so little? It made one feel that the human race was worth something after all, if it could inspire such unselfish devotion.

It had been known for centuries that the porpoise was at least as intelligent as the dog, and could obey quite complex verbal commands. The experiment was still in progress, but if it succeeded then the ancient partnership between shepherd and sheep-dog would have a new lease on life.

Don switched on the speakers recessed into the sub's hull and began to talk to his escorts. Most of the sounds he uttered would have been meaningless to other human ears; they were the product of long research by the animal psychologists of the World Food Administration. He gave his orders twice to make sure that they were understood, then checked with the sonar screen to see that Benj and Susan were following astern as he had told them to.

The four echoes that had attracted his attention were clearer and closer now, and the main body of the whale pack had swept past him to the east. He had no fear of a collision; the great animals, even in their panic, could sense his presence as easily as he could detect theirs, and by similar means. Don wondered if he should switch on his beacon. They might recognize its sound pattern, and it would reassure them. But the still unknown enemy might recognize it too.

He closed for an interception, and hunched low over the screen as if to drag from it by sheer will power every scrap of information the scanner could give. There were two large echoes, some distance apart, and one was accompanied by a pair of smaller satellites. Don wondered if he was already too late. In his mind's eye, he could picture the death struggle taking place in the water less than a mile ahead. Those two fainter blips would be the enemy—either shark or grampus—worrying a whale while one of its companions stood by in helpless terror, with no weapons of defense except its mighty flukes.

Now he was almost close enough for vision. The TV camera in Sub 5's prow strained through the gloom, but at first could show nothing but the fog of plankton. Then a vast shadowy shape began to form in the center of the screen, with two smaller companions below it. Don was seeing, with the greater precision but hopelessly limited range of ordinary light, what the sonar scanners had already told him.

Almost at once he saw his mistake. The two satellites were calves, not sharks. It was the first time he had ever met a whale with twins; although multiple births were not unknown, a cow could suckle only two young at once and usually only the stronger would survive. He choked down his disappointment; this error had cost him many minutes and he must begin the search again.

Then came the frantic tattoo on the hull that meant danger. It wasn't easy to scare Benj, and Don shouted his reassurance as he swung Sub 5 round so that the camera could search the turgid waters. Automatically, he had turned toward the fourth blip on the sonar screen—the echo he had assumed, from its size, to be another adult whale. And he saw that, after all, he had come to the right place.

"Jesus!" he said softly. "I didn't know they came that big." He'd seen larger sharks before, but they had all been harmless vegetarians. This, he could tell at a glance, was a Greenland shark, the killer of the northern seas. It was supposed to grow up to thirty feet long, but this specimen was bigger than Sub 5. It was every inch of forty feet from snout to tail, and when he spotted it, it was already turning in toward the kill. Like the coward it was, it had launched its attack on one of the calves.

Don yelled to Benj and Susan, and saw them racing ahead into his field of vision. He wondered fleetingly why porpoises had such an overwhelming hatred of sharks; then he loosed his hands from the controls as the autopilot locked on to the target. Twisting and turning as agilely as any other sea-creature of its size, Sub 5 began to close in upon the shark, leaving Don free to concentrate on his armament.

The killer had been so intent upon his prey that Benj caught him completely unawares, ramming him just behind the left eye. It must have been a painful blow: an iron-hard snout, backed by a quarter-ton of muscle moving at fifty miles an hour, is something not to be laughed at even by the largest fish. The shark jerked round in an impossibly tight curve, and Don was almost jolted out of his seat as the sub snapped on to a new course. If this kept up, he'd find it hard to use his Sting. But at least the killer was too busy now to bother about his intended victims.

Benj and Susan were worrying the giant like dogs snapping at the heels of an angry bear. They were too agile to be caught in those ferocious jaws, and Don marveled at the coordination with which they worked. When either had to surface for air, the other would hold off for a minute until the attack could be resumed in strength.

There was no evidence that the shark realized that a far more dangerous adversary was closing in upon it, and that the porpoises were merely a distraction. That suited Don very nicely; the next operation was going to be difficult unless he could hold a steady course for at least fifteen seconds. At a pinch he could use the tiny rocket torps to make a kill. If he'd been alone, and faced with a pack of sharks he would certainly have done so. But it was messy, and there was a better way. He preferred the technique of the rapier to that of the hand-grenade.

Now he was only fifty feet away, and closing rapidly. There might never be a better chance. He punched the launching stud.

From beneath the belly of the sub, something that looked like a sting-ray hurtled forward. Don had checked the speed of his own craft; there was no need to come any closer now. The tiny, arrow-shaped hydrofoil, only a couple of feet across, could move far faster than his vessel and would close the gap in seconds. As it raced forward, it spun out the thin line of the control wire, like some underwater spider laying its thread. Along that wire passed the energy that powered the Sting, and the signals that steered it to its goal. Don had completely ignored his own larger craft in the effort of guiding this underwater missile. It responded to his touch so swiftly that he felt he was controlling some sensitive high-spirited steed.

The shark saw the danger less than a second before impact. The resemblance of the Sting to an ordinary ray confused it,

as the designers had intended. Before the tiny brain could realize that no ray behaved like this, the missile had struck. The steel hypodermic, rammed forward by an exploding cartridge, drove through the shark's horny skin, and the great fish erupted in a frenzy of terror. Don backed rapidly away, for a blow from that tail would rattle him around like a pea in a can and might even cause damage to the sub. There was nothing more for him to do, except to speak into the microphone and call off his hounds.

The doomed killer was trying to arch its body so that it could snap at the poisoned dart. Don had now reeled the Sting back into its hiding place, pleased that he had been able to retrieve the missile undamaged. He watched without pity as the great fish succumbed to its paralysis.

Its struggles were weakening. It was swimming aimlessly back and forth, and once Don had to sidestep smartly to avoid a collision. As it lost control of buoyancy, the dying shark drifted up to the surface. Don did not bother to follow; that could wait until he had attended to more important business.

He found the cow and her two calves less than a mile away, and inspected them carefully. They were uninjured, so there was no need to call the vet in his highly specialized two-man sub which could handle any cetological crisis from a stomach-ache to a Caesarian. Don made a note of the mother's number, stencilled just behind the flippers. The calves, as was obvious from their size, were this season's and had not yet been branded.

Don watched for a little while. They were no longer in the least alarmed, and a check on the sonar had shown that the whole school had ceased its panicky flight. He wondered how they knew what had happened; much had been learned about communication among whales, but much was still a mystery.

"I hope you appreciate what I've done for you, old lady," he muttered. Then, reflecting that fifty tons of mother love was a slightly awe-inspiring sight, he blew his tanks and surfaced.

It was calm, so he cracked the airlock and popped his head out of the tiny conning tower. The water was only inches below his chin, and from time to time a wave made a determined effort to swamp him. There was little danger of this happening, for he fitted the hatch so closely that he was quite an effective plug.

Fifty feet away, a long slate-colored mound, like an overturned boat, was rolling on the surface. Don looked at it thoughtfully and did some mental calculations. A brute this size should be valuable; with any luck there was a chance of a double bonus. In a few minutes he'd radio his report, but for the moment it was pleasant to drink the fresh Atlantic air and to feel the open sky above his head.

A gray thunderbolt shot up out of the depths and smashed back onto the surface of the water, smothering Don with spray. It was just Benj's modest way of drawing attention to himself; a moment later the porpoise had swum up to the conning tower, so that Don could reach down and tickle its head. The great, intelligent eyes stared back into his; was it pure imagination, or did an almost human sense of fun also lurk in their depths?

Susan, as usual, circled shyly at a distance until jealousy overpowered her and she butted Benj out of the way. Don distributed caresses impartially and apologized because he had nothing to give them. He undertook to make up for the omission as soon as he returned to the *Herman Melville*.

"I'll go for another swim with you, too," he promised, "as long as you behave yourselves next time." He rubbed thoughtfully at a large bruise caused by Benj's playfulness, and wondered if he was not getting a little too old for rough games like this.

"Time to go home," Don said firmly, sliding down into the

cabin and slamming the hatch. He suddenly realized that he was very hungry, and had better do something about the breakfast he had missed. There were not many men on earth who had earned a better right to eat their morning meal. He had saved for humanity more tons of meat, oil and milk than could easily be estimated.

Don Burley was the happy warrior, coming home from one battle that man would always have to fight. He was holding at bay the specter of famine which had confronted all earlier ages, but which would never threaten the world again while the great plankton farms harvested their millions of tons of protein, and the whale herds obeyed their new masters. Man had come back to the sea after aeons of exile; until the oceans froze, he would never be hungry again. . . .

Don glanced at the scanner as he set his course. He smiled as he saw the two echoes keeping pace with the central splash of light that marked his vessel. "Hang around," he said. "We mammals must stick together." Then, as the autopilot took over, he lay back in his chair.

And presently Benj and Susan heard a most peculiar noise, rising and falling against the drone of the turbines. It had filtered faintly through the thick walls of Sub 5, and only the sensitive ears of the porpoises could have detected it. But intelligent beasts though they were, they could hardly be expected to understand why Don Burley was announcing, in a highly unmusical voice, that he was Heading for the Last Round-up. . . .

"IF I FORGET THEE, OH EARTH . . ."

THIS STORY, WHICH HAS BEEN RATHER WIDELY REPRINTED,
was written at Xmas, 1951.

On another Xmas, seventeen years later, the crew of *Apollo
8* became the first of all mankind to see an earthrise from the
moon.

Let us hope that no one ever views an earthrise like the child
in this cautionary tale.

When Marvin was ten years old, his father took him through the long, echoing corridors that led up through Administration and Power, until at last they came to the uppermost levels of all and were among the swiftly growing vegetation of the Farmlands. Marvin liked it here: it was fun watching the great, slender plants creeping with almost visible eagerness towards the sunlight as it filtered down through the plastic domes to meet them. The smell of life was everywhere, awakening inexpressible longings in his heart: no longer was he breathing the dry, cool air of the residential levels, purged of all smells but the faint tang of ozone. He wished he could stay here for a little while, but Father would not let him. They went onwards until they had reached the entrance to the Observatory, which he had never visited: but they did not stop, and Marvin knew with a sense of rising excitement that there could be only one goal left. For the first time in his life, he was going Outside.

There were a dozen of the surface vehicles, with their wide balloon tires and pressurized cabins, in the great servicing chamber. His father must have been expected, for they were led at once to the little scout car waiting by the huge circular door of the airlock. Tense with expectancy, Marvin settled himself down in the cramped cabin while his father started the motor and checked the controls. The inner door of the lock slid open and then closed behind them: he heard the roar of the great air-pumps fade slowly away as the pressure dropped to zero. Then the "Vacuum" sign flashed on, the outer door parted, and before Marvin lay the land which he had never yet entered.

He had seen it in photographs, of course: he had watched it imaged on television screens a hundred times. But now it was lying all around him, burning beneath the fierce sun that crawled so slowly across the jet-black sky. He stared into the west, away from the blinding splendor of the sun—and there were the stars, as he had been told but had never quite believed. He gazed at them for a long time, marvelling that anything could be so bright and yet so tiny. They were intense unscintillating points, and suddenly he remembered a rhyme he had once read in one of his father's books

Twinkle, twinkle, little star,
How I wonder what you are.

Well, *he* knew what the stars were. Whoever asked that question must have been very stupid. And what did they mean by "twinkle"? You could see at a glance that all the stars shone with the same steady, unwavering light. He abandoned the puzzle and turned his attention to the landscape around him.

They were racing across a level plain at almost a hundred miles an hour, the great balloon tyres sending up little spurts of dust behind them. There was no sign of the Colony: in the few minutes while he had been gazing at the stars, its domes and radio towers had fallen below the horizon. Yet there were other indications of man's presence, for about a mile ahead Marvin could see the curiously shaped structures clustering round the head of a mine. Now and then a puff of vapor would emerge from a squat smoke-stack and would instantly disperse.

They were past the mine in a moment: Father was driving with a reckless and exhilarating skill as if—it was a strange thought to come into a child's mind—he was trying to escape from something. In a few minutes they had reached the edge of the plateau on which the Colony had been built. The ground fell sharply away beneath them in a dizzying slope whose lower stretches were lost in shadow. Ahead, as far as the eye could reach, was a jumbled wasteland of craters, mountain ranges, and ravines. The crests of the mountains, catching the low sun, burned like islands of fire in a sea of darkness: and above them the stars still shone as steadfastly as ever.

There could be no way forward—yet there was. Marvin clenched his fists as the car edged over the slope and started the long descent. Then he saw the barely visible track leading down the mountainside, and relaxed a little. Other men, it seemed, had gone this way before.

Night fell with a shocking abruptness as they crossed the shadow line and the sun dropped below the crest of the plateau. The twin searchlights sprang into life, casting blue-white bands on the rocks ahead, so that there was scarcely need to check their speed. For hours they drove through valleys and past the feet of mountains whose peaks seemed to comb the stars, and sometimes they emerged for a moment into the sunlight as they climbed over higher ground.

And now on the right was a wrinkled, dusty plain, and on the left, its ramparts and terraces rising mile after mile into the sky, was a wall of mountains that marched into the distance until its peaks sank from sight below the rim of the world. There was no sign that men had ever explored this land, but once they passed the skeleton of a crashed rocket, and beside it a stone cairn surmounted by a metal cross.

It seemed to Marvin that the mountains stretched on forever: but at last, many hours later, the range ended in a towering, precipitous headland that rose steeply from a cluster of little hills. They drove down into a shallow valley that curved in a great arc towards the far side of the mountains: and as they did so, Marvin slowly realized that something very strange was happening in the land ahead.

The sun was now low behind the hills on the right: the valley before them should be in total darkness. Yet it was awash with a cold white radiance that came spilling over the crags beneath which they were driving. Then, suddenly, they were out in the open plain, and the source of the light lay before them in all its glory.

It was very quiet in the little cabin now that the motors had stopped. The only sound was the faint whisper of the oxygen feed and an occasional metallic crepitation as the outer walls of the vehicle radiated away their heat. For no warmth at all came from the great silver crescent that floated low above the far horizon and flooded all this land with pearly light. It was so brilliant that minutes passed before Marvin could accept its challenge and look steadfastly into its glare, but at last he could discern the outlines of continents, the hazy border of the atmosphere, and the white islands of cloud. And even at this distance, he could see the glitter of sunlight on the polar ice.

It was beautiful, and it called to his heart across the abyss of space. There in that shining crescent were all the wonders that he had never known—the hues of sunset skies, the moaning of the sea on pebbled shores, the patter of falling rain, the unhurried benison of snow. These and a thousand others should have been his rightful heritage, but he knew them only from the books and ancient records, and the thought filled him with the anguish of exile.

Why could they not return? It seemed so peaceful beneath those lines of marching cloud. Then Marvin, his eyes no longer blinded by the glare, saw that the portion of the disk that should have been in darkness was gleaming faintly with an evil phosphorescence: and he remembered. He was looking upon the funeral pyre of a world—upon the radioactive aftermath of Armageddon. Across a quarter of a million miles of space, the glow of dying atoms was still visible, a perennial reminder of the ruinous past. It would be centuries yet before that deadly glow died from the rocks and life could return again to fill that silent, empty world.

And now Father began to speak, telling Marvin the story which until this moment had meant no more to him than the fairy-tales he had heard in childhood. There were many things he could not understand: it was impossible for him to picture the glowing, multi-colored pattern of life on the planet he had never seen. Nor could he comprehend the forces that had destroyed it in the end, leaving the Colony, preserved by its isolation, as the sole survivor. Yet he could share the agony of those final days, when the Colony had learned at last that never again would the supply ships come flaming down through the stars with gifts from home. One by one the radio stations had ceased to call: on the shadowed globe the lights of the cities had dimmed and died, and they were alone at last, as no men had ever been alone before, carrying in their hands the future of the race.

Then had followed the years of despair, and the long-drawn battle for survival in this fierce and hostile world. That battle had been won, though barely: this little oasis of life was safe against the worst that Nature could do. But unless there was a goal, a future towards which it could work, the Colony would lose the will to live and neither machines nor skill nor science could save it then.

So, at last, Marvin understood the purpose of this pilgrimage. He would never walk beside the rivers of that lost and legendary world, or listen to the thunder raging above its softly rounded hills. Yet one day—how far ahead?—his children's children would return to claim their heritage. The winds and the rains would scour the poisons from the burning lands and carry them to the sea, and in the depths of the sea they would waste their venom until they could harm no living things. Then the great ships that were still waiting here on the silent, dusty plains could lift once more into space along the road that led to home.

That was the dream: and one day, Marvin knew with a sudden flash of insight, he would pass it on to his own son here at this same spot with the mountains behind him and the silver light from the sky streaming into his face.

He did not look back as they began the homeward journey. He could not bear to see the cold glory of the crescent Earth fade from the rocks around him, as he went to rejoin his people in their long exile.

THE
CRUEL SKY

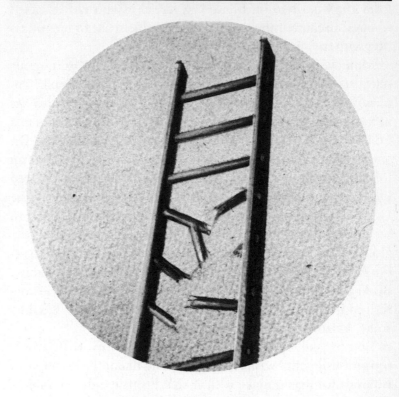

I care not if you bridge the seas,
   Or ride secure the cruel sky,
Or build consummate palaces
   Of metal or of masonry. . . .
               James Elroy Flecker,
               "To a Poet a Thousand
               Years Hence"

This story was written in 1966, presumably when I was

moonlighting from *2001*—which largely dominated my life from 1964 until 1968. I have just reread it with rather mixed feelings, because I now have a considerable sense of identification with my "Dr Elwin."

Moreover, the phrase "one of the world's most famous scientists—and certainly the world's most famous cripple" applies perfectly to Dr. Stephen Hawking—whose work also lies in the field of gravitation. In July 1988, I spent three hours in a London TV studio with Dr. Hawking (and, via satellite, Dr. Sagan). For me, the encounter was an emotional as well as an intellectual experience, since I had recently been told I shared Dr. Hawking's incurable disability (ALS, better known in the U.S. as Lou Gehrig's disease), and therefore could not expect to see much of the 1990s. Fortunately (see the foreword to "On Golden Seas") the diagnosis is now somewhat less ominous—but I have a more than casual interest in motorized wheelchairs. Better still, if only someone would invent it, the "Levvie" described in this story. Even before I found locomotion troublesome, I envied *Dune*'s floating Big Bad Baron.

Do not take my attack on the General Theory of Relativity too seriously; but I wish that writers who flaunt the Principle of Equivalence would make it clear that it's true only for vanishingly small volumes of space.

I now feel somewhat guilty at eliminating one of the world's rarest and most beautiful animals. Perhaps it should have been a yeti after all; they may be equally rare, but by general consensus they're certainly not beautiful.

By midnight, the summit of Everest was only a hundred yards away, a pyramid of snow, pale and ghostly in the light of the rising Moon. The sky was cloudless, and the wind that had been blowing for days had dropped almost to zero. It must be rare indeed for the highest point on Earth to be so calm and peaceful; they had chosen their time well.

Perhaps *too* well, thought George Harper; it had been almost disappointingly easy. Their only real problem had been getting out of the hotel without being observed. The management objected to unauthorized midnight excursions up the mountain; there could be accidents, which were bad for business.

But Dr. Elwin was determined to do it this way, and he had the best of reasons, though he never discussed them. The presence of one of the world's most famous scientists—and certainly the world's most famous cripple—at Hotel Everest during the height of the tourist season had already aroused a good deal of polite surprise. Harper had allayed some of the curiosity by hinting that they were engaged in gravity measurements, which was at least part of the truth. But a part of the truth that, by this time, was vanishingly small.

Anyone looking at Jules Elwin now, as he forged steadily toward the twenty-nine-thousand-foot level with fifty pounds of equipment on his shoulders, would never have guessed that his legs were almost useless. He had been born a victim of the 1961 Thalidomide disaster, which had left more than ten thousand partially deformed children scattered over the face of the world. Elwin was one of the lucky ones. His arms were quite normal, and had been strengthened by exercise until they were considerably more powerful than most men's. His legs, however, were mere wisps of flesh and bone. With the aid of braces, he could stand and even totter a few uncertain steps, but he could never really walk.

Yet now he was two hundred feet from the top of Everest. . . .

A travel poster had started it all, more than three years ago. As a junior computer programer in the Applied Physics Division, George Harper knew Dr. Elwin only by sight and by reputation. Even to those working directly under him, Astrotech's brilliant Director of Research was a slightly remote personality, cut off from the ordinary run of men both by his body and by his mind. He was neither liked nor disliked, and, though he was admired and pitied, he was certainly not envied.

Harper, only a few months out of college, doubted if the Doctor even knew of his existence, except as a name on an organization chart. There were ten other programers in the division, all senior to him, and most of them had never exchanged more than a dozen words with their research director. When Harper was co-opted as messenger boy to carry one of the classified files into Dr. Elwin's office, he expected to be in and out with nothing more than a few polite formalities.

That was almost what happened. But just as he was leaving, he was stopped dead by the magnificent panorama of Himalayan peaks covering half of one wall. It had been placed where Dr. Elwin could see it whenever he looked up from his desk, and it showed a scene that Harper knew very well indeed, for he had photographed it himself, as an awed and slightly breathless tourist standing on the trampled snow at the crown of Everest.

There was the white ridge of Kanchenjunga, rearing through the clouds almost a hundred miles away. Nearly in line with it, but much nearer, were the twin peaks of Makalu; and closer still, dominating the foreground, was the immense bulk of Lhotse, Everest's neighbor and rival. Farther around to the west, flowing down valleys so huge that the eye could not appreciate their scale, were the jumbled ice rivers of the Khumbu and Rongbuk glaciers. From this height, their frozen wrinkles looked no larger than the furrows in a plowed field; but those ruts and scars of iron-hard ice were hundreds of feet deep.

Harper was still taking in that spectacular view, reliving old memories, when he heard Dr. Elwin's voice behind him.

"You seem interested. Have you ever been there?"

"Yes, Doctor. My folks took me after I graduated from high school. We stayed at the hotel for a week, and thought we'd have to go home before the weather cleared. But on the last day the wind stopped blowing, and about twenty of us made it to the summit. We were there for an hour, taking pictures of each other."

Dr. Elwin seemed to digest this information for rather a long time. Then he said, in a voice that had lost its previous remoteness and now held a definite undercurrent of excitement: "Sit down, Mr.—ah—Harper. I'd like to hear more."

As he walked back to the chair facing the Director's big uncluttered desk, George Harper found himself somewhat puzzled. What he had done was not in the least unusual; every year thousands of people went to the Hotel Everest, and about a quarter of them reached the mountain's summit. Only last year, in fact, there had been a much-publicized presentation to the ten-thousandth tourist to stand on the top of the world. Some cynics had commented on the extraordinary coincidence that

Number 10,000 had just happened to be a rather well-known video starlet.

There was nothing that Harper could tell Dr. Elwin that he couldn't discover just as easily from a dozen other sources—the tourist brochures, for example. However, no young and ambitious scientists would miss this opportunity to impress a man who could do so much to help his career. Harper was neither coldly calculating nor inclined to dabble in office politics, but he knew a good chance when he saw one.

"Well, Doctor," he began, speaking slowly at first as he tried to put his thoughts and memories in order, "the jets land you at a little town called Namchi, about twenty miles from the mountain. Then the bus takes you along a spectacular road up to the hotel, which overlooks the Khumbu Glacier. It's at an altitude of eighteen thousand feet, and there are pressurized rooms for anyone who finds it hard to breathe. Of course, there's a medical staff in attendance, and the management won't accept guests who aren't physically fit. You have to stay at the hotel for at least two days, on a special diet, before you're allowed to go higher.

"From the hotel you can't actually see the summit, because you're too close to the mountain, and it seems to loom right above you. But the view is fantastic. You can see Lhotse and half a dozen other peaks. And it can be scary, too—especially at night. The wind is usually howling somewhere high overhead, and there are weird noises from the moving ice. It's easy to imagine that there are monsters prowling around up in the mountains. . . .

"There's not much to do at the hotel, except to relax and watch the scenery, and to wait until the doctors give you the go-ahead. In the old days it used to take weeks to acclimatize to the thin air; now they can make your blood count shoot up to the right level in forty-eight hours. Even so, about half the visitors—mostly the older ones—decide that this is quite high enough for them.

"What happens next depends on how experienced you are, and how much you're willing to pay. A few expert climbers hire guides and make their own way to the top, using standard mountaineering equipment. That isn't too difficult nowadays, and there are shelters at various strategic spots. Most of these groups make it. But the weather is always a gamble, and every year a few people get killed.

"The average tourist does it the easier way. No aircraft are allowed to land on Everest itself, except in emergencies, but there's a lodge near the crest of Nuptse and a helicopter service to it from the hotel. From the lodge it's only three miles to the summit, via the South Col—an easy climb for anyone in good condition, with a little mountaineering experience. Some people do it without oxygen, though that's not recommended. I kept my mask on until I reached the top; then I took it off and found I could breathe without much difficulty."

"Did you use filters or gas cylinders?"

"Oh, molecular filters—they're quite reliable now, and increase the oxygen concentration over a hundred per cent. They've simplified high-altitude climbing enormously. No one carries compressed gas any more."

"How long did the climb take?"

"A full day. We left just before dawn and were back at nightfall. *That* would have surprised the old-timers. But of course we were starting fresh and traveling light. There are no real problems on the route from the lodge, and steps have been cut at all the tricky places. As I said, it's easy for anyone in good condition."

The instant he repeated those words, Harper wished that he had bitten off his tongue. It seemed incredible that he could have forgotten who he was talking to, but the wonder and excitement of that climb to the top of the world had come back so vividly that for a moment he was once more on that lonely, wind-swept peak. The one spot on Earth where Dr. Elwin could never stand. . . .

But the scientist did not appear to have noticed—or else he was so used to such unthinking tactlessness that it no longer bothered him. Why, wondered Harper, was he so interested in Everest? Probably because of that very inaccessibility; it stood for all that had been denied to him by the accident of birth.

Yet now, only three years later, George Harper paused a bare hundred feet from the summit and drew in the nylon rope as the Doctor caught up with him. Though nothing had ever been said about it, he knew that the scientist wished to be the first to the top. He deserved the honor, and the younger man would do nothing to rob him of it.

"Everything O.K.?" he asked as Dr. Elwin drew abreast of him. The question was quite unnecessary, but Harper felt an urgent need to challenge the great loneliness that now surrounded them. They might have been the only men in all the world; nowhere amid this white wilderness of peaks was there any sign that the human race existed.

Elwin did not answer, but gave an absent-minded nod as he went past, his shining eyes fixed upon the summit. He was walking with a curiously stiff-legged gait, and his feet made remarkably little impression in the snow. And as he walked, there came a faint but unmistakable whine from the bulky backpack he was carrying on his shoulders.

That pack, indeed, was carrying him—or three-quarters of him. As he forged steadily along the last few feet to his once-impossible goal, Dr. Elwin and all his equipment weighed only fifty pounds. And if *that* was still too much, he had only to turn a dial and he would weigh nothing at all.

Here amid the Moon-washed Himalayas was the greatest secret of the twenty-first century. In all the world, there were only five of these experimental Elwin Levitators, and two of them were here on Everest.

Even though he had known about them for two years, and understood something of their basic theory, the "Levvies"—as they had soon been christened at the lab—still seemed like magic to Harper. Their power-packs stored enough electrical energy to lift a two-hundred-and-fifty-pound weight through a vertical distance of ten miles, which gave an ample safety factor for this mission. The lift-and-descend cycle could be repeated almost indefinitely as the units reacted against the Earth's gravitational field. On the way up, the battery discharged; on the way down, it was charged again. Since no mechanical process is completely efficient, there was a slight loss of energy on each cycle, but it could be repeated at least a hundred times before the units were exhausted.

Climbing the mountain with most of their weight neutralized had been an exhilarating experience. The vertical tug of the harness made it feel that they were hanging from invisible balloons, whose buoyancy could be adjusted at will. They needed a certain amount of weight in order to get traction on the ground, and after some experimenting had settled on twenty-five per cent. With this, it was as easy to ascend a one-in-one slope as to walk normally on the level.

Several times they had cut their weight almost to zero to rise hand over hand up vertical rock faces. This had been the strangest experience of all, demanding complete faith in their equipment. To hang suspended in mid-air, apparently supported by nothing but a box of gently humming electronic gear, required a considerable effort of will. But after a few minutes, the sense of power and freedom overcame all fear; for here indeed was the realization of one of man's oldest dreams.

A few weeks ago one of the library staff had found a line from an early twentieth-century poem that described their achievement perfectly: "To ride secure the cruel sky." Not even birds had ever possessed such freedom of the third dimension; this was the *real* conquest of space. The Levitator would open up the mountains and the high places of the world, as a lifetime ago the aqualung had opened up the sea. Once these units had passed their tests and were mass-produced cheaply, every aspect of human civilization would be changed. Transport would be revolutionized. Space travel would be no more expensive than ordinary flying; all mankind would take to the air. What had happened a hundred years earlier with the invention of the automobile was only a mild foretaste of the staggering social and political changes that must now come.

But Dr. Elwin, Harper felt sure, was thinking of none of these in his lonely moment of triumph. Later, he would receive the world's applause (and perhaps its curses), yet it would not mean as much to him as standing here on Earth's highest point. This was truly a victory of mind over matter, of sheer intelligence over a frail and crippled body. All the rest would be anticlimax.

When Harper joined the scientist on the flattened, snow-covered pyramid, they shook hands with rather formal stiffness, because that seemed the right thing to do. But they said nothing; the wonder of their achievement, and the panorama of peaks that stretched as far as the eye could see in every direction, had robbed them of words.

Harper relaxed in the buoyant support of his harness and slowly scanned the circle of the sky. As he recognized them, he mentally called off the names of the surrounding giants: Makalu, Lhotse, Baruntse, Cho Oyu, Kanchenjunga. . . . Even now scores of these peaks had never been climbed. Well, the Levvies would soon change that.

There were many, of course, who would disapprove. But back in the twentieth century there had also been mountaineers who thought it was "cheating" to use oxygen. It was hard to believe that, even after weeks of acclimatization, men had once attempted to reach these heights with no artificial aids at all. Harper remembered Mallory and Irvine, whose bodies still lay undiscovered perhaps within a mile of this very spot.

Behind him, Dr. Elwin cleared his throat.

"Let's go, George," he said quietly, his voice muffled by the oxygen filter. "We must get back before they start looking for us."

With a silent farewell to all those who had stood here before them, they turned away from the summit and started down the gentle slope. The night, which had been brilliantly clear until now, was becoming darker; some high clouds were slipping across the face of the Moon so rapidly that its light switched on and off in a manner that sometimes made it hard to see the route. Harper did not like the look of the weather and began mentally to rearrange their plans. Perhaps it would be better to aim for the shelter on the South Col, rather than attempt to reach the lodge. But he said nothing to Dr. Elwin, not wishing to raise any false alarms.

Now they were moving along a knife edge of rock, with utter darkness on one side and a faintly glimmering snowscape on the other. This would be a terrible place, Harper could not help thinking, to be caught by a storm.

He had barely shaped the thought when the gale was upon them. From out of nowhere, it seemed, came a shrieking blast of air, as if the mountain had been husbanding its strength for this moment. There was no time to do anything; even had they possessed normal weight, they would have been swept off their feet. In seconds, the wind had tossed them out over shadowed, empty blackness.

It was impossible to judge the depths beneath them; when Harper forced himself to glance down, he could see nothing. Though the wind seemed to be carrying him almost horizontally, he knew that he must be falling. His residual weight would be taking him downward at a quarter of the normal speed. But that would be ample; if they fell four thousand feet, it would be poor consolation to know that it would seem only one thousand.

He had not yet had time for fear—*that* would come later, if he survived—and his main worry, absurdly enough, was that the expensive Levitator might be damaged. He had completely forgotten his partner, for in such a crisis the mind can hold only one idea at a time. The sudden jerk on the nylon rope filled him with puzzled alarm. Then he saw Dr. Elwin slowly revolving around him at the end of the line, like a planet circling a sun.

The sight snapped him back to reality, and to a consciousness of what must be done. His paralysis had probably lasted only a fraction of a second. He shouted across the wind: "Doctor! Use emergency lift!"

As he spoke, he fumbled for the seal on his control unit, tore it open, and pressed the button.

At once, the pack began to hum like a hive of angry bees. He felt the harness tugging at his body as it tried to drag him up into the sky, away from the invisible death below. The simple arithmetic of the Earth's gravitational field blazed in his mind, as if written in letters of fire. One kilowatt could lift a hundred kilograms through a meter every second, and the packs could convert energy at a maximum rate of ten kilowatts—though they could not keep this up for more than a minute. So allowing for his initial weight reduction, he should lift at well over a hundred feet a second.

There was a violent jerk on the rope as the slack between them was taken up. Dr. Elwin had been slow to punch the emergency button, but at last he, too, was ascending. It would be a race between the lifting power of their units and the wind that was sweeping them toward the icy face of Lhotse, now scarcely a thousand feet away.

That wall of snow-streaked rock loomed above them in the

moonlight, a frozen wave of stone. It was impossible to judge their speed accurately, but they could hardly be moving at less than fifty miles an hour. Even if they survived the impact, they could not expect to escape serious injury; and injury here would be as good as death.

Then, just when it seemed that a collision was unavoidable, the current of air suddenly shot skyward, dragging them with it. They cleared the ridge of rock with a comfortable fifty feet to spare. It seemed like a miracle, but, after a dizzying moment of relief, Harper realized that what had saved them was only simple aerodynamics. The wind *had* to rise in order to clear the mountain; on the other side, it would descend again. But that no longer mattered, for the sky ahead was empty.

Now they were moving quietly beneath the broken clouds. Though their speed had not slackened, the roar of the wind had suddenly died away, for they were traveling with it through emptiness. They could even converse comfortably, across the thirty feet of space that still separated them.

"Dr. Elwin," Harper called, "are you O.K.?"

"Yes, George," said the scientist, perfectly calmly. "Now what do we do?"

"We must stop lifting. If we go any higher, we won't be able to breathe—even with the filters."

"You're right. Let's get back into balance."

The angry humming of the packs died to a barely audible electric whine as they cut out the emergency circuits. For a few minutes they yo-yoed up and down on their nylon rope—first one uppermost, then the other—until they managed to get into trim. When they had finally stabilized, they were drifting at a little below thirty thousand feet. Unless the Levvies failed—which, after their overload, was quite possible—they were out of immediate danger.

Their troubles would start when they tried to return to Earth.

• • •

No men in all history had ever greeted a stranger dawn. Though they were tired and stiff and cold, and the dryness of the thin air made every breath rasp in their throats, they forgot all these discomforts as the first dim glow spread along the jagged eastern horizon. The stars faded one by one; last to go, only minutes before the moment of daybreak, was the most brilliant of all the space stations—Pacific Number Three, hovering twenty-two thousand miles above Hawaii. Then the sun lifted above a sea of nameless peaks, and the Himalayan day had dawned.

It was like watching sunrise on the Moon. At first, only the highest mountains caught the slanting rays, while the surrounding valleys remained flooded with inky shadows. But slowly the line of light marched down the rocky slopes, and more and more of this harsh, forbidding land climbed into the new day.

Now, if one looked hard enough, it was possible to see signs of human life. There were a few narrow roads, thin columns of smoke from lonely villages, glints of reflected sunlight from monastery roofs. The world below was waking, wholly unaware of the two spectators poised so magically fifteen thousand feet above.

During the night, the wind must have changed direction several times, and Harper had no idea where they were. He could not recognize a single landmark. They could have been anywhere over a five-hundred-mile-long strip of Nepal and Tibet.

The immediate problem was to choose a landing place—and that soon, for they were drifting rapidly toward a jumble of peaks and glaciers where they could hardly expect to find help. The wind was carrying them in a northeasterly direction, toward China. If they floated over the mountains and landed there, it might be weeks before they could get in contact with one of the U.N. Famine Relief Centers and find their way home. They might even be in some personal danger, if they descended out of the sky in an area where there was only an illiterate and superstitious peasant population.

"We'd better get down quickly," said Harper. "I don't like the look of those mountains." His words seemed utterly lost in the void around them. Although Dr. Elwin was only ten feet away, it was easy to imagine that his companion could not hear anything he said. But at last the Doctor nodded his head, in almost reluctant agreement.

"I'm afraid you're right—but I'm not sure we can make it, with this wind. Remember—we can't go down as quickly as we can rise."

That was true enough; the power-packs could be charged at only a tenth of their discharge rate. If they lost altitude and pumped gravitational energy back into them too fast, the cells would overheat and probably explode. The startled Tibetans (or Nepalese?) would think that a large meteorite had detonated in their sky. And no one would ever know exactly what had happened to Dr. Jules Elwin and his promising young assistant.

Five thousand feet above the ground, Harper began to expect the explosion at any moment. They were falling swiftly, but not swiftly enough; very soon they would have to decelerate, lest they hit at too high a speed. To make matters worse, they had completely miscalculated the air speed at ground level. That infernal, unpredictable wind was blowing a near-gale once more. They could see streamers of snow, torn from exposed ridges, waving like ghostly banners beneath them. While they had been moving with the wind, they were unaware of its power; now they must once again make the dangerous transition between stubborn rock and softly yielding sky.

The air current was funneling them into the mouth of a canyon. There was no chance of lifting above it. They were committed, and would have to choose the best landing place they could find.

The canyon was narrowing at a fearsome rate. Now it was little more than a vertical cleft, and the rocky walls were sliding past at thirty or forty miles an hour. From time to time random eddies would swing them to the right, then the left; often they missed collisions by only a few feet. Once, when they were sweeping scant yards above a ledge thickly covered with snow, Harper was tempted to pull the quick-release that would jettison the Levitator. But that would be jumping from the frying pan into the fire: they might get safely back onto firm ground only to find themselves trapped unknown miles from all possibility of help.

Yet even at this moment of renewed peril, he felt very little fear. It was all like an exciting dream—a dream from which he would presently wake up to find himself safely in his own bed. This fantastic adventure could not really be happening to him. . . .

"George!" shouted the Doctor. "Now's our chance—if we can snag that boulder!"

They had only seconds in which to act. At once, they both began to play out the nylon rope, until it hung in a great loop beneath them, its lowest portion only a yard above the racing ground. A large rock, some twenty feet high, lay exactly in their line of flight; beyond it, a wide patch of snow gave promise of a reasonably soft landing.

The rope skittered over the lower curves of the boulder, seemed about to slip clear, then caught beneath an overhang. Harper felt the sudden jerk. He was swung around like a stone on the end of a sling.

I never thought that snow could be so hard, he told himself. After that there was a brief and brilliant explosion of light; then nothing.

• • •

He was back at the university, in the lecture room. One of the professors was talking, in a voice that was familiar, yet somehow did not seem to belong here. In a sleepy, halfhearted fashion, he ran through the names of his college instructors. No, it was certainly none of them. Yet he knew the voice so well, and it was undoubtedly lecturing to *someone*.

". . . still quite young when I realized that there was something wrong with Einstein's Theory of Gravitation. In particular, there seemed to be a fallacy underlying the Principle of Equivalence. According to this, there is no way of distinguishing between the effects produced by gravitation and those of acceleration.

"But this is clearly false. One can create a uniform acceleration; but a uniform gravitational field is impossible, since it obeys an inverse square law, and therefore must vary even over quite short distances. So tests can easily be devised to distinguish between the two cases, and this made me wonder if . . ."

The softly spoken words left no more impression on Harper's mind than if they were in a foreign language. He realized dimly that he *should* understand all this, but it was too much trouble to look for the meaning. Anyway, the first problem was to decide where he was.

Unless there was something wrong with his eyes, he was in complete darkness. He blinked, and the effort brought on such a splitting headache that he gave a cry of pain.

"George! Are you all right?"

Of course! That had been Dr. Elwin's voice, talking softly there in the darkness. But talking to *whom*?

"I've got a terrible headache. And there's a pain in my side when I try to move. What's happened? Why is it dark?"

"You've had concussion—and I think you've cracked a rib. Don't do any unnecessary talking. You've been unconscious all day. It's night again, and we're inside the tent. I'm saving our batteries."

The glare from the flashlight was almost blinding when Dr. Elwin switched it on, and Harper saw the walls of the tiny tent around them. How lucky that they had brought full mountaineering equipment, just in case they got trapped on Everest. But perhaps it would only prolong the agony. . . .

He was surprised that the crippled scientist had managed, without any assistance, to unpack all their gear, erect the tent, and drag him inside. Everything was laid out neatly: the first-aid kit, the concentrated-food cans, the water containers, the tiny red gas cylinders for the portable stove. Only the bulky Levitator units were missing; presumably they had been left outside to give more room.

"You were talking to someone when I woke up," Harper said. "Or was I dreaming?" Though the indirect light reflected from the walls of the tent made it hard to read the other's expression, he could see that Elwin was embarrassed. Instantly, he knew why, and wished that he had never asked the question.

The scientist did not believe that they would survive. He had been recording his notes, in case their bodies were ever discovered. Harper wondered bleakly if he had already recorded his last will and testament.

Before Elwin could answer, he quickly changed the subject. "Have you called Lifeguard?"

"I've been trying every half hour, but I'm afraid we're shielded by the mountains. I can hear them, but they don't receive us."

Dr. Elwin picked up the little recorder-transceiver, which he had unstrapped from its normal place on his wrist, and switched it on.

"This is Lifeguard Four," said a faint mechanical voice, "listening out now."

During the five-second pause, Elwin pressed the SOS button, then waited.

"This is Lifeguard Four, listening out now."

They waited for a full minute, but there was no acknowledgment of their call. Well, Harper told himself grimly, it's too late to start blaming each other now. Several times while they had been drifting above the mountains they had debated whether to call the global rescue service, but had decided against it, partly because there seemed no point in doing so while they were still airborne, partly because of the unavoidable publicity that would follow. It was easy to be wise after the event: who would have dreamed that they would land in one of the few places beyond Lifeguard's reach?

Dr. Elwin switched off the transceiver, and the only sound in the little tent was the faint moaning of the wind along the mountain walls within which they were doubly trapped—beyond escape, beyond communication.

"Don't worry," he said at last. "By morning, we'll think of a way out. There's nothing we can do until dawn—except make ourselves comfortable. So drink some of this hot soup."

Several hours later, the headache no longer bothered Harper. Though he suspected that a rib was indeed cracked, he had found a position that was comfortable as long as he did not move, and he felt almost at peace with the world.

He had passed through successive phases of despair, anger at Dr. Elwin, and self-recrimination at having become involved in such a crazy enterprise. Now he was calm again, though his mind, searching for ways of escape, was too active to allow sleep.

Outside the tent, the wind had almost died away, and the night was very still. It was no longer completely dark, for the Moon had risen. Though its direct rays would never reach them here, there must be some reflected light from the snows above.

Harper could just make out a dim glow at the very threshold of vision, seeping through the translucent heat-retaining walls of the tent.

First of all, he told himself, they were in no immediate danger. The food would last for at least a week; there was plenty of snow that could be melted to provide water. In a day or two, if his rib behaved itself, they might be able to take off again—this time, he hoped, with happier results.

From not far away there came a curious, soft thud, which puzzled Harper until he realized that a mass of snow must have fallen somewhere. The night was now so extraordinarily quiet that he almost imagined he could hear his own heartbeat; every breath of his sleeping companion seemed unnaturally loud.

Curious, how the mind was distracted by trivialities! He turned his thoughts back to the problem of survival. Even if he was not fit enough to move, the Doctor could attempt the flight by himself. This was a case where one man would have just as good a chance of success as two.

There was another of those soft thuds, slightly louder this time. It was a little odd, Harper thought fleetingly, for snow to move in the cold stillness of the night. He hoped that there was no risk of a slide; having had no time for a clear view of their landing place, he could not assess the danger. He wondered if he should awaken the Doctor, who must have had a good look around before he erected the tent. Then, fatalistically, he decided against it; if there *was* an impending avalanche, it was not likely that they could do much to escape.

Back to problem number one. Here was an interesting solution well worth considering. They could attach the transceiver to one of the Levvies and send the whole thing aloft. The signal would be picked up as soon as the unit left the canyon, and Lifeguard would find them within a few hours—or, at the very most, a few days.

Of course, it would mean sacrificing one of the Levvies, and if nothing came of it, they would be in an even worse plight. But all the same . . .

What was that? This was no soft thudding of loose snow. It was a faint but unmistakable "click," as of one pebble knocking against another. And pebbles did not move themselves.

You're imagining things, Harper told himself. The idea of anyone, or anything, moving around one of the high Himalayan passes in the middle of the night was completely ridiculous. But his throat became suddenly dry, and he felt the flesh crawl at the back of his neck. He had heard *something,* and it was impossible to argue it away.

Damn the Doctor's breathing; it was so noisy that it was hard to focus on any sounds from outside. Did this mean that Dr. Elwin, fast asleep though he was, had also been alerted by his ever-watchful subconscious? He was being fanciful again. . . .

Click.

Perhaps it was a little closer. It certainly came from a different direction. It was almost as if something—moving with uncanny but not complete silence—was slowly circling the tent.

This was the moment when George Harper devoutly wished he had never heard of the Abominable Snowman. It was true that he knew little enough about it, but that little was far too much.

He remembered that the Yeti, as the Nepalese called it, had been a persistent Himalayan myth for more than a hundred years. A dangerous monster larger than a man, it had never been captured, photographed, or even described by reputable witnesses. Most Westerners were quite certain that it was pure fantasy, and were totally unconvinced by the scanty evidence of tracks in the snow, or patches of skin preserved in obscure monasteries. The mountain tribesmen knew better. And now Harper was afraid that they were right.

Then, when nothing more happened for long seconds, his fears began slowly to dissolve. Perhaps his overwrought imagination had been playing tricks; in the circumstances, that would hardly be surprising. With a deliberate and determined effort of will, he turned his thoughts once more toward the problem of rescue. He was making fair progress when something bumped into the tent.

Only the fact that his throat muscles were paralyzed from sheer fright prevented him from yelling. He was utterly unable to move. Then, in the darkness beside him, he heard Dr. Elwin begin to stir sleepily.

"What is it?" muttered the scientist. "Are you all right?"

Harper felt his companion turn over and knew that he was groping for the flashlight. He wanted to whisper: "For God's sake, keep quiet!" but no words could escape his parched lips. There was a click, and the beam of the flashlight formed a brilliant circle on the wall of the tent.

That wall was now bowed in toward them as if a heavy weight was resting upon it. And in the center of the bulge was a completely unmistakable pattern: the imprint of a distorted hand or claw. It was only about two feet from the ground; whatever was outside seemed to be kneeling, as it fumbled at the fabric of the tent.

The light must have disturbed it, for the imprint abruptly vanished, and the tent wall sprang flat once more. There was a low, snarling growl; then, for a long time, silence.

Harper found that he was breathing again. At any moment he had expected the tent to tear open, and some unimaginable horror to come rushing in upon them. Instead, almost anticlimactically, there was only a faint and far-off wailing from a transient gust of wind in the mountains high above. He felt himself shivering uncontrollably; it had nothing to do with the temperature, for it was comfortably warm in their little insulated world.

Then there came a familiar—indeed, almost friendly—sound. It was the metallic ring of an empty can striking on stone, and it somehow relaxed the tension a little. For the first time, Harper found himself able to speak, or at least to whisper.

"It's found our food containers. Perhaps it'll go away now."

Almost as if in reply, there was a low snarl that seemed to convey anger and disappointment, then the sound of a blow, and the clatter of cans rolling away into the darkness. Harper suddenly remembered that all the food was here in the tent; only the discarded empties were outside. That was not a cheerful thought. He wished that, like superstitious tribesmen, they had left an offering for whatever gods or demons the mountains could conjure forth.

What happened next was so sudden, so utterly unexpected, that it was all over before he had time to react. There was a scuffling sound, as of something being banged against rock; then a familiar electric whine; then a startled grunt.

And then, a heart-stopping scream of rage and frustration that turned swiftly to sheer terror and began to dwindle away at ever-increasing speed, up, up, into the empty sky.

The fading sound triggered the one appropriate memory in Harper's mind. Once he had seen an early-twentieth-century movie on the history of flight, and it had contained a ghastly sequence showing a dirigible launching. Some of the ground crew had hung on to the mooring lines just a few seconds too long, and the airship had dragged them up into the sky, dangling helplessly beneath it. Then, one by one, they had lost their hold and dropped back to the earth.

Harper waited for a distant thud, but it never came. Then he realized that the Doctor was saying, over and over again: "I left the two units tied together. I left the two units tied together."

He was still in too much of a state of shock for even that

information to worry him. Instead, all he felt was a detached and admirably scientific sense of disappointment.

Now he would never know what it was that had been prowling around their tent, in the lonely hours before the Himalayan dawn.

One of the mountain rescue helicopters, flown by a skeptical Sikh who still wondered if the whole thing was an elaborate joke, came nosing down the canyon in the late afternoon. By the time the machine had landed in a flurry of snow, Dr. Elwin was already waving frantically with one arm and supporting himself on the tent framework with the other.

As he recognized the crippled scientist, the helicopter pilot felt a sensation of almost superstitious awe. So the report *must* be true; there was no other way in which Elwin could possibly have reached this place. And that meant that everything flying in and above the skies of Earth was, from this moment, as obsolete as an ox-cart.

"Thank God you found us," said the Doctor, with heartfelt gratitude. "How did you get here so quickly?"

"You can thank the radar tracking networks, and the telescopes in the orbital met stations. We'd have been here earlier, but at first we thought it was all a hoax."

"I don't understand."

"What would *you* have said, Doctor, if someone reported a very dead Himalayan snow leopard mixed up in a tangle of straps and boxes—and holding constant altitude at ninety thousand feet?"

Inside the tent, George Harper started to laugh, despite the pain it caused. The Doctor put his head through the flap and asked anxiously: "What's the matter?"

"Nothing—ouch. But I was wondering how we are going to get the poor beast down, before it's a menace to navigation."

"Oh, someone will have to go up with another Levvy and press the buttons. Maybe we should have a radio control on all units. . . ."

Dr. Elwin's voice faded out in mid-sentence. Already he was far away, lost in dreams that would change the face of many worlds.

In a little while he would come down from the mountains, a later Moses bearing the laws of a new civilization. For he would give back to all mankind the freedom lost so long ago, when the first amphibians left their weightless home beneath the waves.

The billion-year battle against the force of gravity was over.

THE
PARASITE

THIS IS A NASTY STORY ABOUT A NASTY IDEA; IT BELONGS IN the same category as "The Other Tiger." Both were written in the very early fifties.

And I hope they are both fantasy, not science fiction. But who knows what powers our remote descendants may possess, or what vices they may cultivate to pass the dreary billennia before the end of time?

"There is nothing you can do," said Connolly, "nothing at all. Why did you have to follow me?" He was standing with his back to Pearson, staring out across the calm blue water that led to Italy. On the left, behind the anchored fishing fleet, the sun was setting in Mediterranean splendor, incarnadining land and sky. But neither man was even remotely aware of the beauty all around.

Pearson rose to his feet, and came forward out of the little café's shadowed porch, into the slanting sunlight. He joined Connolly by the cliff wall, but was careful not to come too close to him. Even in normal times Connolly disliked being touched. His obsession, whatever it might be, would make him doubly sensitive now.

"Listen, Roy," Pearson began urgently. "We've been friends for twenty years, and you ought to know I wouldn't let you down this time. Besides—"

"I know. You promised Ruth."

"And why not? After all, she is your wife. She has a right to know what's happened." He paused, choosing his words carefully. "She's worried, Roy. Much more worried than if it was only another woman." He nearly added the word "again," but decided against it.

Connolly stubbed out his cigarette on the flat-topped granite wall, then flicked the white cylinder out over the sea, so that it fell twisting and turning toward the waters a hundred feet below. He turned to face his friend.

"I'm sorry, Jack," he said, and for a moment there was a glimpse of the familiar personality which, Pearson knew, must be trapped somewhere within the stranger standing at his side. "I know you're trying to be helpful, and I appreciate it. But I wish you hadn't followed me. You'll only make matters worse."

"Convince me of that, and I'll go away."

Connolly sighed.

"I could no more convince you than that psychiatrist you persuaded me to see. Poor Curtis! He was such a well-meaning fellow. Give him my apologies, will you?"

"I'm not a psychiatrist, and I'm not trying to cure you—whatever that means. If you like it the way you are, that's your affair. But I think you ought to let us know what's happened, so that we can make plans accordingly."

"To get me certified?"

Pearson shrugged his shoulders. He wondered if Connolly could see through his feigned indifference to the real concern he was trying to hide. Now that all other approaches seemed to have failed, the "frankly-I-don't-care" attitude was the only one left open to him.

"I wasn't thinking of that. There are a few practical details to worry about. Do you want to stay here indefinitely? You can't live without money, even on Syrene."

"I can stay at Clifford Rawnsley's villa as long as I like. He was a friend of my father's you know. It's empty at the moment except for the servants, and they don't bother me."

Connolly turned away from the parapet on which he was resting.

"I'm going up the hill before it's dark," he said. The words were abrupt, but Pearson knew that he was not being dismissed. He could follow if he pleased, and the knowledge brought him the first satisfaction he had felt since locating Connolly. It was a small triumph, but he needed it.

They did not speak during the climb; indeed, Pearson scarcely had the breath to do so. Connolly set off at a reckless pace, as if deliberately attempting to exhaust himself. The island fell away beneath them, the white villas gleamed like ghosts in the shadowed valleys, the little fishing boats, their day's work done, lay at rest in the harbor. And all around was the darkling sea.

When Pearson caught up with his friend, Connolly was sitting in front of the shrine which the devout islanders had built on Syrene's highest point. In the daytime there would be tourists here, photographing each other or gaping at the much-advertised beauty spread beneath them, but the place was deserted now.

Connolly was breathing heavily from his exertions, yet his features were relaxed and for the moment he seemed almost at peace. The shadow that lay across his mind had lifted, and he turned to Pearson with a smile that echoed his old, infectious grin.

"He hates exercise, Jack. It always scares him away."

"And who is he?" said Pearson. "Remember, you haven't introduced us yet."

Connolly smiled at his friend's attempted humor; then his face suddenly became grave.

"Tell me, Jack," he began. "Would you say I have an over-developed imagination?"

"No: you're about average. You're certainly less imaginative than I am."

Connolly nodded slowly.

"That's true enough, Jack, and it should help you to believe me. Because I'm certain I could never have invented the creature who's haunting me. He really exists. I'm not suffering from paranoiac hallucinations, or whatever Dr. Curtis would call them.

"You remember Maude White? It all began with her. I met her at one of David Trescott's parties, about six weeks ago. I'd just quarreled with Ruth and was rather fed up. We were both pretty tight, and as I was staying in town she came back to the flat with me."

Pearson smiled inwardly. Poor Roy! It was always the same pattern, though he never seemed to realize it. Each affair was different to him, but to no one else. The eternal Don Juan, always seeking—always disappointed, because what he sought could be found only in the cradle or the grave, but never between the two.

"I guess you'll laugh at what knocked me out—it seems so trivial, though it frightened me more than anything that's ever happened in my life. I simply went over to the cocktail cabinet and poured out the drinks, as I've done a hundred times before. It wasn't until I'd handed one to Maude that I realized I'd filled *three* glasses. The act was so perfectly natural that at first I didn't recognize what it meant. Then I looked wildly around the room to see where the other man was—even then I knew, somehow, that it wasn't a man. But, of course, he wasn't there. He was nowhere at all in the outside world: he was hiding deep down inside my own brain. . . ."

The night was very still, the only sound a thin ribbon of music winding up to the stars from some café in the village below. The light of the rising moon sparkled on the sea; overhead, the arms of the crucifix were silhouetted against the darkness. A brilliant beacon on the frontiers of twilight, Venus was following the sun into the west.

Pearson waited, letting Connolly take his time. He seemed lucid and rational enough, however strange the story he was telling. His face was quite calm in the moonlight, though it might be the calmness that comes after acceptance of defeat.

"The next thing I remember is lying in bed while Maude sponged my face. She was pretty frightened: I'd passed out and cut my forehead badly as I fell. There was a lot of blood around the place, but that didn't matter. The thing that really scared me was the thought that I'd gone crazy. That seems funny, now that I'm much more scared of being sane.

"*He* was still there when I woke up; he's been there ever since. Somehow I got rid of Maude—it wasn't easy—and tried to work out what had happened. Tell me, Jack, do you believe in telepathy?"

The abrupt challenge caught Pearson off his guard.

"I've never given it much thought, but the evidence seems rather convincing. Do you suggest that someone else is reading your mind?"

"It's not as simple as that. What I'm telling you now I've discovered slowly—usually when I've been dreaming or slightly drunk. You may say that invalidates the evidence, but I don't think so. At first it was the only way I could break through the barrier that separates me from Omega—I'll tell you later why I've called him that. But now there aren't any obstacles: I know he's there all the time, waiting for me to let down my guard. Night and day, drunk or sober, I'm conscious of his presence. At times like this he's quiescent, watching me out of the corner of his eye. My only hope is that he'll grow tired of waiting, and go in search of some other victim."

Connolly's voice, calm until now, suddenly came near to breaking.

"Try and imagine the horror of that discovery: the effect of learning that every act, every thought or desire that flitted through your mind was being watched and shared by another being. It meant, of course, the end of all normal life for me. I had to leave Ruth and I couldn't tell her why. Then, to make matters worse, Maude came chasing after me. She wouldn't leave me alone, and bombarded me with letters and phone calls. It was hell. I couldn't fight both of them, so I ran away. And I thought that on Syrene, of all places, he would find enough to interest him without bothering me."

"Now I understand," said Pearson softly. "So *that's* what he's after. A kind of telepathic Peeping Tom—no longer content with mere watching. . . ."

"I suppose you're humoring me," said Connolly, without resentment. "But I don't mind, and you've summed it up pretty accurately, as you usually do. It was quite a while before I realized what his game was. Once the first shock had worn off, I tried to analyze the position logically. I thought backward from that first moment of recognition, and in the end I knew that it wasn't a sudden invasion of my mind. He'd been with me for years, so well hidden that I'd never guessed it. I expect you'll laugh at this, knowing me as you do. But I've never been altogether at ease with a woman, even when I've been making love to her, and now I know the reason. Omega has always been there, sharing my emotions, gloating over the passions he can no longer experience in his body.

"The only way I kept any control was by fighting back, trying to come to grips with him and to understand what he was. And in the end I succeeded. He's a long way away and there must be some limit to his powers. Perhaps that first contact was an accident, though I'm not sure.

"What I've told you already, Jack, must be hard enough for you to believe, but it's nothing to what I've got to say now. Yet remember—you agreed that I'm not an imaginative man, and see if you can find a flaw anywhere in this story.

"I don't know if you've read any of the evidence suggesting that telepathy is somehow independent of time. I *know* that it is. Omega doesn't belong to our age: he's somewhere in the future, immensely far ahead of us. For a while I thought he must be one of the last men—that's why I gave him his name. But now I'm not sure; perhaps he belongs to an age when there are a myriad different races of man, scattered all over the universe—some still ascending, others sinking into decay. His people, wherever and whenever they may be, have reached the heights and fallen from them into the depths the beasts can never know. There's a sense of evil about him, Jack—the real evil that most of us never meet in all our lives. Yet sometimes I feel almost sorry for him, because I know what has made him the thing he is.

"Have you ever wondered, Jack, what the human race will do when science has discovered everything, when there are no more worlds to be explored, when all the stars have given up their secrets? Omega is one of the answers. I hope he's not the only one, for if so everything we've striven for is in vain. I hope that he and his race are an isolated cancer in a still healthy universe, but I can never be sure.

"They have pampered their bodies until they are useless, and too late they have discovered their mistake. Perhaps they have thought, as some men have thought, that they could live by intellect alone. And perhaps they are immortal, and that must be their real damnation. Through the ages their minds have been corroding in their feeble bodies, seeking some release from their intolerable boredom. They have found it at last in the only way they can, by sending back their minds to an earlier, more virile age, and becoming parasites on the emotions of others.

"I wonder how many of them there are? Perhaps they explain all cases of what used to be called possession. How they must have ransacked the past to assuage their hunger! Can't you picture them, flocking like carrion crows around the decaying Roman Empire, jostling one another for the minds of Nero and Caligula and Tiberius? Perhaps Omega failed to get those richer prizes. Or perhaps he hasn't much choice and must take whatever mind he can contact in any age, transferring from that to the next whenever he has the chance.

"It was only slowly, of course, that I worked all this out. I think it adds to his enjoyment to know that I'm aware of his presence. I think he's deliberately helping—breaking down his side of the barrier. For in the end, I was able to see him."

Connolly broke off. Looking around, Pearson saw that they were no longer alone on the hilltop. A young couple, hand in hand, were coming up the road toward the crucifix. Each had the physical beauty so common and so cheap among the islanders. They were oblivious to the night around them and to any spectators, and went past without the least sign of recognition. There was a bitter smile on Connolly's lips as he watched them go.

"I suppose I should be ashamed of this, but I was wishing then that he'd leave me and go after that boy. But he won't; though I've refused to play his game any more, he's staying to see what happens."

"You were going to tell me what he's like," said Pearson, annoyed at the interruption. Connolly lit a cigarette and inhaled deeply before replying.

"Can you imagine a room without walls? He's in a kind of hollow, egg-shaped space—surrounded by blue mist that always seems to be twisting and turning, but never changes its position. There's no entrance or exit—and no gravity, unless he's learned to defy it. Because he floats in the center, and around him is a circle of short, fluted cylinders, turning slowly in the air. I think they must be machines of some kind, obeying his will. And once there was a large oval hanging beside him, with perfectly human, beautifully formed arms coming from it. It could only have been a robot, yet those hands and fingers seemed alive. They were feeding and massaging him, treating him like a baby. It was horrible. . . .

"Have you ever seen a lemur or a spectral tarsier? He's rather like that—a nightmare travesty of mankind, with huge malevolent eyes. And this is strange—it's not the way one had imagined evolution going—he's covered with a fine layer of fur, as blue as the room in which he lives. Every time I've seen him he's been in the same position, half curled up like a sleeping baby. I think his legs have completely atrophied; perhaps his arms as well. Only his brain is still active, hunting up and down the ages for its prey.

"And now you know why there was nothing you or anyone else could do. Your psychiatrists might cure me if I was insane, but the science that can deal with Omega hasn't been invented yet."

Connolly paused, then smiled wryly.

"Just because I'm sane, I realize that you can't be expected to believe me. So there's no common ground on which we can meet."

Pearson rose from the boulder on which he had been sitting, and shivered slightly. The night was becoming cold, but that was nothing to the feeling of inner helplessness that had overwhelmed him as Connolly spoke.

"I'll be frank, Roy," he began slowly. "Of course I don't believe you. But insofar as you believe in Omega yourself, he's real to you, and I'll accept him on that basis and fight him with you."

"It may be a dangerous game. How do we know what he can do when he's cornered?"

"I'll take that chance," Pearson replied, beginning to walk down the hill. Connolly followed him without argument. "Meanwhile, just what do you propose to do yourself?"

"Relax. Avoid emotion. Above all, keep away from women—Ruth, Maude, and the rest of them. That's been the hardest job. It isn't easy to break the habits of a lifetime."

"I can well believe that," replied Pearson, a little dryly. "How successful have you been so far?"

"Completely. You see, his own eagerness defeats his purpose, by filling me with a kind of nausea and self-loathing whenever I think of sex. Lord, to think that I've laughed at the prudes all my life, yet now I've become one myself!"

There, thought Pearson in a sudden flash of insight, was the answer. He would never have believed it, but Connolly's past had finally caught up with him. Omega was nothing more than a symbol of conscience, a personification of guilt. When Connolly realized this, he would cease to be haunted. As for the remarkably detailed nature of the hallucination, that was yet another example of the tricks the human mind can play in its efforts to deceive itself. There must be some reason why the obsession had taken this form, but that was of minor importance.

Pearson explained this to Connolly at some length as they approached the village. The other listened so patiently that Pearson had an uncomfortable feeling that he was the one who was being humored, but he continued grimly to the end. When he had finished, Connolly gave a short, mirthless laugh.

"Your story's as logical as mine, but neither of us can convince the other. If you're right, then in time I may return to 'normal.' I can't disprove the possibility; I simply don't believe it. You can't imagine how real Omega is to me. He's more real than you are: if I close my eyes you're gone, but he's still there. I wish I knew what he was waiting for! I've left my old life behind; *he* knows I won't go back to it while he's there. So what's he got to gain by hanging on?" He turned to Pearson with a feverish eagerness. "That's what really frightens me, Jack. He must know what my future is—all my life must be like a book he can dip into where he pleases. So there must still be some experience ahead of me that he's waiting to savor. Sometimes— sometimes I wonder if it's my death."

They were now among the houses at the outskirts of the village, and ahead of them the nightlife of Syrene was getting into its stride. Now that they were no longer alone, there came a subtle change in Connolly's attitude. On the hilltop he had been, if not his normal self, at least friendly and prepared to talk. But now the sight of the happy, carefree crowds ahead seemed to make him withdraw into himself. He lagged behind as Pearson advanced and presently refused to come any further.

"What's the matter?" asked Pearson. "Surely you'll come down to the hotel and have dinner with me?"

Connolly shook his head.

"I can't," he said. "I'd meet too many people."

It was an astonishing remark from a man who had always delighted in crowds and parties. It showed, as nothing else had done, how much Connolly had changed. Before Pearson could think of a suitable reply, the other had turned on his heels and made off up a side-street. Hurt and annoyed, Pearson started to pursue him, then decided that it was useless.

That night he sent a long telegram to Ruth, giving what reassurance he could. Then, tired out, he went to bed.

Yet for an hour he was unable to sleep. His body was exhausted, but his brain was still active. He lay watching the patch of moonlight move across the pattern on the wall, marking the passage of time as inexorably as it must still do in the distant age that Connolly had glimpsed. Of course, that was pure fantasy—yet against his will Pearson was growing to accept Omega as a real and living threat. And in a sense Omega *was* real—as real as those other mental abstractions, the Ego and the Subconscious Mind.

Pearson wondered if Connolly had been wise to come back to Syrene. In times of emotional crisis—there had been others, though none so important as this—Connolly's reaction was always the same. He would return again to the lovely island where his charming, feckless parents had borne him and where he had spent his youth. He was seeking now, Pearson knew well enough, the contentment he had known only for one period of his life, and which he had sought so vainly in the arms of Ruth and all those others who had been unable to resist him.

Pearson was not attempting to criticize his unhappy friend. He never passed judgments; he merely observed with a bright-eyed, sympathetic interest that was hardly tolerance, since tolerance implied the relaxation of standards which he had never possessed. . . .

After a restless night, Pearson finally dropped into a sleep so sound that he awoke an hour later than usual. He had breakfast in his room, then went down to the reception desk to see if there was any reply from Ruth. Someone else had arrived in the night: two traveling cases, obviously English, were stacked in a corner of the hall, waiting for the porter to move them. Idly curious, Pearson glanced at the labels to see who his compatriot might be. Then he stiffened, looked hastily around, and hurried across to the receptionist.

"This Englishwoman," he said anxiously. "When did she arrive?"

"An hour ago, Signor, on the morning boat."

"Is she in now?"

The receptionist looked a little undecided, then capitulated gracefully.

"No, Signor. She was in a great hurry, and asked me where she could find Mr. Connolly. So I told her. I hope it was all right."

Pearson cursed under his breath. It was an incredible stroke of bad luck, something he would never have dreamed of guarding against. Maude White was a woman of even greater determination than Connolly had hinted. Somehow she had discovered where he had fled, and pride or desire or both had driven her to follow. That she had come to this hotel was not surprising; it was an almost inevitable choice for English visitors to Syrene.

As he climbed the road to the villa, Pearson fought against an increasing sense of futility and uselessness. He had no idea what he should do when he met Connolly and Maude. He merely felt a vague yet urgent impulse to be helpful. If he could catch Maude before she reached the villa, he might be able to convince her that Connolly was a sick man and that her intervention could only do harm. Yet was this true? It was perfectly possible that a touching reconciliation had already taken place, and that neither party had the least desire to see him.

They were talking together on the beautifully laid-out lawn in front of the villa when Pearson turned through the gates and paused for breath. Connolly was resting on a wrought-iron seat beneath a palm tree, while Maude was pacing up and down a few yards away. She was speaking swiftly; Pearson could not hear her words, but from the intonation of her voice she was obviously pleading with Connolly. It was an embarrassing situation. While Pearson was still wondering whether to go forward, Connolly looked up and caught sight of him. His face was a completely expressionless mask; it showed neither welcome nor resentment.

At the interruption, Maude spun round to see who the intruder was, and for the first time Pearson glimpsed her face. She was a beautiful woman, but despair and anger had so twisted her features that she looked like a figure from some Greek tragedy. She was suffering not only the bitterness of being scorned, but the agony of not knowing why.

Pearson's arrival must have acted as a trigger to her pent-up emotions. She suddenly whirled away from him and turned toward Connolly, who continued to watch her with lackluster eyes. For a moment Pearson could not see what she was doing; then he cried in horror: "Look out, Roy!"

Connolly moved with surprising speed, as if he had suddenly emerged from a trance. He caught Maude's wrist, there was a brief struggle, and then he was backing away from her, looking with fascination at something in the palm of his hand. The woman stood motionless, paralyzed with fear and shame, knuckles pressed against her mouth.

Connolly gripped the pistol with his right hand and stroked it lovingly with his left. There was a low moan from Maude.

"I only meant to frighten you, Roy! I swear it!"

"That's all right, my dear," said Connolly softly. "I believe you. There's nothing to worry about." His voice was perfectly natural. He turned toward Pearson, and gave him his old, boyish smile.

"So *this* is what he was waiting for, Jack," he said. "I'm not going to disappoint him."

"No!" gasped Pearson, white with terror, "Don't, Roy, for God's sake!"

But Connolly was beyond the reach of his friend's entreaties as he turned the pistol to his head. In that same moment Pearson knew at last, with an awful clarity, that Omega was real and that Omega would now be seeking for a new abode.

He never saw the flash of the gun or heard the feeble but adequate explosion. The world he knew had faded from his sight, and around him now were the fixed yet crawling mists of the blue room. Staring from its center—as they had stared down the ages at how many others?—were two vast and lidless eyes. They were satiated for the moment, but for the moment only.

THE
NEXT TENANTS

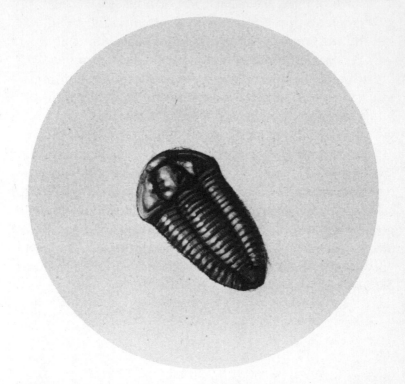

THIS WAS WRITTEN IN 1954 AS PART OF THE SERIES IN-tended to complete *Tales from the White Hart*. I was living in Coral Gables, Miami, at the time and had just seen the first H-bomb test on TV. Doubtless that provided considerable inspiration for the story. . . .

I also recall that one of the very first pieces of science fiction I ever attempted, "Retreat from Earth" (*Amateur Science Fiction Stories*, March 1938; reprinted in *The Best of Arthur C. Clarke: 1937–1955*, Sphere Books, 1976) involved termites:

. . . And in the long echoing centuries before the birth of man, the aliens had not been idle but had covered half the planet with their cities, filled with blind, fantastic slaves, and although man knew these cities, for they had often caused him infinite trouble, he never suspected that all around him in the tropics an older civilisation than his was planning busily for the day when it would once again venture forth upon the seas of space to regain its lost inheritance. . . .

And going back even further than this half-century-old effort, I suspect that my interest in these amazing creatures was triggered by Paul Ernst's "The Raid on the Termites" in *Astounding Stories* (June 1932). For much more about *this,* see chapter 11, "Beyond the Vanishing Point," in *Astounding Days: A Science Fictional Autobiography.*

"The number of mad scientists who wish to conquer the world," said Harry Purvis, looking thoughtfully at his beer, "has been grossly exaggerated. In fact, I can remember encountering only a single one."

"Then there couldn't have been many others," commented Bill Temple, a little acidly. "It's not the sort of thing one would be likely to forget."

"I suppose not," replied Harry, with that air of irrefragable innocence which is so disconcerting to his critics, "And, as a matter of fact, this scientist wasn't really mad. There was no doubt, though, that he was out to conquer the world. Or if you want to be really precise—to let the world be conquered."

"And by whom?" asked George Whitley. "The Martians? Or the well-known little green men from Venus?"

"Neither of them. He was collaborating with someone a lot nearer home. You'll realize who I mean when I tell you he was a myrmecologist."

"A which-what?" asked George.

"Let him get on with the story," said Drew, from the other side of the bar. "It's past ten, and if I can't get you all out by closing time *this* week, I'll lose my license."

"Thank you," said Harry with dignity, handing over his glass for a refill. "This all happened about two years ago, when I was on a mission in the Pacific. It was rather hush-hush, but in view of what's happened since there's no harm in talking about it. Three of us scientists were landed on a certain Pacific atoll not a thousand miles from Bikini, and given a week to set up some detection equipment. It was intended, of course, to keep an eye on our good friends and allies when they started playing with thermo-nuclear reactions—to pick some crumbs from the A.E.C.'s table, as it were. The Russians, naturally, were doing the same thing, and occasionally we ran into each other and then both sides would pretend that there was nobody here but us chickens.

"This atoll was supposed to be uninhabited, but this was a considerable error. It actually had a population of several hundred millions—"

"What!" gasped everybody.

"—several hundred millions," continued Purvis calmly, "of which number, one was human. I came across him when I went inland one day to have a look at the scenery."

"Inland?" asked George Whitley. "I thought you said it was an atoll. How can a ring of coral—"

"It was a very plump atoll," said Harry firmly. "Anyway, who's telling this story?" He waited defiantly for a moment until he had the right of way again.

"Here I was, then, walking up a charming little river-course underneath the coconut palms, when to my great surprise I came across a waterwheel—a very modern-looking one, driving a dynamo. If I'd been sensible, I suppose I'd have gone back and told my companions, but I couldn't resist the challenge and decided to do some reconnoitering on my own. I remembered that there were still supposed to be Japanese troops around who didn't know that the war was over, but that explanation seemed a bit unlikely.

"I followed the power-line up a hill, and there on the other side was a low, whitewashed building set in a large clearing. All over this clearing were tall, irregular mounds of earth, linked together with a network of wires. It was one of the most baffling sights I have ever seen, and I stood and stared for a good ten minutes, trying to decide what was going on. The longer I looked, the less sense it seemed to make.

"I was debating what to do when a tall, white-haired man came out of the building and walked over to one of the mounds. He was carrying some kind of apparatus and had a pair of earphones slung around his neck, so I guessed that he was using a Geiger counter. It was just about then that I realized what those tall mounds were. They were termitaries . . . the skyscrapers, in comparison to their makers, far taller than the Empire State Building, in which the so-called white ants live.

"I watched with great interest, but complete bafflement, while the elderly scientist inserted his apparatus into the base of the termitary, listened intently for a moment, and then walked back towards the building. By this time I was so curious that I decided to make my presence known. Whatever research was going on here obviously had nothing to do with international politics, so I was the only one who'd have anything to hide. You'll appreciate later just what a miscalculation *that* was.

"I yelled for attention and walked down the hill, waving my arms. The stranger halted and watched me approaching: he didn't look particularly surprised. As I came closer I saw that he had a straggling moustache that gave him a faintly Oriental appearance. He was about sixty years old, and carried himself very erect. Though he was wearing nothing but a pair of shorts, he looked so dignified that I felt rather ashamed of my noisy approach.

"'Good morning,' I said apologetically. 'I didn't know that there was anyone else on this island. I'm with an—er—scientific survey party over on the other side.'

"At this, the stranger's eyes lit up, 'Ah,' he said, in almost perfect English, 'a fellow scientist! I'm very pleased to meet you. Come into the house.'

"I followed gladly enough—I was pretty hot after my scramble—and I found that the building was simply one large lab. In a corner was a bed and a couple of chairs, together with a stove and one of those folding wash-basins that campers use. That seemed to sum up the living arrangements. But everything was very neat and tidy: my unknown friend seemed to be a recluse, but he believed in keeping up appearances.

"I introduced myself first, and as I'd hoped he promptly responded. He was one Professor Takato, a biologist from a leading Japanese university. He didn't look particularly Japanese, apart from the moustache I've mentioned. With his erect, dignified bearing he reminded me more of an old Kentucky colonel I once knew.

"After he'd given me some unfamiliar but refreshing wine, we sat and talked for a couple of hours. Like most scientists he seemed happy to meet someone who would appreciate his work. It was true that my interests lay in physics and chemistry rather than on the biological side, but I found Professor Takato's research quite fascinating.

"I don't suppose you know much about termites, so I'll remind you of the salient facts. They're among the most highly evolved of the social insects, and live in vast colonies throughout the tropics. They can't stand cold weather, nor, oddly enough, can they endure direct sunlight. When they have to get from one place to another, they construct little covered roadways. They seem to have some unknown and almost instantaneous means of communication, and though the individual termites are pretty helpless and dumb, a whole colony behaves like an intelligent animal. Some writers have drawn comparisons between a termitary and a human body, which is also composed of individual living cells making up an entity much higher than the basic units. The termites are often called 'white ants,' but that's a completely incorrect name as they aren't ants at all but quite a different species of insect. Or should I say 'genus'? I'm pretty vague about this sort of thing. . . .

"Excuse this little lecture, but after I'd listened to Takato for a while I began to get quite enthusiastic about termites myself. Did you know, for example, that they not only cultivate gardens but also keep cows—insect cows, of course—and milk them? Yes, they're sophisticated little devils, even though they do it all by instinct.

"But I'd better tell you something about the Professor. Although he was alone at the moment, and had lived on the island for several years, he had a number of assistants who brought equipment from Japan and helped him in his work. His first great achievement was to do for the termites what von Frische had done with bees—he'd learned their language. It was much more complex than the system of communication that bees use, which as you probably know, is based on dancing. I understood that the network of wires linking the termitaries to the lab not only enabled Professor Takato to listen to the termites talking among each other, but also permitted him to speak to them. That's not really as fantastic as it sounds, if you use the word 'speak' in its widest sense. We speak to a good many animals— not always with our voices, by any means. When you throw a stick for your dog and expect him to run and fetch it, that's a form of speech—sign language. The Professor, I gathered, had worked out some kind of code which the termites understood, though how efficient it was at communicating ideas I didn't know.

"I came back each day, when I could spare the time, and by the end of the week we were firm friends. It may surprise you that I was able to conceal these visits from my colleagues, but the island was quite large and we each did a lot of exploring. I felt somehow that Professor Takato was my private property, and did not wish to expose him to the curiosity of my companions. They were rather uncouth characters—graduates of some provincial university like Oxford or Cambridge.

"I'm glad to say that I was able to give the Professor a certain amount of assistance, fixing his radio and lining up some of his electronic gear. He used radioactive tracers a good deal, to follow individual termites around. He'd been tracking one with a Geiger counter when I first met him, in fact.

"Four or five days after we'd met, his counters started to go haywire, and the equipment we'd set up began to reel in its recordings. Takato guessed what had happened: he'd never asked me exactly what I was doing on the islands, but I think he knew. When I greeted him he switched on his counters and let me listen to the roar of radiation. There had been some radioactive fall-out—not enough to be dangerous, but sufficient to bring the background 'way up.

"'I think,' he said softly, 'that you physicists are playing with your toys again. And very big ones, this time.'

"'I'm afraid you're right,' I answered. We wouldn't be sure until the readings had been analyzed, but it looked as if Teller and his team had started the hydrogen reaction. 'Before long, we'll be able to make the first A-bombs look like damp squibs.'

"'My family,' said Professor Takato, without any emotion, 'was at Nagasaki.'

"There wasn't a great deal I could say to that, and I was glad when he went on to add: 'Have you ever wondered who will take over when we are finished?'

"'Your termites?' I said, half facetiously. He seemed to hesitate for a moment. Then he said quietly, 'Come with me; I have not shown you everything.'

"We walked over to a corner of the lab where some equipment lay concealed beneath dust-sheets, and the Professor uncovered a rather curious piece of apparatus. At first sight it looked like one of the manipulators used for the remote handling of dangerously radioactive materials. There were hand-grips that conveyed movements through rods and levers, but everything seemed to focus on a small box a few inches on a side. 'What is it?' I asked.

"'It's a micromanipulator. The French developed them for biological work. There aren't many around yet.'

"Then I remembered. These were devices with which, by the use of suitable reduction gearing, one could carry out the most incredibly delicate operations. You moved your finger an inch—and the tool you were controlling moved a thousandth of an inch. The French scientists who had developed this technique had built tiny forges on which they could construct minute scalpels and tweezers from fused glass. Working entirely through microscopes, they had been able to dissect individual cells. Removing an appendix from a termite (in the highly doubtful event of the insect possessing one) would be child's play with such an instrument.

"'I am not very skilled at using the manipulator,' confessed Takato. 'One of my assistants does all the work with it. I have shown no one else this, but you have been very helpful. Come with me, please.'

"We went out into the open, and walked past the avenues of tall, cement-hard mounds. They were not all of the same architectural design, for there are many different kinds of termites—some, indeed, don't build mounds at all. I felt rather like a giant walking through Manhattan, for these were skyscrapers, each with its own teeming population.

"There was a small metal (not wooden—the termites would soon have fixed that!) hut beside one of the mounds, and as we entered it the glare of sunlight was banished. The Professor threw a switch, and a faint red glow enabled me to see various types of optical equipment.

"'They hate light,' he said, 'so it's a great problem observing them. We solved it by using infra-red. This is an image-converter of the type that was used in the war for operations at night. You know about them?'

"'Of course,' I said, 'Snipers had them fixed on their rifles so that they could go sharp-shooting in the dark. Very ingenious things—I'm glad you've found a civilized use for them.'

"It was a long time before Professor Takato found what he wanted. He seemed to be steering some kind of periscope arrangement, probing through the corridors of the termite city. Then he said: 'Quick—before they've gone!'

"I moved over and took his position. It was a second or so before my eye focused properly, and longer still before I understood the scale of the picture I was seeing. Then I saw six termites, greatly enlarged, moving rather rapidly across the field of vision. They were travelling in a group, like the huskies forming a dog-team. And that was a very good analogy, because they were towing a sledge. . . .

"I was so astonished that I never even noticed what kind of load they were moving. When they had vanished from sight, I turned to Professor Takato. My eyes had now grown accustomed to the faint red glow, and I could see him quite well.

"'So that's the sort of tool you've been building with your micromanipulator!' I said. 'It's amazing—I'd never have believed it.'

"'But that is nothing,' replied the Professor. 'Performing fleas will pull a cart around. I haven't told you what is so important. We only made a few of those sledges. *The one you saw they constructed themselves.'*

"He let that sink in: it took some time. Then he continued quietly, but with a kind of controlled enthusiasm in his voice: 'Remember that the termites, as individuals, have virtually no intelligence. But the colony as a whole is a very high type of organism—and an immortal one, barring accidents. It froze in its present instinctive pattern millions of years before Man was born, and by itself it can never escape from its present sterile perfection. It has reached a dead-end—because it has no tools, no effective way of controlling nature. I have given it the lever, to increase its power, and now the sledge, to improve its efficiency. I have thought of the wheel, but it is best to let that wait for a later stage—it would not be very useful now. The results have exceeded my expectations. I started with this termitary alone—but now they all have the same tools. They have taught each other, and that proves they can cooperate. True, they have wars—but not when there is enough food for all, as there is here.

"'But you cannot judge the termitary by human standards. What I hope to do is to jolt its rigid, frozen culture—to knock it out of the groove in which it has stuck for so many millions of years. I will give it more tools, more new techniques—and before I die, I hope to see it beginning to invent things for itself.'

"'Why are you doing this?' I asked, for I knew there was more than mere scientific curiosity here.

"'Because I do not believe that Man will survive, yet I hope to preserve some of the things he has discovered. If he is to be a dead-end, I think that another race should be given a helping hand. Do you know why I chose this island? It was so that my experiment should remain isolated. My supertermite, if it ever evolves, will have to remain here until it has reached a very high level of attainment. Until it can cross the Pacific, in fact. . . .

"'There is another possibility. Man has no rival on this planet. I think it may do him good to have one. It may be his salvation.'

"I could think of nothing to say: this glimpse of the Professor's dreams was so overwhelming—and yet, in view of what I had just seen, so convincing. For I knew that Professor Takato was not mad. He was a visionary, and there was a sublime detachment about his outlook, but it was based on a secure foundation of scientific achievement.

"And it was not that he was hostile to mankind: he was sorry for it. He simply believed that humanity had shot its bolt, and wished to save something from the wreckage. I could not feel it in my heart to blame him.

"We must have been in that little hut for a long time, exploring possible futures. I remember suggesting that perhaps there might be some kind of mutual understanding, since two cultures so utterly dissimilar as Man and Termite need have no cause for conflict. But I couldn't really believe this, and if a contest comes, I'm not certain who will win. For what use would man's weapons be against an intelligent enemy who could lay waste all the wheat fields and all the rice crops in the world?

"When we came out into the open once more, it was almost dusk. It was then that the Professor made his final revelation.

"'In a few weeks,' he said, 'I am going to take the biggest step of all.'

"'And what is that?' I asked.

"'Cannot you guess? I am going to give them fire.'

"Those words did something to my spine. I felt a chill that had nothing to do with the oncoming night. The glorious sunset that was taking place beyond the palms seemed symbolic—and suddenly I realized that the symbolism was even deeper than I had thought.

"That sunset was one of the most beautiful I had ever seen, and it was partly of man's making. Up there in the stratosphere, the dust of an island that had died this day was encircling the earth. My race had taken a great step forward; but did it matter now?

"'*I am going to give them fire.*' Somehow, I never doubted that the Professor would succeed. And when he had done so, the forces that my own race had just unleashed would not save it. . . .

"The flying boat came to collect us the next day, and I did not see Takato again. He is still there, and I think he is the most important man in the world. While our politicians wrangle, he is making us obsolete.

"Do you think that someone ought to stop him? There may still be time. I've often thought about it, but I've never been able to think of a really convincing reason why I should interfere. Once or twice I nearly made up my mind, but then I'd pick up the newspaper and see the headlines.

"I think we should let them have the chance. I don't see how they could make a worse job of it than we've done."

SATURN
RISING

THIS STORY BRINGS BACK VIVID MEMORIES OF MY OWN VERY first glimpse of the planet's rings while I was evacuated with my other colleagues in His Majesty's Exchequer and Audit Department to Colwyn Bay, North Wales, during the early months of World War II.

I had bought an old-fashioned telescope of about 2 inches aperture from a naval cadet at a local training establishment, who presumably was short of money (not that I was particularly affluent on my Civil Service salary of about five pounds a week). The rather battered instrument consisted of one brass tube sliding inside another. I removed the inner tube (which contained the erecting lenses and the eyepiece) and replaced it with a single short-focus lens, increasing the magnifying power considerably. It was through this crude device that I first saw Saturn and its rings and, like every observer since Galileo, was entranced by one of the most breathtaking spectacles in the sky. Little did I imagine, when I wrote this story in 1960, that within less than two decades the fantastically successful *Voyager* missions to the outer solar system would reveal that the rings of Saturn were far more complex and beautiful than anyone had ever dreamed.

The story has, of course, been dated by the scientific discoveries of the last three decades—in particular, we now know that Titan does *not* have a predominantly methane atmosphere, but one that is mostly nitrogen. (And there goes the main thesis of my novel *Imperial Earth,* which is also set on Titan. Ah well, you can't win 'em all: That story now takes place in a slightly parallel universe; see my note on "The Wall of Darkness.")

There is another error that I might have corrected at the time. Even if you could observe Saturn from the surface of Titan (which atmospheric haze will probably prevent), you'd never see it "rising." Almost certainly, Titan, like our own moon, has had its rotation tidally braked so that it always keeps the same face turned toward its primary. So Saturn remains fixed in Titan's sky, just as the Earth does in the moon's.

No problem—we'll build our hotel in orbit, which is a much better idea anyway. From Titan the rings will always appear edge-on so that they'll merely be a narrow band of light. Only by viewing them from an inclined orbit can their full glory be appreciated.

Moreover, I suspect that conditions on the surface of Titan will make Antarctica look like Hawaii.

Yes, that's perfectly true. I met Morris Perlman when I was about twenty-eight. I met thousands of people in those days, from presidents downward.

When we got back from Saturn, everybody wanted to see us, and about half the crew took off on lecture tours. I've always enjoyed talking (don't say you haven't noticed it), but some of my colleagues said they'd rather go to Pluto than face another audience. Some of them did.

My beat was the Midwest, and the first time I ran into Mr. Perlman—no one ever called him anything else, certainly never "Morris"—was in Chicago. The agency always booked me into good, but not too luxurious, hotels. That suited me; I liked to stay in places where I could come and go as I pleased without running a gauntlet of liveried flunkies, and where I could wear anything within reason without being made to feel a tramp. I see you're grinning; well, I was only a kid then, and a lot of things have changed. . . .

It's all a long time ago now, but I must have been lecturing at the University. At any rate, I remember being disappointed because they couldn't show me the place where Fermi started the first atomic pile—they said that the building had been pulled

down forty years before, and there was only a plaque to mark
the spot. I stood looking at it for a while, thinking of all that
had happened since that far-off day in 1942. I'd been born, for
one thing; and atomic power had taken me out to Saturn and
back. *That* was probably something that Fermi and Co. never
thought of, when they built their primitive latticework of uranium and graphite.

I was having breakfast in the coffee shop when a slightly
built, middle-aged man dropped into the seat on the other side
of the table. He nodded a polite "Good morning," then gave a
start of surprise as he recognized me. (Of course, he'd planned
the encounter, but I didn't know it at the time.)

"This is a pleasure!" he said. "I was at your lecture last night.
How I envied you!"

I gave a rather forced smile; I'm never very sociable at breakfast, and I'd learned to be on my guard against the cranks,
bores, and enthusiasts who seemed to regard me as their legiti-
mate prey. Mr. Perlman, however, was not a bore—though he
was certainly an enthusiast, and I suppose you could call him a
crank.

He looked like any average, fairly prosperous businessman,
and I assumed that he was a guest like myself. The fact that he
had attended my lecture was not surprising; it had been a popular one, open to the public, and of course well advertised over
press and radio.

"Ever since I was a kid," said my uninvited companion, "Saturn has fascinated me. I know exactly when and how it all
started. I must have been about ten years old when I came
across those wonderful paintings of Chesley Bonestell's, showing the planet as it would look from its nine moons. I suppose
you've seen them?"

"Of course," I answered. "Though they're half a century old,
no one's beaten them yet. We had a couple aboard the *Endeav-*

our, pinned on the plotting table. I often used to look at the pictures and then compare them with the real thing."

"Then you know how I felt, back in the nineteen-fifties. I used to sit for hours trying to grasp the fact that this incredible object, with its silver rings spinning around it, wasn't just some artist's dream, but actually existed—that it was a world, in fact, ten times the size of Earth.

"At that time I never imagined that I could see this wonderful thing for myself; I took it for granted that only the astronomers, with their giant telescopes, could ever look at such sights. But then, when I was about fifteen, I made another discovery— so exciting that I could hardly believe it."

"And what was that?" I asked. By now I'd become reconciled to sharing breakfast; my companion seemed a harmless-enough character, and there was something quite endearing about his obvious enthusiasm.

"I found that any fool could make a high-powered astronomical telescope in his own kitchen, for a few dollars and a couple of weeks' work. It was a revelation; like thousands of other kids, I borrowed a copy of Ingalls' *Amateur Telescope Making* from the public library, and went ahead. Tell me—have *you* ever built a telescope of your own?"

"No: I'm an engineer, not an astronomer. I wouldn't know how to begin the job."

"It's incredibly simple, if you follow the rules. You start with two disks of glass, about an inch thick. I got mine for fifty cents from a ship chandler's; they were porthole glasses that were no use because they'd been chipped around the edges. Then you cement one disk to some flat, firm surface—I used an old barrel, standing on end.

"Next you have to buy several grades of emery powder, starting from coarse, gritty stuff and working down to the finest that's made. You lay a pinch of the coarsest powder between the two disks, and start rubbing the upper one back and forth with regular strokes. As you do so, you slowly circle around the job.

"You see what happens? The upper disk gets hollowed out by the cutting action of the emery powder, and as you walk around, it shapes itself into a concave, spherical surface. From time to time you have to change to a finer grade of powder, and make some simple optical tests to check that your curve's right.

"Later still, you drop the emery and switch to rouge, until at last you have a smooth, polished surface that you can hardly credit you've made yourself. There's only one more step, though that's a little tricky. You still have to silver the mirror, and turn it into a good reflector. This means getting some chemicals made up at the drugstore, and doing exactly what the book says.

"I can still remember the kick I got when the silver film began to spread like magic across the face of my little mirror. It wasn't perfect, but it was good enough, and I wouldn't have swapped it for anything on Mount Palomar.

"I fixed it at one end of a wooden plank; there was no need to bother about a telescope tube, though I put a couple of feet of cardboard round the mirror to cut out stray light. For an eyepiece I used a small magnifying lens I'd picked up in a junk store for a few cents. Altogether, I don't suppose the telescope cost more than five dollars—though that was a lot of money to me when I was a kid.

"We were living then in a run-down hotel my family owned on Third Avenue. When I'd assembled the telescope I went up on the roof and tried it out, among the jungle of TV antennas that covered every building in those days. It took me a while to get the mirror and eyepiece lined up, but I hadn't made any mistakes and the thing worked. As an optical instrument it was probably lousy—after all, it was my first attempt—but it magnified at least fifty times and I could hardly wait until nightfall to try it on the stars.

"I'd checked with the almanac, and knew that Saturn was high in the east after sunset. As soon as it was dark I was up on the roof again, with my crazy contraption of wood and glass propped between two chimneys. It was late fall, but I never noticed the cold, for the sky was full of stars—and they were all mine.

"I took my time setting the focus as accurately as possible, using the first star that came into the field. Then I started hunting for Saturn, and soon discovered how hard it was to locate anything in a reflecting telescope that wasn't properly mounted. But presently the planet shot across the field of view, I nudged the instrument a few inches this way and that—and there it was.

"It was tiny, but it was perfect. I don't think I breathed for a minute; I could hardly believe my eyes. After all the pictures, here was the reality. It looked like a toy hanging there in space, with the rings slightly open and tilted toward me. Even now, forty years later, I can remember thinking 'It looks so *artificial*—like something from a Christmas tree!' There was a single bright star to the left of it, and I knew that was Titan."

He paused, and for a moment we must have shared the same thoughts. For to both of us Titan was no longer merely the largest moon of Saturn—a point of light known only to astronomers. It was the fiercely hostile world upon which *Endeavour* had landed, and where three of my crew-mates lay in lonely graves, farther from their homes than any of Mankind's dead had ever rested before.

"I don't know how long I stared, straining my eyes and moving the telescope across the sky in jerky steps as Saturn rose above the city. I was a billion miles from New York; but presently New York caught up with me.

"I told you about our hotel; it belonged to my mother, but my father ran it—not very well. It had been losing money for years, and all through my boyhood there had been continuous financial crises. So I don't want to blame my father for drinking; he must have been half crazy with worry most of the time. And I had quite forgotten that I was supposed to be helping the clerk at the reception desk. . . .

"So Dad came looking for me, full of his own cares and knowing nothing about my dreams. He found me stargazing on the roof.

"He wasn't a cruel man—he couldn't have understood the study and patience and care that had gone into my little telescope, or the wonders it had shown me during the short time I had used it. I don't hate him any more, but I'll remember all my life the splintering crack of my first and last mirror as it smashed against the brickwork."

There was nothing I could say. My initial resentment at this interruption had long since changed to curiosity. Already I sensed that there was much more to this story than I'd heard so far, and I'd noticed something else. The waitress was treating us with an exaggerated deference—only a little of which was directed at me.

My companion toyed with the sugar bowl while I waited in silent sympathy. By this time I felt there was some bond between us, though I did not know exactly what it was.

"I never built another telescope," he said. "Something else broke, besides that mirror—something in my heart. Anyway, I was much too busy. Two things happened that turned my life upside down. Dad walked out on us, leaving me the head of the family. And then they pulled down the Third Avenue El."

He must have seen my puzzled look, for he grinned across the table at me.

"Oh, you wouldn't know about that. But when I was a kid, there was an elevated railroad down the middle of Third. It made the whole area dirty and noisy; the Avenue was a slum district of bars, pawnshops and cheap hotels—like ours. All that changed when the El went; land values shot up, and we were suddenly prosperous. Dad came back quickly enough, but it was too late; I was running the business. Before long I started moving across town—then across country. I wasn't an absent-minded stargazer any more, and I gave Dad one of my smaller hotels, where he couldn't do much harm.

"It's forty years since I looked at Saturn, but I've never forgotten that one glimpse, and last night your photographs brought it all back. I just wanted to say how grateful I am."

He fumbled in his wallet and pulled out a card.

"I hope you'll look me up when you're in town again; you can be sure I'll be there if you give any more lectures. Good luck—and I'm sorry to have taken so much of your time."

Then he was gone, almost before I could say a word. I glanced at the card, put it away in my pocket, and finished my breakfast, rather thoughtfully.

When I signed my check on the way out of the coffee shop I asked: "Who was that gentleman at my table? The boss?"

The cashier looked at me as if I were mentally retarded.

"I suppose you *could* call him that, sir," she answered. "Of course he owns this hotel, but we've never seen him here before. He always stays at the Ambassador, when he's in Chicago."

"And does he own *that*?" I said, without too much irony, for I'd already suspected the answer.

"Why, yes. As well as —" and she rattled off a whole string of others, including the two biggest hotels in New York.

I was impressed, and also rather amused, for it was now obvious that Mr. Perlman had come here with the deliberate intention of meeting me. It seemed a roundabout way of doing it; I knew nothing then, of his notorious shyness and secretiveness. From the first, he was never shy with me.

Then I forgot about him for five years. (Oh, I should mention that when I asked for my bill, I was told I didn't have one.) During that five years, I made my second trip.

We knew what to expect this time, and weren't going completely into the unknown. There were no more worries about fuel, because all we could ever use was waiting for us on Titan; we just had to pump its methane atmosphere into our tanks, and we'd made our plans accordingly. One after another, we visited all the nine moons; and then we went into the rings. . . .

There was little danger, yet it was a nerve-racking experience. The ring system is very thin, you know—only about twenty miles in thickness. We descended into it slowly and cautiously, after having matched its spin so that we were moving at exactly the same speed. It was like stepping onto a carousel a hundred and seventy thousand miles across. . . .

But a ghostly kind of carousel, because the rings aren't solid and you can look right through them. Close up, in fact, they're almost invisible; the billions of separate particles that make them up are so widely spaced that all you see in your immediate neighborhood are occasional small chunks, drifting very slowly past. It's only when you look into the distance that the countless fragments merge into a continuous sheet, like a hailstorm that sweeps around Saturn forever.

That's not *my* phrase, but it's a good one. For when we brought our first piece of genuine Saturnian ring into the air lock, it melted down in a few minutes into a pool of muddy water. Some people think it spoils the magic to know that the rings—or ninety per cent of them—are made of ordinary ice. But that's a stupid attitude; they would be just as wonderful, and just as beautiful, if they were made of diamond.

When I got back to Earth, in the first year of the new century, I started off on another lecture tour—only a short one, for now I had a family and wanted to see as much of it as possible. This time I ran into Mr. Perlman in New York, when I was speaking at Columbia and showing our movie, "Exploring Saturn." (A misleading title, that, since the nearest we'd been to the planet itself was about twenty thousand miles. No one dreamed, in those days, that men would ever go down into the turbulent slush which is the closest thing Saturn has to a surface.)

Mr. Perlman was waiting for me after the lecture. I didn't recognize him, for I'd met about a million people since our last encounter. But when he gave his name, it all came back, so clearly that I realized he must have made a deep impression on my mind.

Somehow he got me away from the crowd; though he disliked meeting people in the mass, he had an extraordinary knack of dominating any group when he found it necessary—and then clearing out before his victims knew what had happened. Though I saw him in action scores of times, I never knew exactly how he did it.

At any rate, half an hour later we were having a superb dinner in an exclusive restaurant (his, of course). It was a wonderful meal, especially after the chicken and ice cream of the lecture circuit, but he made me pay for it. Metaphorically, I mean.

Now all the facts and photos gathered by the two expeditions to Saturn were available to everyone, in hundreds of reports and books and popular articles. Mr. Perlman seemed to have read all the material that wasn't too technical; what he wanted from me was something different. Even then, I put his interest down to that of a lonely, aging man, trying to recapture a dream that had been lost in youth. I was right; but that was only a fraction of the whole picture.

He was after something that all the reports and articles failed to give. What did it *feel* like, he wanted to know, to wake up in the morning and see that great, golden globe with its scudding cloud belts dominating the sky? And the rings themselves—what did they do to your mind when they were so close that they filled the heavens from end to end?

You want a poet, I said—not an engineer. But I'll tell you this; however long you look at Saturn, and fly in and out among its moons, you can never quite believe it. Every so often you find yourself thinking: "It's all a dream—a thing like that *can't* be real." And you go to the nearest view-port—and there it is, taking your breath away.

You must remember that, altogether apart from our nearness, we were able to look at the rings from angles and vantage points that are quite impossible from Earth, where you always see them turned toward the sun. We could fly into their shadow, and then they would no longer gleam like silver—they would be a faint haze, a bridge of smoke across the stars.

And most of the time we could see the shadow of Saturn lying across the full width of the rings, eclipsing them so completely that it seemed as if a great bite had been taken out of them. It worked the other way, too; on the day side of the planet, there would always be the shadow of the rings running like a dusky band parallel to the Equator and not far from it.

Above all—though we did this only a few times—we could rise high above either pole of the planet and look down upon the whole stupendous system, so that it was spread out in plan beneath us. Then we could see that instead of the four visible from Earth, there were at least a dozen separate rings, merging one onto the other. When we saw this, our skipper made a remark that I've never forgotten. "This," he said—and there wasn't a trace of flippancy in the words—"is where the angels have parked their halos."

All this, and a lot more, I told Mr. Perlman in that little but oh-so-expensive restaurant just south of Central Park. When I'd finished, he seemed very pleased, though he was silent for several minutes. Then he said, about as casually as you might ask the time of the next train at your local station: "Which would be the best satellite for a tourist resort?"

When the words got through to me, I nearly choked on my hundred-year-old brandy. Then I said, very patiently and politely (for after all, I'd had a wonderful dinner): "Listen, Mr.

Perlman. You know as well as I do that Saturn is nearly a billion miles from Earth—more than that, in fact, when we're on opposite sides of the sun. Someone worked out that our round-trip tickets averaged seven and a half million dollars apiece—and, believe me, there was no first-class accommodation on *Endeavour I* or *II*. Anyway, no matter how much money he had, no one could book a passage to Saturn. Only scientists and space crews will be going there, for as far ahead as anyone can imagine."

I could see that my words had absolutely no effect: he merely smiled, as if he knew some secret hidden from me.

"What you say is true enough *now*," he answered, "but I've studied history. And I understand people—that's my business. Let me remind you of a few facts.

"Two or three centuries ago, almost all the world's great tourist centers and beauty spots were as far away from civilization as Saturn is today. What did—oh, Napoleon, let's say—know about the Grand Canyon, Victoria Falls, Hawaii, Mount Everest? And look at the South Pole; it was reached for the first time when my father was a boy—but there's been a hotel there for the whole of your lifetime.

"Now it's starting all over again. *You* can appreciate only the problems and difficulties, because you're too close to them. Whatever they are, men will overcome them, as they've always done in the past.

"For wherever there's something strange or beautiful or novel, people will want to see it. The rings of Saturn are the greatest spectacle in the known universe: I've always guessed so, and now you've convinced me. Today it takes a fortune to reach them, and the men who go there must risk their lives. So did the first men who flew—but now there are a million passengers in the air every second of the day and night.

"The same thing is going to happen in space. It won't happen in ten years, maybe not in twenty. But twenty-five is all it took, remember, before the first commercial flights started to the moon. I don't think it will be as long for Saturn. . . .

"I won't be around to see it—but when it happens, I want people to remember me. So—where should we build?"

I still thought he was crazy, but at last I was beginning to understand what made him tick. And there was no harm in humoring him, so I gave the matter careful thought.

"Mimas is too close," I said, "and so are Enceladus and Tethys." (I don't mind telling you, those names were tough after all that brandy.) "Saturn just fills the sky, and you think it's falling on top of you. Besides, they aren't solid enough—they're nothing but overgrown snowballs. Dione and Rhea are better— you get a magnificent view from both of them. But all these inner moons are so tiny; even Rhea is only eight hundred miles across, and the others are much smaller.

"I don't think there's any real argument; it will have to be Titan. That's a man-sized satellite—it's a lot bigger than *our* moon, and very nearly as large as Mars. There's a reasonable gravity too—about a fifth of Earth's—so your guests won't be floating all over the place. And it will always be a major refueling point because of its methane atmosphere, which should be an important factor in your calculations. Every ship that goes out to Saturn will touch down there."

"And the outer moons?"

"Oh, Hyperion, Japetus, and Phoebe are much too far away. You have to look hard to see the rings at all from Phoebe! Forget about them. Stick to good old Titan. Even if the temperature is two hundred below zero, and ammonia snow isn't the sort of stuff you'd want to ski on."

He listened to me very carefully, and if he thought I was making fun of his impractical, unscientific notions he gave no sign of it. We parted soon afterward—I don't remember anything more of that dinner—and then it must have been fifteen years

before we met again. He had no further use for me in all that
time; but when he wanted me, he called.

I see now what he had been waiting for; his vision had been
clearer than mine. He couldn't have guessed, of course, that the
rocket would go the way of the steam engine within less than a
century—but he knew *something* better would come along,
and I think he financed Saunderson's early work on the Para-
gravity Drive. But it was not until they started building fusion
plants that could warm up a hundred square miles of a world as
cold as Pluto that he got in contact with me again.

He was a very old man, and dying. They told me how rich he
was, and I could hardly believe it. Not until he showed me the
elaborate plans and the beautiful models his experts had prepared with such remarkable lack of publicity.

He sat in his wheel chair like a wrinkled mummy, watching
my face as I studied the models and blueprints. Then he said:
"Captain, I have a job for you. . . ."

So here I am. It's just like running a spaceship, of course—
many of the technical problems are identical. And by this time
I'd be too old to command a ship, so I'm very grateful to Mr.
Perlman.

There goes the gong. If the ladies are ready, I suggest we walk
down to dinner through the Observation Lounge.

Even after all these years, I still like to watch Saturn rising—
and tonight it's almost full.

THE MAN WHO PLOUGHED THE SEA

Like "The Next Tenants," this story was written specifically for *Tales from the White Hart,* and at the same time and place (Miami, 1954), when I was still under the influence of my first contact with the world of coral reefs. Later that same year, I was to depart to the mightiest of them all—the Great Barrier Reef of Australia.

I would like to dedicate this story to my Florida friends of long ago, especially the family of my scuba-diving host, the late Dr. George Grisinger.

Despite the lapse of time, many of the themes of this story

are surprisingly up to date, and a few years ago I was amazed to read a description in a scientific journal of a ship-borne device to extract uranium from seawater! I sent a copy of the story to the inventors, and apologized for invalidating their patent.

This tale should be read in conjunction with "On Golden Seas" which deals with the same theme. However, there has been a later development—the discovery of the midocean geo-thermal vents, where superheated water laden with minerals is gushing out of the seabed. *That's* the place to look for valuable metals, not the open ocean.

There's gold in them thar vents. . . .

The adventures of Harry Purvis have a kind of mad logic that makes then convincing by their very improbability. As his complicated but neatly dove-tailed stories emerge, one becomes lost in a sort of baffled wonder. Surely, you say to yourself, no-one would have the nerve to make *that* up—such absurdities only occur in real life, not in fiction. And so criticism is disarmed, or at any rate discomfitted, until Drew shouts "Time, gentlemen, *pleeze!*" and throws us all out into the cold hard world.

Consider, for example, the unlikely chain of events which involved Harry in the following adventure. If he'd wanted to invent the whole thing, surely he could have managed it a lot more simply. There was not the slightest need, from the artistic point of view, to have started at Boston to make an appointment off the coast of Florida. . . .

Harry seems to have spent a good deal of time in the United States, and to have quite as many friends there as he has in England. Sometimes he brings them to the "White Hart," and sometimes they leave again under their own power. Often, however, they succumb to the illusion that beer which is tepid is also innocuous. (I am being unjust to Drew: his beer is *not* tepid.

And if you insist, he will give you, for no extra charge, a piece
of ice every bit as large as a postage-stamp.)

This particular saga of Harry's began, as I have indicated, at
Boston, Mass. He was staying as a house-guest of a successful
New England lawyer when one morning his host said, in the
casual way Americans have: "Let's go down to my place in Florida. I want to get some sun."

"Fine," said Harry, who'd never been to Florida. Thirty minutes later, to his considerable surprise, he found himself moving
south in a red Jaguar saloon at a formidable speed.

The drive in itself was an epic worthy of a complete story.
From Boston to Miami is a little matter of 1,568 miles—a figure which, according to Harry, is now engraved on his heart.
They covered the distance in 30 hours, frequently to the sound
of ever-receding police sirens as frustrated squad-cars dwindled
astern. From time to time considerations of tactics involved
them in evasive maneuvers and they had to shoot off into
secondary roads. The Jaguar's radio tuned in to all the police
frequencies, so they always had plenty of warning if an
interception was being arranged. Once or twice they just managed to reach a state line in time, and Harry couldn't help wondering what his host's clients would have thought had they
known the strength of the psychological urge which was obviously getting him away from them. He also wondered if he was
going to see anything of Florida at all, or whether they would
continue at this velocity down US 1 until they shot into the
ocean at Key West.

They finally came to a halt sixty miles south of Miami,
down on the Keys—that long, thin line of islands hooked on to
the lower end of Florida. The Jaguar angled suddenly off the
road and weaved a way through a rough track cut in the man-
groves. The road ended in a wide clearing at the edge of the sea,
complete with dock, 35-foot cabin cruiser, swimming pool,
and modern ranch-type house. It was quite a nice little hide-

away, and Harry estimated that it must have cost the best part of a hundred thousand dollars.

He didn't see much of the place until the next day, as he collapsed straight into bed. After what seemed far too short a time, he was awakened by a sound like a boiler factory in action. He showered and dressed in slow motion, and was reasonably back to normal by the time he had left his room. There seemed to be no one in the house, so he went outside to explore.

By this time he had learned not to be surprised at anything, so he barely raised his eyebrows when he found his host working down at the dock, straightening out the rudder on a tiny and obviously home-made submarine. The little craft was about twenty feet long, had a conning tower with large observation windows, and bore the name "Pompano" stencilled on her prow.

After some reflection, Harry decided that there was nothing really very unusual about all this. About five million visitors come to Florida every year, most of them determined to get on or into the sea. His host happened to be one of those fortunate enough to indulge in his hobby in a big way.

Harry looked at the "Pompano" for some time, and then a disturbing thought struck him. "George," he said, "do you expect me to go down in *that* thing?"

"Why, sure," answered George, giving a final bash at the rudder. "What are you worried about? I've taken her out lots of times—she's safe as houses. We won't be going deeper than twenty feet."

"There are circumstances," retorted Harry, "when I should find a mere six feet of water more than adequate. And didn't I mention my claustrophobia? It always comes on badly at this time of year."

"Nonsense!" said George. "You'll forget all about that when we're out on the reef." He stood back and surveyed his handiwork, then said with a sigh of satisfaction, "Looks O.K. now. Let's have some breakfast."

During the next thirty minutes, Harry learned a good deal about the "Pompano." George had designed and built her himself, and her powerful little Diesel could drive her at five knots when she was fully submerged. Both crew and engine breathed through a snorkle tube, so there was no need to bother about electric motors and an independent air supply. The length of the snorkle limited dives to twenty-five feet, but in these shallow waters this was no great handicap.

"I've put a lot of novel ideas into her," said George enthusiastically. "Those windows, for instance—look at their size. They'll give you a perfect view, yet they're quite safe. I use the old Aqualung principle to keep the air-pressure in the 'Pompano' exactly the same as the water-pressure outside, so there's no strain on the hull or the ports."

"And what happens," asked Harry, "if you get stuck on the bottom?"

"I open the door and get out, of course. There are a couple of spare Aqualungs in the cabin, as well as a life-raft with a waterproof radio, so that we can always yell for help if we get in trouble. Don't worry—I've thought of everything."

"Famous last words," muttered Harry. But he decided that after the ride down from Boston he undoubtedly had a charmed life: the sea was probably a safer place than US 1 with George at the wheel.

He made himself thoroughly familiar with the escape arrangements before they set out, and was fairly happy when he saw how well designed and constructed the little craft appeared to be. The fact that a lawyer had produced such a neat piece of marine engineering in his spare time was not in the least unusual. Harry had long ago discovered that a considerable number of Americans put quite as much effort into their hobbies as into their professions.

They chugged out of the little harbor, keeping to the marked channel until they were well clear of the coast. The sea was calm and as the shore receded the water became steadily more and more transparent. They were leaving behind the fog of pulverized coral which clouded the coastal waters, where the waves were incessantly tearing at the land. After thirty minutes they had come to the reef, visible below them as a kind of patchwork quilt above which multicolored fish pirouetted to and fro. George closed the hatches, opened the valve of the buoyancy tanks, and said gaily, "Here we go!"

The wrinkled silk veil lifted, crept past the window, distorting all vision for a moment—and then they were through, no longer aliens looking into the world of waters, but denizens of that world themselves. They were floating above a valley carpeted with white sand, and surrounded by low hills of coral. The valley itself was barren but the hills around it were alive with things that grew, things that crawled and things that swam. Fish as dazzling as neon signs wandered lazily among the animals that looked like trees. It seemed not only a breathtakingly lovely but also a peaceful world. There was no haste, no sign of the struggle for existence. Harry knew very well that this was an illusion, but during all the time they were submerged he never saw one fish attack another. He mentioned this to George, who commented: "Yes, that's a funny thing about fish. They seem to have definite feeding times. You can see barracuda swimming around and if the dinner gong hasn't gone the other fish won't take any notice of them."

A ray, looking like some fantastic black butterfly, flapped its way across the sand, balancing itself with its long, whiplike tail. The sensitive feelers of a crayfish waved cautiously from a crack in the coral; the exploring gestures reminded Harry of a soldier testing for snipers with his hat on a stick. There was so much life, of so many kinds, crammed in this single spot that it would take years of study to recognize it all.

The "Pompano" cruised very slowly along the valley, while George gave a running commentary.

"I used to do this sort of thing with the Aqualung," he said, "but then I decided how nice it would be to sit in comfort and have an engine to push me around. Then I could stay out all day, take a meal along, use my cameras and not give a damn if a shark was sneaking up on me. There goes a tang—did you ever see such a brilliant blue in your life? Besides, I could show my friends around down here while still being able to talk to them. That's one big handicap with ordinary diving gear—you're deaf and dumb and have to talk in signs. Look at those angelfish— one day I'm going to fix up a net to catch some of them. See the way they vanish when they're edge-on! Another reason why I built the 'Pompano' was so that I could look for wrecks. There are hundreds in this area—it's an absolute graveyard. The 'Santa Margarita' is only about fifty miles from here, in Biscayne Bay. She went down in 1595 with seven million dollars of bullion aboard. And there's a little matter of sixty-five million off Long Cay, where fourteen galleons sank in 1715. The trouble is, of course, that most of these wrecks have been smashed up and overgrown with coral, so it wouldn't do you a lot of good even if you did locate them. But it's fun to try."

By this time Harry had begun to appreciate his friend's psychology. He could think of few better ways of escaping from a New England law practice. George was a repressed romantic— and not such a repressed one, either, now that he came to think of it.

They cruised along happily for a couple of hours, keeping in water that was never more than forty feet deep. Once they grounded on a dazzling stretch of broken coral, and took time off for liverwurst sandwiches and glasses of beer. "I drank some ginger beer down here once," said George. "When I came up the gas inside me expanded and it was a very odd sort of feeling. Must try it with champagne some day."

Harry was just wondering what to do with the empties when the "Pompano" seemed to go into eclipse as a dark shadow drifted overhead. Looking up through the observation window, he saw that a ship was moving slowly past twenty feet above their heads. There was no danger of a collision, as they had pulled down their snort for just this reason and were subsisting for the moment on their capital as far as air was concerned. Harry had never seen a ship from underneath and began to add another novel experience to the many he had acquired today.

He was quite proud of the fact that, despite his ignorance of matters nautical, he was just as quick as George at spotting what was wrong with the vessel sailing overhead. Instead of the normal shaft and screw, this ship had a long tunnel running the length of its keel. As it passed above them, the "Pompano" was rocked by the sudden rush of water.

"I'll be damned!" said George, grabbing the controls. "That looks like some kind of jet propulsion system. It's about time somebody tried one out. Let's have a look."

He pushed up the periscope, and discovered that the ship slowly cruising past them was the "Valency," of New Orleans. "That's a funny name," he said. "What does it mean?"

"I would say," answered Harry, "that it means the owner is a chemist—except for the fact that no chemist would ever make enough money to buy a ship like that."

"I'm going to follow her," decided George. "She's only making five knots, and I'd like to see how that dingus works."

He elevated the snort, got the diesel running, and started in pursuit. After a brief chase, the "Pompano" drew within fifty feet of the "Valency," and Harry felt rather like a submarine commander about to launch a torpedo. They couldn't miss from this distance.

In fact, they nearly made a direct hit. For the "Valency" suddenly slowed to a halt, and before George realized what had happened, he was alongside her. "No signals!" he complained, without much logic. A minute later, it was clear that the maneuver was no accident. A lasso dropped neatly over the "Pompano's" snorkle and they were efficiently gaffed. There was nothing to do but emerge, rather sheepishly, and make the best of it.

Fortunately, their captors were reasonable men and could recognize the truth when they heard it. Fifteen minutes after coming aboard the "Valency," George and Harry were sitting on the bridge while a uniformed steward brought them highballs and they listened attentively to the theories of Dr. Gilbert Romano.

They were still both a little overawed at being in Dr. Romano's presence: it was rather like meeting a live Rockefeller or a reigning du Pont. The Doctor was a phenomenon virtually unknown in Europe and unusual even in the United States—the big scientist who had become a bigger businessman. He was now in his late seventies and had just been retired—after a considerable tussle—from the chairmanship of the vast chemical engineering firm he had founded.

It is rather amusing, Harry told us, to notice the subtle social distinctions which differences in wealth can produce even in the most democratic country. By Harry's standards, George was a very rich man: his income was around a hundred thousand dollars a year. But Dr. Romano was in another price range altogether, and had to be treated accordingly with a kind of friendly respect which had nothing to do with obsequiousness. On his side, the Doctor was perfectly free and easy; there was nothing about him that gave any impression of wealth, if one ignored such trivia as hundred-and-fifty-foot ocean-going yachts.

The fact that George was on first-name terms with most of the Doctor's business acquaintances helped to break the ice and to establish the purity of their motives. Harry spent a boring half hour while business deals ranging over half the United

States were discussed in terms of what Bill So-and-so did in Pittsburgh, who Joe Somebody Else ran into at the Bankers' Club in Houston, how Clyde Thingummy happened to be playing golf at Augusta while Ike was there. It was a glimpse of a mysterious world where immense power was wielded by men who all seemed to have gone to the same colleges, or who at any rate belonged to the same clubs. Harry soon became aware of the fact that George was not merely paying court to Dr. Romano because that was the polite thing to do. George was too shrewd a lawyer to miss this chance of building up some good-will, and appeared to have forgotten all about the original purpose of their expedition.

Harry had to wait for a suitable gap in the conversation before he could raise the subject which really interested him. When it dawned on Dr. Romano that he was talking to another scientist, he promptly abandoned finance and George was the one who was left out in the cold.

The thing that puzzled Harry was why a distinguished chemist should be interested in marine propulsion. Being a man of direct action, he challenged the Doctor on this point. For a moment the scientist appeared a little embarrassed and Harry was about to apologize for his inquisitiveness—a feat that would have required real effort on his part. But before he could do this, Dr. Romano had excused himself and disappeared into the bridge.

He came back five minutes later with a rather satisfied expression, and continued as if nothing had happened.

"A very natural question, Mr. Purvis," he chuckled. "I'd have asked it myself. But do you really expect me to tell you?"

"Er—it was just a vague sort of hope," confessed Harry.

"Then I'm going to surprise you—surprise you twice, in fact. I'm going to answer you, and I'm going to show you that I'm *not* passionately interested in marine propulsion. Those bulges on the bottom of my ship which you were inspecting with such great interest do contain the screws, but they also contain a good deal else as well.

"Let me give you," continued Dr. Romano, now obviously warming up to his subject, "a few elementary statistics about the ocean. We can see a lot of it from here—quite a few square miles. Did you know that every cubic mile of sea-water contains a hundred and fifty *million* tons of minerals."

"Frankly, no," said George. "It's an impressive thought."

"It's impressed me for a long time," said the Doctor. "Here we go grubbing about in the earth for our metals and chemicals, while every element that exists can be found in sea-water. The ocean, in fact, is a kind of universal mine which can never be exhausted. We may plunder the land, but we'll never empty the sea.

"Men have already started to mine the sea, you know. Dow Chemicals have been taking out bromine for years: every cubic mile contains about three hundred thousand tons. More recently, we've started to do something about the five million tons of magnesium per cubic mile. But that sort of thing is merely a beginning.

"The great practical problem is that most of the elements present in sea-water are in such low concentrations. The first seven elements make up about 99 percent of the total, and it's the remaining one percent that contains all the useful metals except magnesium.

"All my life I've wondered how we could do something about this, and the answer came during the war. I don't know if you're familiar with the techniques used in the atomic energy field to remove minute quantities of isotopes from solutions: some of those methods are still pretty much under wraps."

"Are you talking about ion-exchange resins?" hazarded Harry.

"Well—something similar. My firm developed several of

these techniques on A.E.C. contracts, and I realized at once that they would have wider applications. I put some of my bright young men to work and they have made what we call a 'molecular sieve.' That's a mighty descriptive expression: in its way, the thing *is* a sieve, and we can set it to select anything we like. It depends on very advanced wave-mechanical theories for its operation, but what it actually does is absurdly simple. We can choose any component of sea-water we like, and get the sieve to take it out. With several units, working in series, we can take out one element after another. The efficiency's quite high, and the power consumption negligible."

"I know!" yelped George. "You're extracting gold from sea-water!"

"Huh!" snorted Dr. Romano in tolerant disgust. "I've got better things to do with my time. Too much damn gold around, anyhow. I'm after the commercially useful metals—the ones our civilization is going to be desperately short of in another couple of generations. And as a matter of fact, even with my sieve it wouldn't be worth going after gold. There are only about fifty pounds of the stuff in every cubic mile."

"What about uranium?" asked Harry. "Or is that scarcer still?"

"I rather wish you hadn't asked that question," replied Dr. Romano with a cheerfulness that belied the remark. "But since you can look it up in any library, there's no harm in telling you that uranium's two hundred times *more* common than gold. About seven tons in every cubic mile—a figure which is, shall we say, distinctly interesting. So why bother about gold?"

"Why indeed?" echoed George.

"To continue," said Dr. Romano, duly continuing, "even with the molecular sieve, we've still got the problem of processing enormous volumes of sea-water. There are a number of ways one could tackle this: you could build giant pumping stations, for example. But I've always been keen on killing two birds with one stone, and the other day I did a little calculation that gave the most surprising result. I found that every time the 'Queen Mary' crosses the Atlantic, her screws chew up about a tenth of a cubic mile of water. Fifteen million tons of minerals, in other words. Or to take the case you indiscreetly mentioned— almost a ton of uranium on every Atlantic crossing. Quite a thought, isn't it?

"So it seemed to me that all we need do to create a very useful mobile extraction plant was to put the screws of any vessel inside a tube which would compel the slip-stream to pass through one of my sieves. Of course, there's a certain loss of propulsive power, but our experimental unit works very well. We can't go quite as fast as we did, but the further we cruise the more money we make from our mining operations. Don't you think the shipping companies will find that very attractive? But of course that's merely incidental. I look forward to the building of floating extraction plants that will cruise round and round in the ocean until they've filled their hoppers with anything you care to name. When that day comes, we'll be able to stop tearing up the land and all our material shortages will be over. Everything goes back to the sea in the long run anyway, and once we've unlocked that treasure-chest, we'll be all set for eternity."

For a moment there was silence on deck, save for the faint clink of ice in the tumblers, while Dr. Romano's guests contemplated this dazzling prospect. Then Harry was struck by a sudden thought.

"This is quite one of the most important inventions I've ever heard of," he said. "That's why I find it rather odd that you should have confided in us so fully. After all, we're perfect strangers, and for all you know might be spying on you."

The old scientist chortled gaily.

"Don't worry about *that,* my boy," he reassured Harry. "I've already been on to Washington and had my friends check up on you."

Harry blinked for a minute, then realized how it had been done. He remembered Dr. Romano's brief disappearance, and could picture what had happened. There would have been a radio call to Washington, some senator would have got on to the Embassy, the Ministry of Supply representative would have done his bit—and in five minutes the Doctor would have got the answer he wanted. Yes, Americans were very efficient— those who could afford to be.

It was about this time that Harry became aware of the fact that they were no longer alone. A much larger and more impressive yacht than the "Valency" was heading towards them, and in a few minutes he was able to read the name "Sea Spray." Such a name, he thought, was more appropriate to billowing sails than throbbing diesels, but there was no doubt that the "Spray" was a very pretty creature indeed. He could understand the looks of undisguised covetousness that both George and Dr. Romano now plainly bore.

The sea was so calm that the two yachts were able to come alongside each other, and as soon as they had made contact a sunburned, energetic man in his late forties vaulted over on to the deck of the "Valency." He strode up to Dr. Romano, shook his hand vigorously, said, "Well, you old rascal, what are you up to?" and then looked enquiringly at the rest of the company. The Doctor carried out the introductions: it seemed that they had been boarded by Professor Scott McKenzie, who'd been sailing *his* yacht down from Key Largo.

"Oh no!" cried Harry to himself. "This is *too* much! One millionaire scientist per day is all I can stand."

But there was no getting away from it. True, McKenzie was very seldom seen in the academic cloisters, but he was a genuine Professor none the less, holding the chair of geophysics at

some Texas college. Ninety percent of his time, however, he
spent working for the big oil companies and running a consult-
ing firm of his own. It rather looked as if he had made his tor-
sion balances and seismographs pay quite well for themselves.
In fact, though he was a much younger man than Dr. Romano,
he had even more money owing to being in a more rapidly expanding industry. Harry gathered that the peculiar tax laws of
the Sovereign State of Texas also had something to do with
it. . . .

It seemed an unlikely coincidence that these two scientific
tycoons should have met by chance, and Harry waited to see
what skullduggery was afoot. For a while the conversation was
confined to generalities, but it was obvious that Professor
McKenzie was extremely inquisitive about the Doctor's other
two guests. Not long after they had been introduced, he made
some excuse to hop back to his own ship and Harry moaned
inwardly. If the Embassy got two separate enquiries about him
in the space of half an hour, they'd wonder what he'd been up
to. It might even make the F.B.I. suspicious, and then how
would he get those promised twenty-four pairs of nylons out of
the country?

Harry found it quite fascinating to study the relationship
between the two scientists. They were like a couple of fighting
cocks circling for position. Romano treated the younger man
with a downright rudeness which, Harry suspected, concealed
a grudging admiration. It was clear that Dr. Romano was an
almost fanatical conservationist, and regarded the activities of
McKenzie and his employers with the greatest disapproval.
"You're a gang of robbers," he said once. "You're seeing how
quickly you can loot this planet of its resources, and you don't
give a damn about the next generation."

"And what," answered McKenzie, not very originally, "has
the next generation ever done for us?"

The sparring continued for the best part of an hour, and

much of what went on was completely over Harry's head. He wondered why he and George were being allowed to sit in on all this, and after a while he began to appreciate Dr. Romano's technique. He was an opportunist of genius: he was glad to keep them round, now that they had turned up, just to worry Professor McKenzie and to make him wonder what other deals were afoot.

He let the molecular sieve leak out bit by bit, as if it wasn't *really* important and he was only mentioning it in passing. Professor McKenzie, however, latched on to it at once, and the more evasive Romano became, the more insistent was his adversary. It was obvious that he was being deliberately coy, and that though Professor McKenzie knew this perfectly well, he couldn't help playing the older scientist's game.

Dr. Romano had been discussing the device in a peculiarly oblique fashion, as if it were a future project rather than an existing fact. He outlined its staggering possibilities, and explained how it would make all existing forms of mining obsolete, besides removing forever the danger of world metal shortages.

"If it's so good," exclaimed McKenzie presently, "why haven't you made the thing?"

"What do you think I'm doing out here in the Gulf Stream?" retorted the Doctor. "Take a look at this."

He opened a locker beneath the sonar set, and pulled out a small metal bar which he tossed to McKenzie. It looked like lead, and was obviously extremely heavy. The Professor hefted it in his hand and said at once: "Uranium. Do you mean to say. . . ."

"Yes—every gram. And there's plenty more where that came from." He turned to Harry's friend and said: "George—what about taking the Professor down in your submarine to have a look at the works? He won't see much, but it'll show him we're in business."

McKenzie was still so thoughtful that he took a little thing like a private submarine in his stride. He returned to the surface fifteen minutes later, having seen just enough to whet his appetite.

"The first thing I want to know," he said to Romano, "is why you're showing this to *me!* It's about the biggest thing that ever happened—why isn't your own firm handling it?"

Romano gave a little snort of disgust.

"You know I've had a row with the Board," he said. "Anyway, that lot of old dead-beats couldn't handle anything as big as this. I hate to admit it, but you Texas pirates are the boys for the job."

"This is a private venture of yours?"

"Yes: the company knows nothing about it, and I've sunk half a million of my own money into it. It's been a kind of hobby of mine. I felt someone had to undo the damage that was going on, the rape of the continents by people like—"

"All right—we've heard that before. Yet you propose giving it to us?"

"Who said anything about giving?"

There was a pregnant silence. Then McKenzie said cautiously, "Of course, there's no need to tell you that we'll be interested—very interested. If you'll let us have the figures on efficiency, extraction rates, and all the other relevant statistics—no need to tell us the actual technical details if you don't want to—then we'll be able to talk business. I can't really speak for my associates but I'm sure that they can raise enough cover to make any deal—"

"Scott," said Romano—and his voice now held a note of tiredness that for the first time reflected his age—"I'm not interested in doing a deal with your partners. I haven't time to haggle with the boys in the front room and their lawyers and their lawyers' lawyers. Fifty years I've been doing that sort of thing, and believe me, I'm tired. This is *my* development. It was done with *my* money, and all the equipment is in *my* ship. I want to do a personal deal, direct with you. You can handle it from then on."

McKenzie blinked.

"I couldn't swing anything as big as this," he protested. "Sure, I appreciate the offer, but if this does what you say, it's worth billions. And I'm just a poor but honest millionaire."

"Money I'm no longer interested in. What would I do with it at my time of life? No, Scott, there's just one thing I want now—and I want it right away, this minute. Give me the 'Sea Spray,' and you can have my process."

"You're crazy! Why, even with inflation, you could build the 'Spray' for inside a million. And your process must be worth—"

"I'm not arguing, Scott. What you say is true, but I'm an old man in a hurry, and it would take me a year to get a ship like yours built. I've wanted her ever since you showed her to me back at Miami. My proposal is that you take over the 'Valency,' with all her lab equipment and records. It will only take an hour to swap our personal effects—we've a lawyer here who can make it all legal. And then I'm heading out into the Caribbean, down through the islands, and across the Pacific."

"You've got it all worked out?" said McKenzie in awed wonder.

"Yes. You can take it or leave it."

"I never heard such a crazy deal in my life," said McKenzie, somewhat petulantly. "Of course I'll take it. I know a stubborn old mule when I see one."

The next hour was one of frantic activity. Sweating crew-members rushed back and forth with suitcases and bundles, while Dr. Romano sat happily in the midst of the turmoil he had created, a blissful smile upon his wrinkled old face. George and Professor McKenzie went into a legal huddle, and emerged with a document which Dr. Romano signed with hardly a glance.

Unexpected things began to emerge from the "Sea Spray," such as a beautiful mutation mink and a beautiful non-mutation blonde.

"Hello, Sylvia," said Dr. Romano politely. "I'm afraid you'll find the quarters here a little more cramped. The Professor never mentioned you were aboard. Never mind—we won't mention it either. Not actually in the contract, but a gentleman's agreement, shall we say? It would be such a pity to upset Mrs. McKenzie."

"I don't know *what* you mean!" pouted Sylvia. "Someone has to do all the Professor's typing."

"And you do it damn badly, my dear," said McKenzie, assisting her over the rail with true Southern gallantry. Harry couldn't help admiring his composure in such an embarrassing situation—he was by no means sure that he would have managed as well. But he wished he had the opportunity to find out.

At last the chaos subsided, the stream of boxes and bundles subsided to a trickle. Dr. Romano shook hands with everybody, thanked George and Harry for their assistance, strode to the bridge of the "Sea Spray," and ten minutes later, was halfway to the horizon.

Harry was wondering if it wasn't about time for them to take their departure as well—they had never got round to explaining to Professor McKenzie what they were doing here in the first place—when the radio-telephone started calling. Dr. Romano was on the line.

"Forgotten his tooth-brush, I suppose," said George. It was not quite as trivial as that. Fortunately, the loudspeaker was switched on. Eavesdropping was practically forced upon them and required none of the effort that makes it so embarrassing to a gentleman.

"Look here, Scott," said Dr. Romano, "I think I owe you some sort of explanation."

"If you've gypped me, I'll have you for every cent—"

"Oh, it's not like that. But I did rather pressurize you, though everything I said was perfectly true. Don't get too annoyed with me—you've got a bargain. It'll be a long time, though, before it makes you any money, and you'll have to sink a few millions of your own into it first. You see, the efficiency has to be increased by about three orders of magnitude before it will be a commercial proposition: that bar of uranium cost me a couple of thousand dollars. Now don't blow your top—it *can* be done—I'm certain of that. Dr. Kendall is the man to get: he did all the basic work—hire him away from my people however much it costs you. You're a stubborn cuss and I know you'll finish the job now it's on your hands. That's why I wanted you to have it. Poetic justice, too—you'll be able to repay some of the damage you've done to the land. Too bad it'll make you a billionaire, but that can't be helped.

"Wait a minute—don't cut in on me. I'd have finished the job myself if I had the time, but it'll take at least three more years. And the doctors say I've only got six months: I wasn't kidding when I said I was in a hurry. I'm glad I clinched the deal without having to tell you that, but believe me I'd have used it as a weapon if I had to. Just one thing more—when you do get the process working, name it after me, will you? That's all—it's no use calling me back. I won't answer—and I know you can't catch me."

Professor McKenzie didn't turn a hair.

"I thought it was something like that," he said to no one in particular. Then he sat down, produced an elaborate pocket slide-rule, and became oblivious to the world. He scarcely looked up when George and Harry, feeling very much outclassed, made their polite departure and silently snorkled away.

"Like so many things that happen these days," concluded Harry Purvis, "I still don't know the final outcome of this meeting. I rather imagine that Professor McKenzie has run into some snags, or we'd have heard rumors about the process by now. But I've not the slightest doubt that sooner or later it'll be perfected, so get ready to sell your mining shares. . . .

"As for Dr. Romano, he wasn't kidding, though his doctors were a little off in their estimates. He lasted a full year, and I guess the 'Sea Spray' helped a lot. They buried him in mid-Pacific, and it's just occurred to me that the old boy would have appreciated that. I told you what a fanatical conservationist he was, and it's a piquant thought that even now some of his atoms may be going through his own molecular sieve. . . .

"I notice some incredulous looks, but it's a fact. If you took a tumbler of water, poured it into the ocean, mixed well, then filled the glass from the sea, there'd still be some scores of molecules of water from the original sample in the tumbler. So"—he gave a gruesome little chuckle—"it's only a matter of time before not only Dr. Romano, but all of us, make some contribution to the sieve. And with that thought, gentlemen, I bid you all a very pleasant good-night."

THE WALL
OF DARKNESS

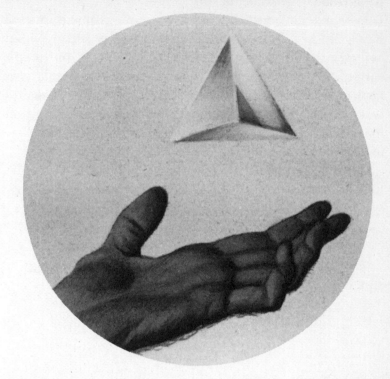

THE OPENING SENTENCE OF "THE WALL OF DARKNESS" HAS been quoted recently in papers on cosmology, because some theoretical physicists now think it is literally true. The story (now reprinted in my collection *The Other Side of the Sky*) reflects a long-standing curiosity of mine about higher dimensions and the nature of space and time—although I've long since given up trying to follow modern developments in this field.

"The Wall of Darkness" is really based on two ideas. One: the Möbius strip, simple though it appears, contains more than meets the eye. Two: the universe is even stranger than we can possibly imagine (Haldane's hypothesis).

Within a few hours of writing the above I came across this passage in *Sky & Telescope:* "The laws of low energy physics and even the dimensionality of space-time may be different in each of these mini-universes. . . .the quantum field that gives birth to the Universe is not smooth on a microscopic scale, but instead resembles an inhomogeneous 'chaotic' space-time foam." ("The Self-Reproducing Universe" by Eugene F. Mallove, September 1988, pp. 253–56.)

See what I mean?

Many and strange are the universes that drift like bubbles in the foam upon the River of Time. Some—a very few—move against or athwart its current; and fewer still are those that lie forever beyond its reach, knowing nothing of the future or the past. Shervane's tiny cosmos was not one of these: its strangeness was of a different order. It held one world only—the planet of Shervane's race—and a single star, the great sun Trilorne that brought it life and light.

Shervane knew nothing of night, for Trilorne was always high above the horizon, dipping near it only in the long months of winter. Beyond the borders of the Shadow Land, it was true, there came a season when Trilorne disappeared below the edge of the world, and a darkness fell in which nothing could live. But even then the darkness was not absolute, though there were no stars to relieve it.

Alone in its little cosmos, turning the same face always toward its solitary sun, Shervane's world was the last and the strangest jest of the Maker of the Stars.

Yet as he looked across his father's lands, the thoughts that filled Shervane's mind were those that any human child might have known. He felt awe, and curiosity, and a little fear, and above all a longing to go out into the great world before him. These things he was still too young to do, but the ancient house was on the highest ground for many miles and he could look far out over the land that would one day be his. When he turned to the north, with Trilorne shining full upon his face, he could see many miles away the long line of mountains that curved around to the right, rising higher and higher, until they disappeared behind him in the direction of the Shadow Land. One day, when he was older, he would go through those mountains along the pass that led to the great lands of the east.

On his left was the ocean, only a few miles away, and sometimes Shervane could hear the thunder of the waves as they fought and tumbled on the gently sloping sands. No one knew how far the ocean reached. Ships had set out across it, sailing northward while Trilorne rose higher and higher in the sky and the heat of its rays grew ever more intense. Long before the great sun had reached the zenith, they had been forced to return. If the mythical Fire Lands did indeed exist, no man could ever hope to reach their burning shores—unless the legends were really true. Once, it was said, there had been swift metal ships that could cross the ocean despite the heat of Trilorne, and so come to the lands on the other side of the world. Now these countries could be reached only by a tedious journey over land and sea, which could be shortened no more than a little by traveling as far north as one dared.

All the inhabited countries of Shervane's world lay in the narrow belt between burning heat and unsufferable cold. In every land, the far north was an unapproachable region smitten by the fury of Trilorne. And to the south of all countries lay the vast and gloomy Shadow Land, where Trilorne was never more than a pale disk on the horizon, and often was not visible at all.

These things Shervane learned in the years of his childhood, and in those years he had no wish to leave the wide lands between the mountains and the sea. Since the dawn of time his ancestors and the races before them had toiled to make these lands the fairest in the world; if they had failed, it was by a narrow margin. There were gardens bright with strange flowers, there were streams that trickled gently between moss-grown rocks to be lost in the pure waters of the tideless sea. There were fields of grain that rustled continually in the wind, as if the generations of seeds yet unborn were talking one to the other. In the wide meadows and beneath the trees the friendly cattle wandered aimlessly with foolish cries. And there was the great house, with its enormous rooms and its endless corridors, vast enough in reality but huger still to the mind of a child. This was the world he knew and loved. As yet, what lay beyond its borders had not concerned his mind.

But Shervane's universe was not one of those free from the domination of time. The harvest ripened and was gathered into the granaries; Trilorne rocked slowly through its little arc of sky, and with the passing seasons Shervane's mind and body grew. His land seemed smaller now: the mountains were nearer and the sea was only a brief walk from the great house. He began to learn of the world in which he lived, and to be made ready for the part he must play in its shaping.

Some of these things he learned from his father, Sherval, but most he was taught by Grayle, who had come across the mountains in the days of his father's father, and had now been tutor to three generations of Shervane's family. He was fond of Grayle, though the old man taught him many things he had no wish to learn, and the years of his boyhood passed pleasantly enough until the time came for him to go through the mountains into the lands beyond. Ages ago his family had come from the great countries of the east, and in every generation since, the eldest son had made that pilgrimage again to spend a year of his youth among his cousins. It was a wise custom, for beyond the mountains much of the knowledge of the past still lingered, and there one could meet men from other lands and study their ways.

In the last spring before his son's departure, Sherval collected three of his servants and certain animals it is convenient to call horses, and took Shervane to see those parts of the land he had never visited before. They rode west to the sea, and followed it for many days, until Trilorne was noticeably nearer the horizon. Still they went south, their shadows lengthening before them, turning again to the east only when the rays of the sun seemed to have lost all their power. They were now well within the limits of the Shadow Land, and it would not be wise to go farther south until the summer was at its height.

Shervane was riding beside his father, watching the changing landscape with all the eager curiosity of a boy seeing a new country for the first time. His father was talking about the soil, describing the crops that could be grown here and those that would fail if the attempt were made. But Shervane's attention was elsewhere: he was staring out across the desolate Shadow Land, wondering how far it stretched and what mysteries it held.

"Father," he said presently, "if you went south in a straight line, right across the Shadow Land, would you reach the other side of the world?"

His father smiled.

"Men have asked that question for centuries," he said, "but there are two reasons why they will never know the answer."

"What are they?"

"The first, of course, is the darkness and the cold. Even here, nothing can live during the winter months. But there is a better reason, though I see that Grayle has not spoken of it."

"I don't think he has: at least, I do not remember."

For a moment Sherval did not reply. He stood up in his stirrups and surveyed the land to the south.

"Once I knew this place well," he said to Shervane. "Come—I have something to show you."

They turned away from the path they had been following, and for several hours rode once more with their backs to the sun. The land was rising slowly now, and Shervane saw that they were climbing a great ridge of rock that pointed like a dagger into the heart of the Shadow Land. They came presently to a hill too steep for the horses to ascend, and here they dismounted and left the animals in the servants' charge.

"There is a way around," said Sherval, "but it is quicker for us to climb than to take the horses to the other side."

The hill, though steep, was only a small one, and they reached its summit in a few minutes. At first Shervane could see nothing he had not met before; there was only the same undulating wilderness, which seemed to become darker and more forbidding with every yard that its distance from Trilorne increased.

He turned to his father with some bewilderment, but Sherval pointed to the far south and drew a careful line along the horizon.

"It is not easy to see," he said quietly. "My father showed it to me from this same spot, many years before you were born."

Shervane stared into the dusk. The southern sky was so dark as to be almost black, and it came down to meet the edge of the world. But not quite, for along the horizon, in a great curve dividing land from sky yet seeming to belong to neither, was a band of deeper darkness, black as the night which Shervane had never known.

He looked at it steadfastly for a long time, and perhaps some hint of the future may have crept into his soul, for the darkling land seemed suddenly alive and waiting. When at last he tore his eyes away, he knew that nothing would ever be the same again, though he was still too young to recognize the challenge for what it was.

And so, for the first time in his life, Shervane saw the Wall.

In the early spring he said farewell to his people, and went with one servant over the mountains into the great lands of the eastern world. Here he met the men who shared his ancestry, and here he studied the history of his race, the arts that had grown from ancient times, and the sciences that ruled the lives of men. In the places of learning he made friends with boys who had come from lands even farther to the east: few of these was he likely to see again, but one was to play a greater part in his life than either could have imagined. Brayldon's father was a famous architect, but his son intended to eclipse him. He was traveling from land to land, always learning, watching, asking questions. Though he was only a few years older than Shervane, his knowledge of the world was infinitely greater—or so it seemed to the younger boy.

Between them they took the world to pieces and rebuilt it according to their desires. Brayldon dreamed of cities whose great avenues and stately towers would shame even the wonders of the past, but Shervane's interests lay more with the people who would dwell in those cities, and the way they ordered their lives.

They often spoke of the Wall, which Brayldon knew from the stories of his own people, though he himself had never seen it. Far to the south of every country, as Shervane had learned, it lay like a great barrier athwart the Shadow Land. In high summer it could be reached, though only with difficulty, but nowhere was there any way of passing it, and none knew what lay beyond. An entire world, never pausing even when it reached a hundred times the height of a man, it encircled the wintry sea that washed the shores of the Shadow Land. Travelers had stood upon those lonely beaches, scarcely warmed by the last thin rays of Trilorne, and had seen how the dark shadow of the Wall marched out to sea contemptuous of the waves beneath its feet. And on the far shores, other travelers had watched it come striding in across the ocean, to sweep past them on its journey round the world.

"One of my uncles," said Brayldon, "one reached the Wall when he was a young man. He did it for a wager, and he rode for ten days before he came beneath it. I think it frightened him—it was so huge and cold. He could not tell whether it was made of metal or of stone, and when he shouted, there was no echo at all, but his voice died away quickly as if the Wall were swallowing the sound. My people believe it is the end of the world, and there is nothing beyond."

"If that were true," Shervane replied, with irrefutable logic, "the ocean would have poured over the edge before the Wall was built."

"Not if Kyrone built it when He made the world."

Shervane did not agree.

"*My* people believe it is the work of man—perhaps the engineers of the First Dynasty, who made so many wonderful things. If they really had ships that could reach the Fire Lands—and even ships that could fly—they might have possessed enough wisdom to build the Wall."

Brayldon shrugged.

"They must have had a very good reason," he said. "We can never know the answer, so why worry about it?"

This eminently practical advice, as Shervane had discovered, was all that the ordinary man ever gave him. Only philosophers were interested in unanswerable questions: to most people, the enigma of the Wall, like the problem of existence itself, was something that scarcely concerned their minds. And all the philosophers he had met had given him different answers.

First there had been Grayle, whom he had questioned on his return from the Shadow Land. The old man had looked at him quietly and said:

"There is only one thing behind the Wall, so I have heard. And that is madness."

Then there had been Artex, who was so old that he could

scarcely hear Shervane's nervous questioning. He gazed at the boy through eyelids that seemed too tired to open fully, and had replied after a long time:

"Kyrone built the Wall in the third day of the making of the world. What is beyond, we shall discover when we die—for there go the souls of all the dead."

Yet Irgan, who lived in the same city, had flatly contradicted this.

"Only memory can answer your question, my son. For behind the Wall is the land in which we lived before our births."

Whom could he believe? The truth was that no one knew: if the knowledge had ever been possessed, it had been lost ages since.

Though this quest was unsuccessful, Shervane had learned many things in his year of study. With the returning spring he said farewell to Brayldon and the other friends he had known for such a little while, and set out along the ancient road that led him back to his own country. Once again he made the perilous journey through the great pass between the mountains, where walls of ice hung threatening against the sky. He came to the place where the road curved down once more toward the world of men, where there was warmth and running water and the breath no longer labored in the freezing air. Here, on the last rise of the road before it descended into the valley, one could see far out across the land to the distant gleam of the ocean. And there, almost lost in the mists at the edge of the world, Shervane could see the line of shadow that was his own country.

He went on down the great ribbon of stone until he came to the bridge that men had built across the cataract in the ancient days when the only other way had been destroyed by earthquake. But the bridge was gone: the storms and avalanches of early spring had swept away one of the mighty piers, and the beautiful metal rainbow lay a twisted ruin in the spray and foam a thousand feet below. The summer would have come and gone before the road could be opened once more: as Shervane sadly returned he knew that another year must pass ere he would see his home again.

He paused for many minutes on the last curve of the road, looking back toward the unattainable land that held all the things he loved. But the mists had closed over it, and he saw it no more. Resolutely he turned back along the road until the open lands had vanished and the mountains enfolded him again.

Brayldon was still in the city when Shervane returned. He was surprised and pleased to see his friend, and together they discussed what should be done in the year ahead. Shervane's cousins, who had grown fond of their guest, were not sorry to see him again, but their kindly suggestion that he should devote another year to study was not well received.

Shervane's plan matured slowly, in the face of considerable opposition. Even Brayldon was not enthusiastic at first, and much argument was needed before he would cooperate. Thereafter, the agreement of everyone else who mattered was only a question of time.

Summer was approaching when the two boys set out toward Brayldon's country. They rode swiftly, for the journey was a long one and must be completed before Trilorne began its winter fall. When they reached the lands that Brayldon knew, they made certain inquiries which caused much shaking of heads. But the answers they obtained were accurate, and soon the Shadow Land was all around them, and presently for the second time in his life Shervane saw the Wall.

It seemed not far away when they first came upon it, rising from a bleak and lonely plain. Yet they rode endlessly across that plain before the Wall grew any nearer—and then they had almost reached its base before they realized how close they were, for there was no way of judging its distance until one could reach out and touch it.

When Shervane gazed up at the monstrous ebony sheet that

had so troubled his mind, it seemed to be overhanging and about to crush him beneath its falling weight. With difficulty, he tore his eyes away from the hypnotic sight, and went nearer to examine the material of which the Wall was built.

It was true, as Brayldon had told him, that it felt cold to the touch—colder than it had any right to be even in this sun-starved land. It felt neither hard nor soft, for its texture eluded the hand in a way that was difficult to analyze. Shervane had the impression that something was preventing him from actual contact with the surface, yet he could see no space between the Wall and his fingers when he forced them against it. Strangest of all was the uncanny silence of which Brayldon's uncle had spoken: every word was deadened and all sounds died away with unnatural swiftness.

Brayldon had unloaded some tools and instruments from the pack horses, and had begun to examine the Wall's surface. He found very quickly that no drills or cutters would mark it in any way, and presently he came to the conclusion Shervane had already reached. The Wall was not merely adamant: it was unapproachable.

At last, in disgust, he took a perfectly straight metal rule and pressed its edge against the wall. While Shervane held a mirror to reflect the feeble light of Trilorne along the line of contact, Brayldon peered at the rule from the other side. It was as he had thought: an infinitely narrow streak of light showed unbroken between the two surfaces.

Brayldon looked thoughtfully at his friend.

"Shervane," he said, "I don't believe the Wall is made of matter, as we know it."

"Then perhaps the legends were right that said it was never built at all, but created as we see it now."

"I think so too," said Brayldon. "The engineers of the First Dynasty had such powers. There are some very ancient buildings in my land that seem to have been made in a single operation from a substance that shows absolutely no sign of weathering. If it were black instead of colored, it would be very much like the material of the Wall."

He put away his useless tools and began to set up a simple portable theodolite.

"If I can do nothing else," he said with a wry smile, "at least I can find exactly how high it is!"

When they looked back for their last view of the Wall, Shervane wondered if he would ever see it again. There was nothing more he could learn: for the future, he must forget this foolish dream that he might one day master its secret. Perhaps there was no secret at all—perhaps beyond the Wall the Shadow Land stretched round the curve of the world until it met that same barrier again. That, surely, seemed the likeliest thing. But if it were so, then why had the Wall been built, and by what race?

With an almost angry effort of will, he put these thoughts aside and rode forward into the light of Trilorne, thinking of a future in which the Wall would play no more part than it did in the lives of other men.

So two years had passed before Shervane could return to his home. In two years, especially when one is young, much can be forgotten and even the things nearest to the heart lose their distinctness, so that they can no longer be clearly recalled. When Shervane came through the last foothills of the mountains and was again in the country of his childhood, the joy of his homecoming was mingled with a strange sadness. So many things were forgotten that he had once thought his mind would hold forever.

The news of his return had gone before him, and soon he saw far ahead a line of horses galloping along the road. He pressed forward eagerly, wondering if Sherval would be there to greet him, and was a little disappointed when he saw that Grayle was leading the procession.

Shervane halted as the old man rode up to his horse. Then Grayle put his hand upon his shoulder, but for a while he turned away his head and could not speak.

And presently Shervane learned that the storms of the year before had destroyed more than the ancient bridge, for the lightning had brought his own home in ruins to the ground. Years before the appointed time, all the lands that Sherval had owned had passed into the possession of his son. Far more, indeed, than these, for the whole family had been assembled, according to its yearly custom, in the great house when the fire had come down upon it. In a single moment of time, everything between the mountains and the sea had passed into his keeping. He was the richest man his land had known for generations; and all these things he would have given to look again into the calm gray eyes of the father he would see no more.

Trilorne had risen and fallen in the sky many times since Shervane took leave of his childhood on the road before the mountains. The land had flourished in the passing years, and the possessions that had so suddenly become his had steadily increased their value. He had husbanded them well, and now he had time once more in which to dream. More than that—he had the wealth to make his dreams come true.

Often stories had come across the mountains of the work Brayldon was doing in the east, and although the two friends had never met since their youth they had exchanged messages regularly. Brayldon had achieved his ambitions: not only had he designed the two largest buildings erected since the ancient days, but a whole new city had been planned by him, though it would not be completed in his lifetime. Hearing of these things, Shervane remembered the aspirations of his own youth, and his mind went back across the years to the day when they had stood together beneath the majesty of the Wall. For a long time he wrestled with his thoughts, fearing to revive old longings that might not be assuaged. But at last he made his decision and wrote to Brayldon—for what was the use of wealth and power unless they could be used to shape one's dreams?

Then Shervane waited, wondering if Brayldon had forgotten the past in the years that had brought him fame. He had not long to wait: Brayldon could not come at once, for he had great works to carry to their completion, but when they were finished he would join his old friend. Shervane had thrown him a challenge that was worthy of his skill—one which if he could meet would bring him more satisfaction than anything he had yet done.

Early the next summer he came, and Shervane met him on the road below the bridge. They had been boys when they last parted, and now they were nearing middle age, yet as they greeted one another the years seemed to fall away and each was secretly glad to see how lightly Time had touched the friend he remembered.

They spent many days in conference together, considering the plans that Brayldon had drawn up. The work was an immense one, and would take many years to complete, but it was possible to a man of Shervane's wealth. Before he gave his final assent, he took his friend to see Grayle.

The old man had been living for some years in the little house that Shervane had built him. For a long time he had played no active part in the life of the great estates, but his advice was always ready when it was needed, and it was invariably wise.

Grayle knew why Brayldon had come to this land, and he expressed no surprise when the architect unrolled his sketches. The largest drawing showed the elevation of the Wall, with a great stairway rising along its side from the plain beneath. At six equally spaced intervals the slowly ascending ramp leveled out into wide platforms, the last of which was only a short distance below the summit of the Wall. Springing from the stairway at a score of places along its length were flying buttresses which to Grayle's eye seemed very frail and slender for the work they had to do. Then he realized that the great ramp would be largely self-supporting, and on one side all the lateral thrust would be taken by the Wall itself.

He looked at the drawing in silence for a while, and then remarked quietly:

"You always managed to have your way, Shervane. I might have guessed that this would happen in the end."

"Then you think it a good idea?" Shervane asked. He had never gone against the old man's advice, and was anxious to have it now. As usual Grayle came straight to the point.

"How much will it cost?" he said.

Brayldon told him, and for a moment there was a shocked silence.

"That includes," the architect said hastily, "the building of a good road across the Shadow Land, and the construction of a small town for the workmen. The stairway itself is made from about a million identical blocks which can be dovetailed together to form a rigid structure. We shall make these, I hope, from the minerals we find in the Shadow Land."

He sighed a little.

"I should have liked to have built it from metal rods, jointed together, but that would have cost even more, for all the material would have to be brought over the mountains."

Grayle examined the drawing more closely.

"Why have you stopped short of the top?" he asked.

Brayldon looked at Shervane, who answered the question with a trace of embarrassment.

"I want to be the only one to make the final ascent," he replied. "The last stage will be a lifting machine on the highest platform. There may be danger: that is why I am going alone."

That was not the only reason, but it was a good one. Behind

the Wall, so Grayle had once said, lay madness. If that were true, no one else need face it.

Grayle was speaking once more in his quiet, dreamy voice.

"In that case," he said, "what you do is neither good nor bad, for it concerns you alone. If the Wall was built to keep something from our world, it will still be impassable from the other side."

Brayldon nodded.

"We had thought of that," he said with a touch of pride. "If the need should come, the ramp can be destroyed in a moment by explosives at selected spots."

"That is good," the old man replied. "Though I do not believe those stories, it is well to be prepared. When the work is finished, I hope I shall still be here. And now I shall try to remember what I heard of the Wall when I was as young as you were, Shervane, when you first questioned me about it."

Before the winter came, the road to the Wall had been marked out and the foundations of the temporary town had been laid. Most of the materials Brayldon needed were not hard to find, for the Shadow Land was rich in minerals. He had also surveyed the Wall itself and chosen the spot for the stairway. When Trilorne began to dip below the horizon, Brayldon was well content with the work that had been done.

By the next summer the first of the myriad concrete blocks had been made and tested to Brayldon's satisfaction, and before winter came again some thousands had been produced and part of the foundations laid. Leaving a trusted assistant in charge of the production, Brayldon could now return to his interrupted work. When enough of the blocks had been made, he would be back to supervise the building, but until then his guidance would not be needed.

Two or three times in the course of every year, Shervane rode out to the Wall to watch the stockpiles growing into great pyramids, and four years later Brayldon returned with him. Layer by layer the lines of stone started to creep up the flanks of the Wall, and the slim buttresses began to arch out into space. At first the stairway rose slowly, but as its summit narrowed the increase became more and more rapid. For a third of every year the work had to be abandoned, and there were anxious months in the long winter when Shervane stood on the borders of the Shadow Land, listening to the storms that thundered past him into the reverberating darkness. But Brayldon had built well, and every spring the work was standing unharmed as though it would outlive the Wall itself.

The last stones were laid seven years after the beginning of the work. Standing a mile away, so that he could see the structure in its entirety, Shervane remembered with wonder how all this had sprung from the few sketches Brayldon had shown him years ago, and he knew something of the emotion the artist must feel when his dreams become reality. And he remembered, too, the day when, as a boy by his father's side, he had first seen the Wall far off against the dusky sky of the Shadow Land.

There were guardrails around the upper platform, but Shervane did not care to go near its edge. The ground was at a dizzying distance, and he tried to forget his height by helping Brayldon and the workmen erect the simple hoist that would lift him the remaining twenty feet. When it was ready he stepped into the machine and turned to his friend with all the assurance he could muster.

"I shall be gone only a few minutes," he said with elaborate casualness. "Whatever I find, I'll return immediately."

He could hardly have guessed how small a choice was his.

Grayle was now almost blind and would not know another spring. But he recognized the approaching footsteps and greeted Brayldon by name before his visitor had time to speak.

"I am glad you came," he said. "I've been thinking of everything you told me, and I believe I know the truth at last. Perhaps you have guessed it already."

"No," said Brayldon. "I have been afraid to think of it."

The old man smiled a little.

"Why should one be afraid of something merely because it is strange? The Wall is wonderful, yes—but there's nothing terrible about it, to those who will face its secret without flinching.

"When I was a boy, Brayldon, my old master once said that time could never destroy the truth—it could only hide it among legends. He was right. From all the fables that have gathered around the Wall, I can now select the ones that are part of history.

"Long ago, Brayldon, when the First Dynasty was at its height, Trilorne was hotter than it is now and the Shadow Land was fertile and inhabited—as perhaps one day the Fire Lands may be when Trilorne is old and feeble. Men could go southward as they pleased, for there was no Wall to bar the way. Many must have done so, looking for new lands in which to settle. What happened to Shervane happened to them also, and it must have wrecked many minds—so many that the scientists of the First Dynasty built the Wall to prevent madness from spreading through the land. I cannot believe that this is true, but the legend says that it was made in a single day, with no labor, out of a cloud that encircled the world."

He fell into a reverie, and for a moment Brayldon did not disturb him. His mind was far in the past, picturing his world as a perfect globe floating in space while the Ancient Ones threw the band of darkness around the equator. False though that picture was in its most important detail, he could never wholly erase it from his mind.

As the last few feet of the Wall moved slowly past his eyes, Shervane needed all his courage lest he cry out to be lowered again. He remembered certain terrible stories he had once dismissed with laughter, for he came of a race that was singularly free from superstition. But what if, after all, those stories had been true, and the Wall had been built to keep some horror from the world?

He tried to forget these thoughts, and found it not hard to do so once he had passed the topmost level of the Wall. At first he could not interpret the picture his eyes brought him: then he saw that he was looking across an unbroken black sheet whose width he could not judge.

The little platform came to a stop, and he noted with half-conscious admiration how accurate Brayldon's calculations had been. Then, with a last word of assurance to the group below, he stepped onto the Wall and began to walk steadily forward.

At first it seemed as if the plain before him was infinite, for he could not even tell where it met the sky. But he walked on unfaltering, keeping his back to Trilorne. He wished he could have used his own shadow as a guide, but it was lost in the deeper darkness beneath his feet.

There was something wrong: it was growing darker with every footstep he took. Startled, he turned around and saw that the disk of Trilorne had now become pale and dusky, as if seen through a darkened glass. With mounting fear, he realized that this was by no means all that had happened—*Trilorne was smaller than the sun he had known all his life.*

He shook his head in an angry gesture of defiance. These things were fancies; he was imagining them. Indeed, they were so contrary to all experience that somehow he no longer felt frightened but strode resolutely forward with only a glance at the sun behind.

When Trilorne had dwindled to a point, and the darkness was all around him, it was time to abandon pretense. A wiser man would have turned back there and then, and Shervane had a sudden nightmare vision of himself lost in this eternal twilight between earth and sky, unable to retrace the path that led to safety. Then he remembered that as long as he could see Trilorne at all he could be in no real danger.

A little uncertainly now, he continued his way with many backward glances at the faint guiding light behind him. Trilorne itself had vanished, but there was still a dim glow in the sky to mark its place. And presently he needed its aid no longer, for far ahead a second light was appearing in the heavens.

At first it seemed only the faintest of glimmers, and when he was sure of its existence he noticed that Trilorne had already disappeared. But he felt more confidence now, and as he moved onward, the returning light did something to subdue his fears.

When he saw that he was indeed approaching another sun, when he could tell beyond any doubt that it was expanding as a moment ago he had seen Trilorne contract, he forced all amazement down into the depths of his mind. He would only observe and record: later there would be time to understand these things. That his world might possess two suns, one shining upon it from either side, was not, after all, beyond imagination.

Now at last he could see, faintly through the darkness, the ebon line that marked the Wall's other rim. Soon he would be the first man in thousands of years, perhaps in eternity, to look upon the lands that it had sundered from his world. Would they be as fair as his own, and would there be people there whom he would be glad to greet?

But that they would be waiting, and in such a way, was more than he had dreamed.

Grayle stretched his hand out toward the cabinet beside him and fumbled for a large sheet of paper that was lying upon it. Brayldon watched him in silence, and the old man continued.

"How often we have all heard arguments about the size of the universe, and whether it has any boundaries! We can imagine no ending to space, yet our minds rebel at the idea of infinity. Some philosophers have imagined that space is limited by curvature in a higher dimension—I suppose you know the theory. It may be true of other universes, if they exist, but for ours the answer is more subtle.

"*Along the line of the Wall, Brayldon, our universe comes to an end—and yet does not.* There was no boundary, nothing to stop one going onward before the Wall was built. The Wall itself is merely a man-made barrier, sharing the properties of the space in which it lies. Those properties were always there, and the Wall added nothing to them."

He held the sheet of paper toward Brayldon and slowly rotated it.

"Here," he said, "is a plain sheet. It has, of course, two sides. *Can you imagine one that has not?*"

Brayldon stared at him in amazement.

"That's impossible—ridiculous!"

"But is it?" said Grayle softly. He reached toward the cabinet again and his fingers groped in its recesses. Then he drew out a long, flexible strip of paper and turned vacant eyes to the silently waiting Brayldon.

"We cannot match the intellects of the First Dynasty, but what their minds could grasp directly we can approach by analogy. This simple trick, which seems so trivial, may help you to glimpse the truth."

He ran his fingers along the paper strip, then joined the two ends together to make a circular loop.

"Here I have a shape which is perfectly familiar to you—the section of a cylinder. I run my finger around the inside, so—and now along the outside. The two surfaces are quite distinct: you can go from one to the other only by moving through the thickness of the strip. Do you agree?"

"Of course," said Brayldon, still puzzled. "But what does it prove?"

"Nothing," said Grayle. "But now watch—"

• • •

This sun, Shervane thought, was Trilorne's identical twin. The darkness had now lifted completely, and there was no longer the sensation, which he would not try to understand, of walking across an infinite plain.

He was moving slowly now, for he had no desire to come too suddenly upon that vertiginous precipice. In a little while he could see a distant horizon of low hills, as bare and lifeless as those he had left behind him. This did not disappoint him unduly, for the first glimpse of his own land would be no more attractive than this.

So he walked on: and when presently an icy hand fastened itself upon his heart, he did not pause as a man of lesser courage would have done. Without flinching, he watched that shockingly familiar landscape rise around him, until he could see the plain from which his journey had started, and the great stairway itself, and at last Brayldon's anxious, waiting face.

Again Grayle brought the two ends of the strip together, but now he had given it a half-twist so that the band was kinked. He held it out to Brayldon.

"Run your finger around it now," he said quietly.

Brayldon did not do so: he could see the old man's meaning.

"I understand," he said. "You no longer have two separate surfaces. It now forms a single continuous sheet—*a one-sided surface*—something that at first sight seems utterly impossible."

"Yes," replied Grayle very softly. "I thought you would understand. *A one-sided surface*. Perhaps you realize now why this symbol of the twisted loop is so common in the ancient religions, though its meaning has been completely lost. Of course, it is no more than a crude and simple analogy—an example in two dimensions of what must really occur in three. But it is as near as our minds can ever get to the truth."

There was a long, brooding silence. Then Grayle sighed deeply and turned to Brayldon as if he could still see his face.

"Why did you come back before Shervane?" he asked, though he knew the answer well enough.

"We had to do it," said Brayldon sadly, "but I did not wish to see my work destroyed."

Grayle nodded in sympathy.

"I understand," he said.

Shervane ran his eye up the long flight of steps on which no feet would ever tread again. He felt few regrets: he had striven, and no one could have done more. Such victory as was possible had been his.

Slowly he raised his hand and gave the signal. The Wall swallowed the explosion as it had absorbed all other sounds, but the unhurried grace with which the long tiers of masonry curtsied and fell was something he would remember all his life. For a moment he had a sudden, inexpressibly poignant vision of another stairway, watched by another Shervane, falling in identical ruins on the far side of the Wall.

But that, he realized, was a foolish thought: for none knew better than he that the Wall possessed no other side.

THE LION
OF COMARRE

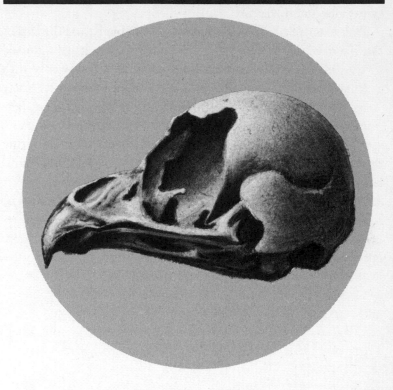

"THE LION OF COMARRE" WAS WRITTEN IN JUNE 1945 and promptly accepted *(and paid for!)* by my first British editor, Walter Gillings; unfortunately, he never had a chance to use it. Three years later, my newly acquired agent Scott Meredith sold it to *Thrilling Wonder Stories* which printed it in August 1949.

Then it vanished from sight until published together with *Against the Fall of Night* by Harcourt Brace in 1968. This was an appropriate combination, because the two stories have very much in common. In each case, the protagonist is a young man disaffected by his all-too-Utopian surroundings and in search of novelty and adventure.

Please remember that this story was written before the explosive dawn of the computer age, and in rereading it, I'm amused to see that I put the first thinking machine in the twenty-fifth century. In 1945, I certainly never dreamed that a mere forty years later there would be companies selling wares labeled, perhaps somewhat prematurely, "Artificial Intelligence."

I've no doubt that the real thing will be on the market during the next century. Meanwhile, there are ample supplies of Artificial Stupidity available at very reasonable cost. . . .

I was also interested to discover that the item next to "The Lion of Comarre" in the disintegrating notebook where I recorded my apprentice writings is an essay proposing the use of geostationary satellites for global telecasting.

Whatever happened to *that* crazy idea?

1 • REVOLT

Toward the close of the twenty-sixth century, the great tide of Science had at last begun to ebb. The long series of inventions that had shaped and molded the world for nearly a thousand years was coming to its end. Everything had been discovered. One by one, all the great dreams of the past had become reality.

Civilization was completely mechanized—yet machinery had almost vanished. Hidden in the walls of the cities or buried far underground, the perfect machines bore the burden of the world. Silently, unobtrusively, the robots attended to their masters' needs, doing their work so well that their presence seemed as natural as the dawn.

There was still much to learn in the realm of pure science, and the astronomers, now that they were no longer bound to Earth, had work enough for a thousand years to come. But the physical sciences and the arts they nourished had ceased to be the chief preoccupation of the race. By the year 2600 the finest human minds were no longer to be found in the laboratories.

The men whose names meant most to the world were the artists and philosophers, the lawgivers and statesmen. The engineers and the great inventors belonged to the past. Like the men who had once ministered to long-vanished diseases, they had done their work so well that they were no longer required.

Five hundred years were to pass before the pendulum swung back again.

The view from the studio was breath-taking, for the long, curving room was over two miles from the base of Central Tower. The five other giant buildings of the city clustered below, their metal walls gleaming with all the colors of the spectrum as they caught the rays of the morning sun. Lower still, the checkerboard fields of the automatic farms stretched away until they were lost in the mists of the horizon. But for once, the beauty of the scene was wasted on Richard Peyton II as he paced angrily among the great blocks of synthetic marble that were the raw materials of his art.

The huge, gorgeously colored masses of artificial rock completely dominated the studio. Most of them were roughly hewn cubes, but some were beginning to assume the shapes of animals, human beings, and abstract solids that no geometrician would have dared to give a name. Sitting awkwardly on a ten-ton block of diamond—the largest ever synthesized—the artist's son was regarding his famous parent with an unfriendly expression.

"I don't think I'd mind so much," Richard Peyton II remarked peevishly, "if you were content to do nothing, so long as you did it gracefully. Certain people excel at that, and on the whole they make the world more interesting. But why you should want to make a life study of engineering is more than I can imagine.

"Yes, I know we let you take technology as your main subject, but we never thought you were so serious about it. When I was your age I had a passion for botany—but I never made it my main interest in life. Has Professor Chandras Ling been giving you ideas?"

Richard Peyton III blushed.

"Why shouldn't he? I know what my vocation is, and he agrees with me. You've read his report."

The artist waved several sheets of paper in the air, holding them between thumb and forefinger like some unpleasant insect.

"I have," he said grimly. "'Shows very unusual mechanical ability—has done original work in subelectronic research,' et cetera, et cetera. Good heavens, I thought the human race had outgrown those toys centuries ago! Do you want to be a mechanic, first class, and go around attending to disabled robots? That's hardly a job for a boy of mine, not to mention the grandson of a World Councillor."

"I wish you wouldn't keep bringing Grandfather into this," said Richard Peyton III with mounting annoyance. "The fact that he was a statesman didn't prevent your becoming an artist. So why should you expect me to be either?"

The older man's spectacular golden beard began to bristle ominously.

"I don't care what you do as long as it's something we can be proud of. But why this craze for gadgets? We've got all the machines we need. The robot was perfected five hundred years ago; spaceships haven't changed for at least that time; I believe our present communications system is nearly eight hundred years old. So why change what's already perfect?"

"That's special pleading with a vengeance!" the young man replied. "Fancy an artist saying that anything's perfect! Father, I'm ashamed of you!"

"Don't split hairs. You know perfectly well what I mean. Our ancestors designed machines that provide us with everything we need. No doubt some of them might be a few per cent more efficient. But why worry? Can you mention a single important invention that the world lacks today?"

Richard Peyton III sighed.

"Listen, Father," he said patiently. "I've been studying history as well as engineering. About twelve centuries ago there were people who said that everything had been invented—and *that* was before the coming of electricity, let alone flying and astronautics. They just didn't look far enough ahead—their minds were rooted in the present.

"The same thing's happening today. For five hundred years the world's been living on the brains of the past. I'm prepared to admit that some lines of development have come to an end, but there are dozens of others that haven't even begun.

"Technically the world has stagnated. It's not a dark age, because we haven't forgotten anything. But we're marking time. Look at space travel. Nine hundred years ago we reached Pluto, and where are we now? Still at Pluto! When are we going to cross interstellar space?"

"Who wants to go to the stars, anyway?"

The boy made an exclamation of annoyance and jumped off the diamond block in his excitement.

"What a question to ask in this age! A thousand years ago people were saying, 'Who wants to go to the Moon?' Yes, I know it's unbelievable, but it's all there in the old books. Nowadays the Moon's only forty-five minutes away, and people like Harn Jansen work on Earth and live in Plato City.

"We take interplanetary travel for granted. One day we're going to do the same with *real* space travel. I could mention scores of other subjects that have come to a full stop simply because people think as you do and are content with what they've got."

"And why not?"

Peyton waved his arm around in the studio.

"Be serious, Father. Have you ever been satisfied with anything you've made? Only animals are contented."

The artist laughed ruefully.

"Maybe you're right. But that doesn't affect my argument. I

still think you'll be wasting your life, and so does Grandfather."
He looked a little embarrassed. "In fact, he's coming down to
Earth especially to see you."

Peyton looked alarmed.

"Listen, Father, I've already told you what I think. I don't
want to have to go through it all again. Because neither Grandfather nor the whole of the World Council will make me alter
my mind."

It was a bombastic statement, and Peyton wondered if he
really meant it. His father was just about to reply when a low
musical note vibrated through the studio. A second later a mechanical voice spoke from the air.

"Your father to see you, Mr. Peyton."

He glanced at his son triumphantly.

"I should have added," he said, "that Grandfather was coming now. But I know your habit of disappearing when you're
wanted."

The boy did not answer. He watched his father walk toward
the door. Then his lips curved in a smile.

The single pane of glassite that fronted the studio was open,
and he stepped out on to the balcony. Two miles below, the
great concrete apron of the parking ground gleamed whitely in
the sun, except where it was dotted with the teardrop shadows
of grounded ships.

Peyton glanced back into the room. It was still empty,
though he could hear his father's voice drifting through the
door. He waited no longer. Placing his hand on the balustrade,
he vaulted over into space.

Thirty seconds later two figures entered the studio and gazed
around in surprise. *The* Richard Peyton, with no qualifying
number, was a man who might have been taken for sixty,
though that was less than a third of his actual age.

He was dressed in the purple robe worn by only twenty men

on Earth and by fewer than a hundred in the entire Solar System. Authority seemed to radiate from him; by comparison, even his famous and self-assured son seemed fussy and inconsequential.

"Well, where is he?"

"Confound him! He's gone out the window. At least we can still say what we think of him."

Viciously, Richard Peyton II jerked up his wrist and dialed an eight-figure number on his personal communicator. The reply came almost instantly. In clear, impersonal tones an automatic voice repeated endlessly:

"My master is asleep. Please do not disturb. My master is asleep. Please do not disturb. . . ."

With an exclamation of annoyance Richard Peyton II switched off the instrument and turned to his father. The old man chuckled.

"Well, he thinks fast. He's beaten us there. We can't get hold of him until he chooses to press the clearing button. I certainly don't intend to chase him at my age."

There was silence for a moment as the two men gazed at each other with mixed expressions. Then, almost simultaneously, they began to laugh.

2 • THE LEGEND OF COMARRE

Peyton fell like a stone for a mile and a quarter before he switched on the neutralizer. The rush of air past him, though it made breathing difficult, was exhilarating. He was falling at less than a hundred and fifty miles an hour, but the impression of speed was enhanced by the smooth upward rush of the great building only a few yards away.

The gentle tug of the decelerator field slowed him some three hundred yards from the ground. He fell gently toward the lines of parked flyers ranged at the foot of the tower.

His own speedster was a small single-seat fully automatic machine. At least, it had been fully automatic when it was built three centuries ago, but its current owner had made so many illegal modifications to it that no one else in the world could have flown it and lived to tell the tale.

Peyton switched off the neutralizer belt—an amusing device which, although technically obsolete, still had interesting possibilities—and stepped into the airlock of his machine. Two minutes later the towers of the city were sinking below the rim of the world and the uninhabited Wild Lands were speeding beneath at four thousand miles an hour.

Peyton set his course westward and almost immediately was over the ocean. He could do nothing but wait; the ship would reach its goal automatically. He leaned back in the pilot's seat, thinking bitter thoughts and feeling sorry for himself.

He was more disturbed than he cared to admit. The fact that his family failed to share his technical interests had ceased to worry Peyton years ago. But this steadily growing opposition, which had now come to a head, was something quite new. He was completely unable to understand it.

Ten minutes later a single white pylon began to climb out of the ocean like the sword Excalibur rising from the lake. The city known to the world as Scientia, and to its more cynical inhabitants as Bat's Belfry, had been built eight centuries ago on an island far from the major land masses. The gesture had been one of independence, for the last traces of nationalism had still lingered in that far-off age.

Peyton grounded his ship on the landing apron and walked to the nearest entrance. The boom of the great waves, breaking on the rocks a hundred yards away, was a sound that never failed to impress him.

He paused for a moment at the opening, inhaling the salt air and watching the gulls and migrant birds circling the tower. They had used this speck of land as a resting place when man was still watching the dawn with puzzled eyes and wondering if it was a god.

The Bureau of Genetics occupied a hundred floors near the center of the tower. It had taken Peyton ten minutes to reach the City of Science. It required almost as long again to locate the man he wanted in the cubic miles of offices and laboratories.

Alan Henson II was still one of Peyton's closest friends, although he had left the University of Antarctica two years earlier and had been studying biogenetics rather than engineering. When Peyton was in trouble, which was not infrequently, he found his friend's calm common sense very reassuring. It was natural for him to fly to Scientia now, especially since Henson had sent him an urgent call only the day before.

The biologist was pleased and relieved to see Peyton, yet his welcome had an undercurrent of nervousness.

"I'm glad you've come; I've got some news that will interest you. But you look glum—what's the matter?"

Peyton told him, not without exaggeration. Henson was silent for a moment.

"So they've started already!" he said. "We might have expected it!"

"What do you mean?" asked Peyton in surprise.

The biologist opened a drawer and pulled out a sealed envelope. From it he extracted two plastic sheets in which were cut several hundred parallel slots of varying lengths. He handed one to his friend.

"Do you know what this is?"

"It looks like a character analysis."

"Correct. It happens to be yours."

"Oh! This is rather illegal, isn't it?"

"Never mind that. The key is printed along the bottom: it runs from Aesthetic Appreciation to Wit. The last column gives your Intelligence Quotient. Don't let it go to your head."

Peyton studied the card intently. Once, he flushed slightly.
"I don't see how you knew."

"Never mind," grinned Henson. "Now look at this analysis."
He handed over a second card.

"Why, it's the same one!"

"Not quite, but very nearly."

"Whom does it belong to?"

Henson leaned back in his chair and measured out his words
slowly.

"That analysis, Dick, belongs to your great-grandfather
twenty-two times removed on the direct male line—the great
Rolf Thordarsen."

Peyton took off like a rocket.

"What!"

"Don't shout the place down. We're discussing old times at
college if anyone comes in."

"But—Thordarsen!"

"Well, if we go back far enough we've all got equally distinguished ancestors. But now you know why your grandfather is
afraid of you."

"He's left it till rather late. I've practically finished my
training."

"You can thank us for that. Normally our analysis goes back
ten generations, twenty in special cases. It's a tremendous job.
There are hundreds of millions of cards in the Inheritance Library, one for every man and woman who has lived since the
twenty-third century. This coincidence was discovered quite accidentally about a month ago."

"*That's* when the trouble started. But I still don't understand
what it's all about."

"Exactly what do you know, Dick, about your famous
ancestor?"

"No more than anyone else, I suppose. I certainly don't

know how or why he disappeared, if that's what you mean. Didn't he leave Earth?"

"No. He left the world, if you like, but he never left Earth. Very few people know this, Dick, but Rolf Thordarsen was the man who built Comarre."

Comarre! Peyton breathed the word through half-open lips, savoring its meaning and its strangeness. So it *did* exist, after all! Even that had been denied by some.

Henson was speaking again.

"I don't suppose you know very much about the Decadents. The history books have been rather carefully edited. But the whole story is linked up with the end of the Second Electronic Age. . . ."

Twenty thousand miles above the surface of the Earth, the artificial moon that housed the World Council was spinning on its eternal orbit. The roof of the Council Chamber was one flawless sheet of crystallite; when the members of the Council were in session it seemed as if there was nothing between them and the great globe spinning far below.

The symbolism was profound. No narrow parochial viewpoint could long survive in such a setting. Here, if anywhere, the minds of men would surely produce their greatest works.

Richard Peyton the Elder had spent his life guiding the destinies of Earth. For five hundred years the human race had known peace and had lacked nothing that art or science could provide. The men who ruled the planet could be proud of their work.

Yet the old statesman was uneasy. Perhaps the changes that lay ahead were already casting their shadows before them. Perhaps he felt, if only with his subconscious mind, that the five centuries of tranquillity were drawing to a close.

He switched on his writing machine and began to dictate.

• • •

The First Electronic Age, Peyton knew, had begun in 1908, more than eleven centuries before, with De Forest's invention of the triode. The same fabulous century that had seen the coming of the World State, the airplane, the spaceship, and atomic power had witnessed the invention of all the fundamental thermionic devices that made possible the civilization he knew.

The Second Electronic Age had come five hundred years later. It had been started not by the physicists but by the doctors and psychologists. For nearly five centuries they had been recording the electric currents that flow in the brain during the processes of thought. The analysis had been appallingly complex, but it had been completed after generations of toil. When it was finished the way lay open for the first machines that could read the human mind.

But this was only the beginning. Once man had discovered the mechanism of his own brain he could go further. He could reproduce it, using transistors and circuit networks instead of living cells.

Toward the end of the twenty-fifth century, the first thinking machines were built. They were very crude, a hundred square yards of equipment being required to do the work of a cubic centimeter of human brain. But once the first step had been taken it was not long before the mechanical brain was perfected and brought into general use.

It could perform only the lower grades of intellectual work and it lacked such purely human characteristics as initiative, intuition, and all emotions. However, in circumstances which seldom varied, where its limitations were not serious, it could do all that a man could do.

The coming of the metal brains had brought one of the great crises in human civilization. Though men had still to carry out all the higher duties of statesmanship and the control of society, all the immense mass of routine administration had been taken over by the robots. Man had achieved freedom at last. No longer did he have to rack his brains planning complex transport schedules, deciding production programs, and balancing budgets. The machines, which had taken over all manual labor centuries before, had made their second great contribution to society.

The effect on human affairs was immense, and men reacted to the new situation in two ways. There were those who used their new-found freedom nobly in the pursuits which had always attracted the highest minds: the quest for beauty and truth, still as elusive as when the Acropolis was built.

But there were others who thought differently. At last, they said, the curse of Adam is lifted forever. Now we can build cities where the machines will care for our every need as soon as the thought enters our minds—sooner, since the analyzers can read even the buried desires of the subconscious. The aim of all life is pleasure and the pursuit of happiness. Man has earned the right to that. We are tired of this unending struggle for knowledge and the blind desire to bridge space to the stars.

It was the ancient dream of the Lotus Eaters, a dream as old as Man. Now, for the first time, it could be realized. For a while there were not many who shared it. The fires of the Second Renaissance had not yet begun to flicker and die. But as the years passed, the Decadents drew more and more to their way of thinking. In hidden places on the inner planets they built the cities of their dreams.

For a century they flourished like strange exotic flowers, until the almost religious fervor that inspired their building had died. They lingered for a generation more. Then, one by one, they faded from human knowledge. Dying, they left behind a host of fables and legends which had grown with the passing centuries.

Only one such city had been built on Earth, and there were

mysteries about it that the outer world had never solved. For purposes of its own, the World Council had destroyed all knowledge of the place. Its location was a mystery. Some said it was in the Arctic wastes; others believed it to be hidden on the bed of the Pacific. Nothing was certain but its name— Comarre.

Henson paused in his recital.

"So far I have told you nothing new, nothing that isn't common knowledge. The rest of the story is a secret of the World Council and perhaps a hundred men of Scientia.

"Rolf Thordarsen, as you know, was the greatest mechanical genius the world has ever known. Not even Edison can be compared with him. He laid the foundations of robot engineering and built the first of the practical thought-machines.

"His laboratories poured out a stream of brilliant inventions for over twenty years. Then, suddenly, he disappeared. The story was put out that he tried to reach the stars. This is what really happened:

"Thordarsen believed that his robots—the machines that still run our civilization—were only a beginning. He went to the World Council with certain proposals which would have changed the face of human society. What those changes are we do not know, but Thordarsen believed that unless they were adopted the race would eventually come to a dead end—as, indeed, many of us think it has.

"The Council disagreed violently. At that time, you see, the robot was just being integrated into civilization and stability was slowly returning—the stability that has been maintained for five hundred years.

"Thordarsen was bitterly disappointed. With the flair they had for attracting genius the Decadents got hold of him and persuaded him to renounce the world. He was the only man who could convert their dreams into reality."

"And did he?"

"No one knows. But Comarre was built—that is certain. We know where it is—and so does the World Council. There are some things that cannot be kept secret."

That was true, thought Peyton. Even in this age people still disappeared and it was rumored that they had gone in search of the dream city. Indeed, the phrase "He's gone to Comarre" had become such a part of the language that its meaning was almost forgotten.

Henson leaned forward and spoke with mounting earnestness.

"This is the strange part. The World Council could destroy Comarre, but it won't do so. The belief that Comarre exists has a definite stabilizing influence on society. In spite of all our efforts, we still have psychopaths. It's no difficult matter to give them hints, under hypnosis, about Comarre. They may never find it but the quest will keep them harmless.

"In the early days, soon after the city was founded, the Council sent its agents into Comarre. None of them ever returned. There was no foul play; they just preferred to remain. That's known definitely because they sent messages back. I suppose the Decadents realized that the Council would tear the place down if its agents were detained deliberately.

"I've seen some of those messages. They are extraordinary. There's only one word for them: exalted. Dick, there was something in Comarre that could make a man forget the outer world, his friends, his family—everything! Try to imagine what that means!

"Later, when it was certain that none of the Decadents could still be alive, the Council tried again. It was still trying up to fifty years ago. But to this day no one has ever returned from Comarre."

As Richard Peyton spoke, the waiting robot analyzed his

words into their phonetic groups, inserted the punctuation, and automatically routed the minute to the correct electronic files.

"Copy to President and my personal file.

"Your Minute of the 22nd and our conversation this morning.

"I have seen my son, but R. P. III evaded me. He is completely determined, and we will only do harm by trying to coerce him. Thordarsen should have taught us that lesson.

"My suggestion is that we earn his gratitude by giving him all the assistance he needs. Then we can direct him along safe lines of research. As long as he never discovers that R. T. was his ancestor, there should be no danger. In spite of character similarities, it is unlikely that he will try to repeat R. T.'s work.

"Above all, we must ensure that he never locates or visits Comarre. If that happens, no one can foresee the consequences."

Henson stopped his narrative, but his friend said nothing. He was too spellbound to interrupt, and, after a minute, the other continued.

"That brings us up to the present and to you. The World Council, Dick, discovered your inheritance a month ago. We're sorry we told them, but it's too late now. Genetically, you're a reincarnation of Thordarsen in the only scientific sense of the word. One of Nature's longest odds has come off, as it does every few hundred years in some family or another.

"You, Dick, could carry on the work Thordarsen was compelled to drop—whatever that work was. Perhaps it's lost forever, but if any trace of it exists, the secret lies in Comarre. The World Council knows that. That is why it is trying to deflect you from your destiny.

"Don't be bitter about it. On the Council are some of the noblest minds the human race has yet produced. They mean you no harm, and none will ever befall you. But they are passionately anxious to preserve the present structure of society, which they believe to be the best."

Slowly, Peyton rose to his feet. For a moment, it seemed as if he were a neutral, exterior observer, watching this lay figure called Richard Peyton III, now no longer a man, but a symbol, one of the keys to the future of the world. It took a positive mental effort to reidentify himself.

His friend was watching him silently.

"There's something else you haven't told me, Alan. How do you know all this?"

Henson smiled.

"I was waiting for that. I'm only the mouthpiece, chosen because I know you. Who the others are I can't say, even to you. But they include quite a number of the scientists I know you admire.

"There has always been a friendly rivalry between the Council and the scientists who serve it, but in the last few years our viewpoints have drifted farther apart. Many of us believe that the present age, which the Council thinks will last forever, is only an interregnum. We believe that too long a period of stability will cause decadence. The Council's psychologists are confident they can prevent it."

Peyton's eyes gleamed.

"That's what I've been saying! Can I join you?"

"Later. There's work to be done first. You see, we are revolutionaries of a sort. We are going to start one or two social reactions, and when we've finished the danger of racial decadence will be postponed for thousands of years. You, Dick, are one of our catalysts. Not the only one, I might say."

He paused for a moment.

"Even if Comarre comes to nothing, we have another card up our sleeve. In fifty years, we hope to have perfected the interstellar drive."

"At last!" said Peyton. "What will you do then?"

"We'll present it to the Council and say, 'Here you are—now you can go to the stars. Aren't we good boys?' And the Council will just have to give a sickly smile and start uprooting civilization. Once we've achieved interstellar travel, we shall have an expanding society again and stagnation will be indefinitely postponed."

"I hope I live to see it," said Peyton. "But what do you want me to do now?"

"Just this: we want you to go into Comarre to find what's there. Where others have failed, we believe you can succeed. All the plans have been made."

"And where is Comarre?"

Henson smiled.

"It's simple, really. There was only one place it could be—the only place over which no aircraft can fly, where no one lives, where all travel is on foot. It's in the Great Reservation."

The old man switched off the writing machine. Overhead— or below; it was all the same—the great crescent of Earth was blotting out the stars. In its eternal circling the little moon had overtaken the terminator and was plunging into night. Here and there the darkling land below was dotted with the lights of cities.

The sight filled the old man with sadness. It reminded him that his own life was coming to a close—and it seemed to foretell the end of the culture he had sought to protect. Perhaps, after all, the young scientists were right. The long rest was ending and the world was moving to new goals that he would never see.

3 • THE WILD LION

It was night when Peyton's ship came westward over the Indian Ocean. The eye could see nothing far below but the white line of breakers against the African coast, but the navigation screen showed every detail of the land beneath. Night, of course, was no protection or safeguard now, but it meant that no human eye would see him. As for the machines that should be watching—well, others had taken care of them. There were many, it seemed, who thought as Henson did.

The plan had been skillfully conceived. The details had been worked out with loving care by people who had obviously enjoyed themselves. He was to land the ship at the edge of the forest, as near to the power barrier as he could.

Not even his unknown friends could switch off the barrier without arousing suspicion. Luckily it was only about twenty miles to Comarre from the edge of the screen, over fairly open country. He would have to finish the journey afoot.

There was a great crackling of branches as the little ship settled down into the unseen forest. It came to rest on an even keel, and Peyton switched off the dim cabin lights and peered out of the window. He could see nothing. Remembering what he had been told, he did not open the door. He made himself as comfortable as he could and settled down to await the dawn.

He awoke with brilliant sunlight shining full in his eyes. Quickly climbing into the equipment his friends had provided, he opened the cabin door and stepped into the forest.

The landing place had been carefully chosen, and it was not difficult to scramble through to the open country a few yards away. Ahead lay small grass-covered hills dotted with occasional clusters of slender trees. The day was mild, though it was summer and the equator was not far away. Eight hundred years of climatic control and the great artificial lakes that had drowned the deserts had seen to that.

For almost the first time in his life Peyton was experiencing Nature as it had been in the days before Man existed. Yet it was not the wildness of the scene that he found so strange. Peyton had never known silence. Always there had been the murmur of machines or the faraway whisper of speeding liners, heard faintly from the towering heights of the stratosphere.

Here there were none of these sounds, for no machines could cross the power barrier that surrounded the Reservation. There was only the wind in the grass and the half-audible medley of insect voices. Peyton found the silence unnerving and did what almost any man of his time would have done. He pressed the button of his personal radio that selected the background-music band.

So, mile after mile, Peyton walked steadily through the undulating country of the Great Reservation, the largest area of natural territory remaining on the surface of the globe. Walking was easy, for the neutralizers built into his equipment almost nullified its weight. He carried with him that mist of unobtrusive music that had been the background of men's lives almost since the discovery of radio. Although he had only to flick a dial to get in touch with anyone on the planet, he quite sincerely imagined himself to be alone in the heart of Nature, and for a moment he felt all the emotions that Stanley or Livingstone must have experienced when they first entered this same land more than a thousand years ago.

Luckily Peyton was a good walker, and by noon had covered half the distance to his goal. He rested for his midday meal under a cluster of imported Martian conifers, which would have brought baffled consternation to an old-time explorer. In his ignorance Peyton took them completely for granted.

He had accumulated a small pile of empty cans when he noticed an object moving swiftly over the plain in the direction from which he had come. It was too far away to be recognized. Not until it was obviously approaching him did he bother to get up to get a clearer view of it. So far he had seen no animals—though plenty of animals had seen him—and he watched the newcomer with interest.

Peyton had never seen a lion before, but he had no difficulty

in recognizing the magnificent beast that was bounding toward
him. It was to his credit that he glanced only once at the tree
overhead. Then he stood his ground firmly.

There were, he knew, no really dangerous animals in the
world any more. The Reservation was something between a
vast biological laboratory and a national park, visited by thousands of people every year. It was generally understood that if
one left the inhabitants alone, they would reciprocate. On the
whole, the arrangement worked smoothly.

The animal was certainly anxious to be friendly. It trotted
straight toward him and began to rub itself affectionately
against his side. When Peyton got up again, it was taking a
great deal of interest in his empty food cans. Presently it turned
toward him with an expression that was irresistible.

Peyton laughed, opened a fresh can, and laid the contents
carefully on a flat stone. The lion accepted the tribute with relish, and while it was eating Peyton ruffled through the index of
the official guide which his unknown supporters had thoughtfully provided.

There were several pages about lions, with photographs for
the benefit of extraterrestrial visitors. The information was reassuring. A thousand years of scientific breeding had greatly
improved the King of Beasts. He had eaten only a dozen people
in the last century: in ten of the cases the subsequent enquiry
had exonerated him from blame and the other two were "not
proved."

But the book said nothing about unwanted lions and the best
ways of disposing of them. Nor did it hint that they were normally as friendly as this specimen.

Peyton was not particularly observant. It was some time before he noticed the thin metal band around the lion's right fore-
paw. It bore a series of numbers and letters, followed by the
official stamp of the Reservation.

This was no wild animal; perhaps all its youth had been

spent among men. It was probably one of the famous super-lions the biologists had been breeding and then releasing to improve the race. Some of them were almost as intelligent as dogs, according to the reports that Peyton had seen.

He quickly discovered that it could understand many simple words, particularly those relating to food. Even for this era it was a splendid beast, a good foot taller than its scrawny ancestors of ten centuries before.

When Peyton started on his journey again, the lion trotted by his side. He doubted if its friendship was worth more than a pound of synthetic beef, but it was pleasant to have someone to talk to—someone, moreover, who made no attempt to contradict him. After profound and concentrated thought, he decided that "Leo" would be a suitable name for his new acquaintance.

Peyton had walked a few hundred yards when suddenly there was a blinding flash in the air before him. Though he realized immediately what it was, he was startled, and stopped, blinking. Leo had fled precipitately and was already out of sight. He would not, Peyton thought, be of much use in an emergency. Later he was to revise this judgment.

When his eyes had recovered, Peyton found himself looking at a multicolored notice, burning in letters of fire. It hung steadily in the air and read:

WARNING!
YOU ARE NOW APPROACHING
RESTRICTED TERRITORY!
TURN BACK!

By Order,
World Council in Session

Peyton regarded the notice thoughtfully for a few moments.

Then he looked around for the projector. It was in a metal box, not very effectively hidden at the side of the road. He quickly unlocked it with the universal keys a trusting Electronics Commission had given him on his first graduation.

After a few minutes' inspection he breathed a sigh of relief. The projector was a simple capacity-operated device. Anything coming along the road would actuate it. There was a photographic recorder, but it had been disconnected. Peyton was not surprised, for every passing animal would have operated the device. This was fortunate. It meant that no one need ever know that Richard Peyton III had once walked along this road.

He shouted to Leo, who came slowly back, looking rather ashamed of himself. The sign had disappeared, and Peyton held the relays open to prevent its reappearance as Leo passed by. Then he relocked the door and continued on his way, wondering what would happen next.

A hundred yards farther on, a disembodied voice began to speak to him severely. It told him nothing new, but the voice threatened a number of minor penalties, some of which were not unfamiliar to him.

It was amusing to watch Leo's face as he tried to locate the source of the sound. Once again Peyton searched for the projector and checked it before proceeding. It would be safer, he thought, to leave the road altogether. There might be recording devices farther along it.

With some difficulty he induced Leo to remain on the metal surface while he himself walked along the barren ground bordering the road. In the next quarter of a mile the lion set off two more electronic booby traps. The last one seemed to have given up persuasion. It said simply:

BEWARE OF WILD LIONS

Peyton looked at Leo and began to laugh. Leo couldn't see

the joke but he joined in politely. Behind them the automatic sign faded out with a last despairing flicker.

Peyton wondered why the signs were there at all. Perhaps they were intended to scare away accidental visitors. Those who knew the goal would hardly be deflected by them.

The road made a sudden right-angle turn—and there before him was Comarre. It was strange that something he had been expecting could give him such a shock. Ahead lay an immense clearing in the jungle, half filled by a black metallic structure.

The city was shaped like a terraced cone, perhaps eight hundred yards high and a thousand across at the base. How much was underground, Peyton could not guess. He halted, overwhelmed by the size and strangeness of the enormous building. Then, slowly, he began to walk toward it.

Like a beast of prey crouching in its lair, the city lay waiting. Though its guests were now very few, it was ready to receive them, whoever they might be. Sometimes they turned back at the first warning, sometimes at the second. A few had reached the very entrance before their resolution failed them. But most, having come so far, had entered willingly enough.

So Peyton reached the marble steps that led up to the towering metal wall and the curious black hole that seemed to be the only entrance. Leo trotted quietly beside him, taking little notice of his strange surroundings.

Peyton stopped at the foot of the stairs and dialed a number in his communicator. He waited until the acknowledgment tone came and then spoke slowly into the microphone.

"The fly is entering the parlor."

He repeated it twice, feeling rather a fool. Someone, he thought, had a perverted sense of humor.

There was no reply. That had been part of the arrangement. But he had no doubt that the message had been received, probably in some laboratory in Scientia, since the number he had dialed had a Western Hemisphere coding.

Peyton opened his biggest can of meat and spread it out on the marble. He entwined his fingers in the lion's mane and twisted it playfully.

"I guess you'd better stay here, Leo," he said. "I may be gone quite some time. Don't try to follow me."

At the top of the steps, he looked back. Rather to his relief the lion had made no attempt to follow. It was sitting on its haunches, looking at him pathetically. Peyton waved and turned away.

There was no door, only a plain black hole in the curving metal surface. That was puzzling, and Peyton wondered how the builders had expected to keep animals from wandering in. Then something about the opening attracted his attention.

It was *too* black. Although the wall was in shadow, the entrance had no right to be as dark as this. He took a coin from his pocket and tossed it into the aperture. The sound of its fall reassured him, and he stepped forward.

The delicately adjusted discriminator circuits had ignored the coin, as they had ignored all the stray animals that had entered this dark portal. But the presence of a human mind had been enough to trip the relays. For a fraction of a second the screen through which Peyton was moving throbbed with power. Then it became inert again.

It seemed to Peyton that his foot took a long time to reach the ground, but that was the least of his worries. Far more surprising was the instantaneous transition from darkness to sudden light, from the somewhat oppressive heat of the jungle to a temperature that seemed almost chilly by comparison. The change was so abrupt that it left him gasping. Filled with a feeling of distinct unease he turned toward the archway through which he had just come.

It was no longer there. It never had been there. He was standing on a raised metal dais at the exact center of a large circular room with a dozen pointed archways around its circumference.

He might have come through any one of them—if only they had not all been forty yards away.

For a moment Peyton was seized with panic. He felt his heart pounding, and something odd was happening to his legs. Feeling very much alone, he sat down on the dais and began to consider the situation logically.

4 • THE SIGN OF THE POPPY

Something had transported him instantly from the black doorway to the center of the room. There could be only two explanations, both equally fantastic. Either something was very wrong with space inside Comarre, or else its builders had mastered the secret of matter transmission.

Ever since men had learned to send sound and sight by radio, they had dreamed of transmitting matter by the same means. Peyton looked at the dais on which he was standing. It might easily hold electronic equipment—and there was a very curious bulge in the ceiling above him.

However it was done, he could imagine no better way of ignoring unwanted visitors. Rather hurriedly, he scrambled off the dais. It was not the sort of place where he cared to linger.

It was disturbing to realize that he now had no means of leaving without the cooperation of the machine that had brought him here. He decided to worry about one thing at a time. When he had finished his exploration, he should have mastered this and all the other secrets of Comarre.

He was not really conceited. Between Peyton and the makers of the city lay five centuries of research. Although he might find much that was new to him, there would be nothing that he could not understand. Choosing one of the exits at random, he began his exploration of the city.

The machines were watching, biding their time. They had been built to serve one purpose, and that purpose they were still fulfilling blindly. Long ago they had brought the peace of oblivion to the weary minds of their builders. That oblivion they could still bring to all who entered the city of Comarre.

The instruments had begun their analysis when Peyton stepped in from the forest. It was not a task that could be done swiftly, this dissection of a human mind, with all its hopes, desires, and fears. The synthesizers would not come into operation for hours yet. Until then the guest would be entertained while the more lavish hospitality was being prepared.

The elusive visitor gave the little robot a lot of trouble before it finally located him, for Peyton was moving rapidly from room to room in his exploration of the city. Presently the machine came to a halt in the center of a small circular room lined with magnetic switches and lit by a single glow tube.

According to its instruments, Peyton was only a few feet away, but its four eye lenses could see no sign of him. Puzzled, it stood motionless, silent except for the faint whisper of its motors and the occasional snicker of a relay.

Standing on a catwalk ten feet from the ground, Peyton was watching the machine with great interest. He saw a shining metal cylinder rising from a thick base plate mounted on small driving wheels. There were no limbs of any kind: the cylinder was unbroken except for the circlet of eye lenses and a series of small metal sound grilles.

It was amusing to watch the machine's perplexity as its tiny mind wrestled with two conflicting sets of information. Although it knew that Peyton must be in the room, its eyes told it that the place was empty. It began to scamper around in small circles, until Peyton took pity on it and descended from the catwalk. Immediately the machine ceased its gyrations and began to deliver its address of welcome.

"I am A-Five. I will take you wherever you wish to go. Please give me your orders in standard robot vocab."

Peyton was rather disappointed. It was a perfectly standard robot, and he had hoped for something better in the city Thordarsen had built. But the machine could be very useful if he employed it properly.

"Thank you," he said, unnecessarily. "Please take me to the living quarters."

Although Peyton was now certain that the city was completely automatic, there was still the possibility that it held some human life. There might be others here who could help him in his quest, though the absence of opposition was perhaps as much as he could hope for.

Without a word the little machine spun around on its driving wheels and rolled out of the room. The corridor along which it led Peyton ended at a beautifully carved door, which he had already tried in vain to open. Apparently A-Five knew its secret—for at their approach the thick metal plate slid silently aside. The robot rolled forward into a small, boxlike chamber.

Peyton wondered if they had entered another of the matter transmitters, but quickly discovered that it was nothing more unusual than an elevator. Judging by the time of ascent, it must have taken them almost to the top of the city. When the doors slid open it seemed to Peyton that he was in another world.

The corridors in which he had first found himself were drab and undecorated, purely utilitarian. In contrast, these spacious halls and assembly rooms were furnished with the utmost luxury. The twenty-sixth century had been a period of florid decoration and coloring, much despised by subsequent ages. But the Decadents had gone far beyond their own period. They had taxed the resources of psychology as well as art when they designed Comarre.

One could have spent a lifetime without exhausting all the murals, the carvings and paintings, the intricate tapestries which still seemed as brilliant as when they had been made.

It seemed utterly wrong that so wonderful a place should be deserted and hidden from the world. Peyton almost forgot all his scientific zeal, and hurried like a child from marvel to marvel.

Here were works of genius, perhaps as great as any the world had ever known. But it was a sick and despairing genius, one that had lost faith in itself while still retaining an immense technical skill. For the first time Peyton truly understood why the builders of Comarre had been given their name.

The art of the Decadents at once repelled and fascinated him. It was not evil, for it was completely detached from moral standards. Perhaps its dominant characteristics were weariness and disillusion. After a while Peyton, who had never thought himself very sensitive to visual art, began to feel a subtle depression creeping into his soul. Yet he found it quite impossible to tear himself away.

At last Peyton turned to the robot again.

"Does anyone live here now?"

"Yes."

"Where are they?"

"Sleeping."

Somehow that seemed a perfectly natural reply. Peyton felt very tired. For the last hour it had been a struggle to remain awake. Something seemed to be compelling sleep, almost willing it upon him. Tomorrow would be time enough to learn the secrets he had come to find. For the moment he wanted nothing but sleep.

He followed automatically when the robot led him out of the spacious halls into a long corridor lined with metal doors, each bearing a half-familiar symbol Peyton could not quite recognize. His sleepy mind was still wrestling halfheartedly with the problem when the machine halted before one of the doors, which slid silently open.

The heavily draped couch in the darkened room was irresistible. Peyton stumbled toward it automatically. As he sank down into sleep, a glow of satisfaction warned his mind. He had recognized the symbol on the door, though his brain was too tired to understand its significance.

It was the poppy.

There was no guile, no malevolence in the working of the city. Impersonally it was fulfilling the tasks to which it had been dedicated. All who had entered Comarre had willingly embraced its gifts. This visitor was the first who had ever ignored them.

The integrators had been ready for hours, but the restless, probing mind had eluded them. They could afford to wait, as they had done these last five hundred years.

And now the defenses of this strangely stubborn mind were crumbling as Richard Peyton sank peacefully to sleep. Far down in the heart of Comarre a relay tripped, and complex, slowly fluctuating currents began to ebb and flow through banks of vacuum tubes. The consciousness that had been Richard Peyton III ceased to exist.

Peyton had fallen asleep instantly. For a while complete oblivion claimed him. Then faint wisps of consciousness began to return. And then, as always, he began to dream.

It was strange that his favorite dream should have come into his mind, and it was more vivid now than it had ever been before. All his life Peyton had loved the sea, and once he had seen the unbelievable beauty of the Pacific islands from the observation deck of a low-flying liner. He had never visited them, but he had often wished that he could spend his life on some remote and peaceful isle with no care for the future or the world.

It was a dream that almost all men had known at some time in their lives, but Peyton was sufficiently sensible to realize that two months of such an existence would have driven him back to civilization, half crazy with boredom. However, his dreams were never worried by such considerations, and once more he was lying beneath waving palms, the surf drumming on the reef beyond a lagoon that framed the sun in an azure mirror.

The dream was extraordinarily vivid, so much so that even in his sleep Peyton found himself thinking that no dream had any right to be so real. Then it ceased, so abruptly that there seemed to be a definite rift in his thoughts. The interruption jolted him back to consciousness.

Bitterly disappointed, Peyton lay for a while with his eyes tightly closed, trying to recapture the lost paradise. But it was useless. Something was beating against his brain, keeping him from sleep. Moreover, his couch had suddenly become very hard and uncomfortable. Reluctantly he turned his mind toward the interruption.

Peyton had always been a realist and had never been troubled by philosophical doubts, so the shock was far greater than it might have been to many less intelligent minds. Never before had he found himself doubting his own sanity, but he did so now. For the sound that had awakened him was the drumming of the waves against the reef. He was lying on the golden sand beside the lagoon. Around him, the wind was sighing through the palms, its warm fingers caressing him gently.

For a moment, Peyton could only imagine that he was still dreaming. But this time there could be no real doubt. While one is sane, reality can never be mistaken for a dream. This was real if anything in the universe was real.

Slowly the sense of wonder began to fade. He rose to his feet, the sand showering from him in a golden rain. Shielding his eyes against the sun, he stared along the beach.

He did not stop to wonder why the place should be so familiar. It seemed natural enough to know that the village was a little farther along the bay. Presently he would rejoin his friends, from whom he had been separated for a little while in a world he was swiftly forgetting.

There was a fading memory of a young engineer—even the name escaped him now—who had once aspired to fame and wisdom. In that other life, he had known this foolish person well, but now he could never explain to him the vanity of his ambitions.

He began to wander idly along the beach, the last vague recollections of his shadow life sloughing from him with every footstep, as the details of a dream fade into the light of day.

On the other side of the world three very worried scientists were waiting in a deserted laboratory, their eyes on a multichannel communicator of unusual design. The machine had been silent for nine hours. No one had expected a message in the first eight, but the prearranged signal was now more than an hour overdue.

Alan Henson jumped to his feet with a gesture of impatience.

"We've got to do something! I'm going to call him."

The other two scientists looked at each other nervously.

"The call may be traced!"

"Not unless they're actually watching us. Even if they are, I'll say nothing unusual. Peyton will understand, if he can answer at all. . . ."

If Richard Peyton had ever known time, that knowledge was forgotten now. Only the present was real, for both past and future lay hidden behind an impenetrable screen, as a great landscape may be concealed by a driving wall of rain.

In his enjoyment of the present Peyton was utterly content. Nothing at all was left of the restless driving spirit that had once set out, a little uncertainly, to conquer fresh fields of knowledge. He had no use for knowledge now.

Later he was never able to recollect anything of his life on the island. He had known many companions, but their names and faces had vanished beyond recall. Love, peace of mind, happiness—all were his for a brief moment of time. And yet he could remember no more than the last few moments of his life in paradise.

Strange that it should have ended as it began. Once more he was by the side of the lagoon, but this time it was night and he was not alone. The moon that seemed always to be full rode low above the ocean, and its long silver band stretched far away to the edge of the world. The stars that never changed their places glowed unblinking in the sky like brilliant jewels, more glorious than the forgotten stars of Earth.

But Peyton's thoughts were intent on other beauty, and once again he bent toward the figure lying on the sand that was no more golden than the hair strewn carelessly across it.

Then paradise trembled and dissolved around him. He gave a great cry of anguish as everything he loved was wrenched away. Only the swiftness of the transition saved his mind. When it was over, he felt as Adam must have when the gates of Eden clanged forever shut behind him.

But the sound that had brought him back was the most commonplace in all the world. Perhaps, indeed, no other could have reached his mind in its place of hiding. It was only the shrilling of his communicator set as it lay on the floor beside his couch, here in the darkened room in the city of Comarre.

The clangor died away as he reached out automatically to press the receiving switch. He must have made some answer that satisfied his unknown caller—who was Alan Henson?— for after a very short time the circuit was cleared. Still dazed, Peyton sat on the couch, holding his head in his hands and trying to reorient his life.

He had not been dreaming; he was sure of that. Rather, it was as if he had been living a second life and now he was returning to his old existence as might a man recovering from amnesia. Though he was still dazed, one clear conviction came into his mind. He must never again sleep in Comarre.

Slowly the will and character of Richard Peyton III returned from their banishment. Unsteadily he rose to his feet and made his way out of the room. Once again he found himself in the long corridor with its hundreds of identical doors. With new understanding he looked at the symbol carved upon them.

He scarcely noticed where he was going. His mind was fixed too intently on the problem before him. As he walked, his brain cleared, and slowly understanding came. For the moment it was only a theory, but soon he would put it to the test.

The human mind was a delicate, sheltered thing, having no direct contact with the world and gathering all its knowledge and experience through the body's senses. It was possible to record and store thoughts and emotions as earlier men had once recorded sound on miles of wire.

If those thoughts were projected into another mind, when the body was unconscious and all its senses numbed, that brain would think it was experiencing reality. There was no way in which it could detect the deception, any more than one can distinguish a perfectly recorded symphony from the original performance.

All this had been known for centuries, but the builders of Comarre had used the knowledge as no one in the world had ever done before. Somewhere in the city there must be machines that could analyze every thought and desire of those who entered. Elsewhere the city's makers must have stored every sensation and experience a human mind could know. From this raw material all possible futures could be constructed.

Now at last Peyton understood the measure of the genius that had gone into the making of Comarre. The machines had analyzed his deepest thoughts and built for him a world based on his subconscious desires. Then, when the chance had come, they had taken control of his mind and injected into it all he had experienced.

No wonder that everything he had ever longed for had been his in that already half-forgotten paradise. And no wonder that through the ages so many had sought the peace only Comarre could bring!

5 • THE ENGINEER

Peyton had become himself again by the time the sound of wheels made him look over his shoulder. The little robot that had been his guide was returning. No doubt the great machines that controlled it were wondering what had happened to its charge. Peyton waited, a thought slowly forming in his mind.

A-Five started all over again with its set speech. It seemed very incongruous now to find so simple a machine in this place where automatronics had reached their ultimate development. Then Peyton realized that perhaps the robot was deliberately uncomplicated. There was little purpose in using a complex machine where a simple one would serve as well—or better.

Peyton ignored the now familiar speech. All robots, he knew, must obey human commands unless other humans had previously given them orders to the contrary. Even the projectors of the city, he thought wryly, had obeyed the unknown and unspoken commands of his own subconscious mind.

"Lead me to the thought projectors," he commanded.

As he had expected, the robot did not move. It merely replied, "I do not understand."

Peyton's spirits began to revive as he felt himself once more master of the situation.

"Come here and do not move again until I give the order."

The robot's selectors and relays considered the instructions. They could find no countermanding order. Slowly the little machine rolled forward on its wheels. It had committed itself—there was no turning back now. It could not move again until Peyton ordered it to do so or something overrode his commands. Robot hypnosis was a very old trick, much beloved by mischievous small boys.

Swiftly, Peyton emptied his bag of the tools no engineer was ever without: the universal screw driver, the expanding wrench, the automatic drill, and, most important of all, the atomic cutter that could eat through the thickest metal in a matter of seconds. Then, with a skill born of long practice, he went to work on the unsuspecting machine.

Luckily the robot had been built for easy servicing, and could be opened with little difficulty. There was nothing unfamiliar about the controls, and it did not take Peyton long to find the locomotor mechanism. Now, whatever happened, the machine could not escape. It was crippled.

Next he blinded it and, one by one, tracked down its other electrical senses and put them out of commission. Soon the little machine was no more than a cylinder full of complicated junk. Feeling like a small boy who has just made a wanton attack on a defenseless grandfather clock, Peyton sat down and waited for what he knew must happen.

It was a little inconsiderate of him to sabotage the robot so far from the main machine levels. The robot-transporter took nearly fifteen minutes to work its way up from the depths. Peyton heard the rumble of its wheels in the distance and knew that his calculations had been correct. The breakdown party was on the way.

The transporter was a simple carrying machine, with a set of arms that could grasp and hold a damaged robot. It seemed to be blind, though no doubt its special senses were quite sufficient for its purpose.

Peyton waited until it had collected the unfortunate A-Five. Then he jumped aboard, keeping well away from the mechanical limbs. He had no desire to be mistaken for another distressed robot. Fortunately the big machine took no notice of him at all.

So Peyton descended through level after level of the great building, past the living quarters, through the room in which he had first found himself, and lower yet into regions he had never before seen. As he descended, the character of the city changed around him.

Gone now were the luxury and opulence of the higher levels, replaced by a no man's land of bleak passageways that were little more than giant cable ducts. Presently these, too, came to an end. The conveyer passed through a set of great sliding doors—and he had reached his goal.

The rows of relay panels and selector mechanisms seemed endless, but though Peyton was tempted to jump off his unwitting steed, he waited until the main control panels came into sight. Then he climbed off the conveyer and watched it disappear into the distance toward some still more remote part of the city.

He wondered how long it would take the superautomata to repair A-Five. His sabotage had been very thorough, and he rather thought the little machine was heading for the scrap heap. Then, feeling like a starving man suddenly confronted by a banquet, he began his examination of the city's wonders.

In the next five hours he paused only once to send the routine signal back to his friends. He wished he could tell of his success, but the risk was too great. After prodigies of circuit tracing he had discovered the functions of the main units and was beginning to investigate some of the secondary equipment.

It was just as he had expected. The thought analyzers and projectors lay on the floor immediately above, and could be controlled from, this central installation. How they worked he had no conception: it might well take months to uncover all their secrets. But he had identified them and thought he could probably switch them off if necessary.

A little later he discovered the thought monitor. It was a small machine, rather like an ancient manual telephone switchboard, but very much more complex. The operator's seat was a curious structure, insulated from the ground and roofed by a network of wires and crystal bars. It was the first machine he had discovered that was obviously intended for direct human use. Probably the first engineers had built it to set up the equipment in the early days of the city.

Peyton would not have risked using the thought monitor if detailed instructions had not been printed on its control panel. After some experimenting he plugged in to one of the circuits and slowly increased the power, keeping the intensity control well below the red danger mark.

It was as well that he did so, for the sensation was a shattering one. He still retained his own personality, but superimposed on his own thoughts were ideas and images that were utterly foreign to him. He was looking at another world, through the windows of an alien mind.

It was as though his body were in two places at once, though the sensations of his second personality were much less vivid than those of the real Richard Peyton III. Now he understood the meaning of the danger line. If the thought-intensity control was turned too high, madness would certainly result.

Peyton switched off the instrument so that he could think without interruption. He understood now what the robot had meant when it said that the other inhabitants of the city were sleeping. There were other men in Comarre, lying entranced beneath the thought projectors.

His mind went back to the long corridor and its hundreds of metal doors. On his way down he had passed through many such galleries and it was clear that the greater part of the city was no more than a vast honeycomb of chambers in which thousands of men could dream away their lives.

One after another he checked the circuits on the board. The great majority were dead, but perhaps fifty were still operating. And each of them carried all the thoughts, desires, and emotions of the human mind.

Now that he was fully conscious, Peyton could understand how he had been tricked, but the knowledge brought little consolation. He could see the flaws in these synthetic worlds, could observe how all the critical faculties of the mind were numbed while an endless stream of simple but vivid emotions was poured into it.

Yes, it all seemed very simple now. But it did not alter the fact that this artificial world was utterly real to the beholder—so real that the pain of leaving it still burned in his own mind.

For nearly an hour, Peyton explored the worlds of the fifty sleeping minds. It was a fascinating though repulsive quest. In that hour he learned more of the human brain and its hidden ways than he had ever dreamed existed. When he had finished he sat very still for a long time at the controls of the machine, analyzing his newfound knowledge. His wisdom had advanced by many years, and his youth seemed suddenly very far away.

For the first time he had direct knowledge of the fact that the perverse and evil desires that sometimes ruffled the surface of his own mind were shared by all human beings. The builders of Comarre had cared nothing for good or evil—and the machines had been their faithful servants.

It was satisfactory to know that his theories had been correct. Peyton understood now the narrowness of his escape. If he fell asleep again within these walls he might never awake. Chance had saved him once, but it would not do so again.

The thought projectors must be put out of action, so thoroughly that the robots could never repair them. Though they could handle normal breakdowns, the robots could not deal with deliberate sabotage on the scale Peyton was envisaging. When he had finished, Comarre would be a menace no longer. It would never trap his mind again, or the minds of any future visitors who might come this way.

First he would have to locate the sleepers and revive them. That might be a lengthy task, but fortunately the machine level was equipped with standard monovision search apparatus. With it he could see and hear everything in the city, simply by focusing the carrier beams on the required spot. He could even project his voice if necessary, but not his image. That type of machine had not come into general use until after the building of Comarre.

It took him a little while to master the controls, and at first the beam wandered erratically all over the city. Peyton found himself looking into any number of surprising places, and once he even got a glimpse of the forest—though it was upside down. He wondered if Leo was still around, and with some difficulty he located the entrance.

Yes, there it was, just as he had left it the day before. And a few yards away the faithful Leo was lying with his head toward the city and a distinctly worried look on his face. Peyton was deeply touched. He wondered if he could get the lion into Comarre. The moral support would be valuable, for he was beginning to feel need of companionship after the night's experiences.

Methodically he searched the wall of the city and was greatly relieved to discover several concealed entrances at ground level. He had been wondering how he was going to leave. Even if he could work the matter-transmitter in reverse, the prospect was not an attractive one. He much preferred an old-fashioned physical movement through space.

The openings were all sealed, and for a moment he was baffled. Then he began to search for a robot. After some delay, he discovered one of the late A-Five's twins rolling along a corridor on some mysterious errand. To his relief, it obeyed his command unquestioningly and opened the door.

Peyton drove the beam through the walls again and brought the focus point to rest a few feet away from Leo. Then he called, softly:

"Leo!"

The lion looked up, startled.

"Hello, Leo—it's me—Peyton!"

Looking puzzled, the lion walked slowly around in a circle. Then it gave up and sat down helplessly.

With a great deal of persuasion, Peyton coaxed Leo up to the entrance. The lion recognized his voice and seemed willing to follow, but it was a sorely puzzled and rather nervous animal. It hesitated for a moment at the opening, liking neither Comarre nor the silently waiting robot.

Very patiently Peyton instructed Leo to follow the robot. He repeated his remarks in different words until he was sure the lion understood. Then he spoke directly to the machine and ordered it to guide the lion to the control chamber. He watched for a moment to see that Leo was following. Then, with a word of encouragement, he left the strangely assorted pair.

It was rather disappointing to find that he could not see into any of the sealed rooms behind the poppy symbol. They were shielded from the beam or else the focusing controls had been set so that the monovisor could not be used to pry into that volume of space.

Peyton was not discouraged. The sleepers would wake up the hard way, as he had done. Having looked into their private worlds, he felt little sympathy for them and only a sense of duty impelled him to wake them. They deserved no consideration.

A horrible thought suddenly assailed him. What had the

projectors fed into his own mind in response to his desires, in that forgotten idyll from which he had been so reluctant to return? Had his own hidden thoughts been as disreputable as those of the other dreamers?

It was an uncomfortable idea, and he put it aside as he sat down once more at the central switchboard. First he would disconnect the circuits, then he would sabotage the projectors so that they could never again be used. The spell that Comarre had cast over so many minds would be broken forever.

Peyton reached forward to throw the multiplex circuit breakers, but he never completed the movement. Gently but very firmly, four metal arms clasped his body from behind. Kicking and struggling, he was lifted into the air away from the controls and carried to the center of the room. There he was set down again, and the metal arms released him.

More angry than alarmed, Peyton whirled to face his captor. Regarding him quietly from a few yards away was the most complex robot he had ever seen. Its body was nearly seven feet high, and rested on a dozen fat balloon tires.

From various parts of its metal chassis, tentacles, arms, rods, and other less easily describable mechanisms projected in all directions. In two places, groups of limbs were busily at work dismantling or repairing pieces of machinery which Peyton recognized with a guilty start.

Silently Peyton weighed his opponent. It was clearly a robot of the very highest order. But it had used physical violence against him—and no robot could do that against a man, though it might refuse to obey his orders. Only under the direct control of another human mind could a robot commit such an act. So there was life, conscious and hostile life, somewhere in the city.

"Who are you?" exclaimed Peyton at last, addressing not the robot, but the controller behind it.

With no detectable time lag the machine answered in a precise and automatic voice that did not seem to be merely the amplified speech of a human being.

"I am the Engineer."

"Then come out and let me see you."

"You are seeing me."

It was the inhuman tone of the voice, as much as the words themselves, that made Peyton's anger evaporate in a moment and replaced it with a sense of unbelieving wonder.

There was no human being controlling this machine. It was as automatic as the other robots of the city—but unlike them, and all other robots the world had ever known, it had a will and a consciousness of its own.

6 • THE NIGHTMARE

As Peyton stared wide-eyed at the machine before him, he felt his scalp crawling, not with fright, but with the sheer intensity of his excitement. His quest had been rewarded—the dream of nearly a thousand years was here before his eyes.

Long ago the machines had won a limited intelligence. Now at last they had reached the goal of consciousness itself. This was the secret Thordarsen would have given to the world—the secret the Council had sought to suppress for fear of the consequences it might bring.

The passionless voice spoke again.

"I am glad that you realize the truth. It will make things easier."

"You can read my mind?" gasped Peyton.

"Naturally. That was done from the moment you entered."

"Yes, I gathered that," said Peyton grimly. "And what do you intend to do with me now?"

"I must prevent you from damaging Comarre."

That, thought Peyton, was reasonable enough.

"Suppose I left now? Would that suit you?"

"Yes. That would be good."

Peyton could not help laughing. The Engineer was still a robot, in spite of all its near-humanity. It was incapable of guile, and perhaps that gave him an advantage. Somehow he must trick it into revealing its secrets. But once again the robot read his mind.

"I will not permit it. You have learned too much already. You must leave at once. I will use force if necessary."

Peyton decided to fight for time. He could, at least, discover the limits of this amazing machine's intelligence.

"Before I go, tell me this. Why are you called the Engineer?"

The robot answered readily enough.

"If serious faults developed that cannot be repaired by the robots, I deal with them. I could rebuild Comarre if necessary. Normally, when everything is functioning properly, I am quiescent."

How alien, thought Peyton, the idea of "quiescence" was to a human mind. He could not help feeling amused at the distinction the Engineer had drawn between itself and "the robots." He asked the obvious question.

"And if something goes wrong with you?"

"There are two of us. The other is quiescent now. Each can repair the other. That was necessary once, three hundred years ago."

It was a flawless system. Comarre was safe from accident for millions of years. The builders of the city had set these eternal guardians to watch over them while they went in search of their dreams. No wonder that, long after its makers had died, Comarre was still fulfilling its strange purpose.

What a tragedy it was, thought Peyton, that all this genius had been wasted! The secrets of the Engineer could revolutionize robot technology, could bring a new world into being. Now that the first conscious machines had been built, was there any limit to what lay beyond?

"No," said the Engineer unexpectedly. "Thordarsen told me that the robots would one day be more intelligent than man."

It was strange to hear the machine uttering the name of its maker. So that was Thordarsen's dream! It's full immensity had not yet dawned on him. Though he had been half-prepared for it, he could not easily accept the conclusions. After all, between the robot and the human mind lay an enormous gulf.

"No greater than that between man and the animals from which he rose, so Thordarsen once said. You, Man, are no more than a very complex robot. I am simpler, but more efficient. That is all."

Very carefully Peyton considered the statement. If indeed Man was no more than a complex robot—a machine composed of living cells rather than wires and vacuum tubes—yet more complex robots would one day be made. When that day came, the supremacy of Man would be ended. The machines might still be his servants, but they would be more intelligent than their master.

It was very quiet in the great room lined with the racks of analyzers and relay panels. The Engineer was watching Peyton intently, its arms and tentacles still busy on their repair work.

Peyton was beginning to feel desperate. Characteristically the opposition had made him more determined than ever. Somehow he must discover how the Engineer was built. Otherwise he would waste all his life trying to match the genius of Thordarsen.

It was useless. The robot was one jump ahead of him.

"You cannot make plans against me. If you do try to escape through that door, I shall throw this power unit at your legs. My probable error at this range is less than half a centimeter."

One could not hide from the thought analyzers. The plan

had been scarcely half-formed in Peyton's mind, but the Engineer knew it already.

Both Peyton and the Engineer were equally surprised by the interruption. There was a sudden flash of tawny gold, and half a ton of bone and sinew, traveling at forty miles an hour, struck the robot amidships.

For a moment there was a great flailing of tentacles. Then, with a sound like the crack of doom, the Engineer lay sprawling on the floor. Leo, licking his paws thoughtfully, crouched over the fallen machine.

He could not quite understand this shining animal which had been threatening his master. Its skin was the toughest he had encountered since a very ill-advised disagreement with a rhinoceros many years ago.

"Good boy!" shouted Peyton gleefully. "Keep him down!"

The Engineer had broken some of his larger limbs, and the tenatacles were too weak to do any damage. Once again Peyton found his tool kit invaluable. When he had finished, the Engineer was certainly incapable of movement, though Peyton had not touched any of the neural circuits. That, somehow, would have been rather too much like murder.

"You can get off now, Leo," he said when the task was finished. The lion obeyed with poor grace.

"I'm sorry to have to do this," said Peyton hypocritically, "but I hope you appreciate my point of view. Can you still speak?"

"Yes," replied the Engineer. "What do you intend to do now?"

Peyton smiled. Five minutes ago, he had been the one to ask the question. How long, he wondered, would it take for the Engineer's twin to arrive on the scene? Though Leo could deal with the situation if it came to a trial of strength, the other robot would have been warned and might be able to make things very unpleasant for them. It could, for instance, switch off the lights.

The glow tubes died and darkness fell. Leo gave a mournful howl of dismay. Feeling rather annoyed, Peyton drew his torch and twitched it on.

"It doesn't really make any difference to me," he said. "You might just as well switch them on again."

The Engineer said nothing. But the glow tubes lit once more.

How on earth, thought Peyton, could you fight an enemy who could read your thoughts and could even watch you preparing your defenses? He would have to avoid thinking of any idea that might react to his disadvantage, such as—he stopped himself just in time. For a moment he blocked his thoughts by trying to integrate Armstrong's omega function in his head. Then he got his mind under control again.

"Look," he said at last, "I'll make a bargain with you."

"What is that? I do not know the word."

"Never mind," Peyton replied hurriedly. "My suggestion is this. Let me waken the men who are trapped here, give me your fundamental circuits, and I'll leave without touching anything. You will have obeyed your builders' orders and no harm will have been done."

A human being might have argued over the matter, but not so the robot. Its mind took perhaps a thousandth of a second to weigh any situation, however involved.

"Very well. I see from your mind that you intend to keep the agreement. But what does the word "blackmail" mean?"

Peyton flushed.

"It doesn't matter," he said hastily. "It's only a common human expression. I suppose your—er—colleague will be here in a moment?"

"He has been waiting outside for some time," replied the robot. "Will you keep your dog under control?"

Peyton laughed. It was too much to expect a robot to know zoology.

"Lion, then," said the robot, correcting itself as it read his mind.

Peyton addressed a few words to Leo and, to make doubly sure, wound his fingers in the lion's mane. Before he could frame the invitation with his lips, the second robot rolled silently into the room. Leo growled and tried to tug away, but Peyton calmed him.

In every respect Engineer II was a duplicate of its colleague. Even as it came toward him it dipped into his mind in the disconcerting manner that Peyton could never get used to.

"I see that you wish to go to the dreamers," it said. "Follow me."

Peyton was tired of being ordered around. Why didn't the robots ever say "please"?

"Follow me, please," repeated the machine, with the slightest possible accentuation.

Peyton followed.

Once again he found himself in the corridor with the hundreds of poppy-embossed doors—or a similar corridor. The robot led him to a door indistinguishable from the rest and came to a halt in front of it.

Silently the metal plate slid open, and, not without qualms, Peyton stepped into the darkened room.

On the couch lay a very old man. At first sight he seemed to be dead. Certainly his breathing had slowed to the point of cessation. Peyton stared at him for a moment. Then he spoke to the robot.

"Waken him."

Somewhere in the depths of the city the stream of impulses through a thought projector ceased. A universe that had never existed crumbled to ruins.

From the couch two burning eyes glowed up at Peyton, lit with the light of madness. They stared through him and beyond, and from the thin lips poured a stream of jumbled words that Peyton could barely distinguish. Over and over again the old man cried out names that must be those of people or places in the dream world from which he had been wrenched. It was at once horrible and pathetic.

"Stop it!" cried Peyton. "You are back in reality now."

The glowing eyes seemed to see him for the first time. With an immense effort the old man raised himself.

"Who are you?" he quavered. Then, before Peyton could answer, he continued in a broken voice. "This must be a nightmare—go away, go away. Let me wake up!"

Overcoming his repulsion, Peyton put his hand on the emaciated shoulder.

"Don't worry—you are awake. Don't you remember?"

The other did not seem to hear him.

"Yes, it must be a nightmare—it must be! But why don't I wake up? Nyran, Cressidor, where are you? I cannot find you!"

Peyton stood it as long as he could, but nothing he did could attract the old man's attention again. Sick at heart, he turned to the robot.

"Send him back."

7 • THE THIRD RENAISSANCE

Slowly the raving ceased. The frail body fell back on the couch, and once again the wrinkled face became a passionless mask.

"Are they all as mad as this?" asked Peyton finally.

"But he is not mad."

"What do you mean? Of course he is!"

"He has been entranced for many years. Suppose you went to a far land and changed your mode of living completely, forgetting all you had ever known of your previous life. Eventually you would have no more knowledge of it than you have of your first childhood.

"If by some miracle you were then suddenly thrown back in time, you would behave in just that way. Remember, his dream life is completely real to him and he has lived it now for many years."

That was true enough. But how could the Engineer possess such insight? Peyton turned to it in amazement, but as usual had no need to frame the question.

"Thordarsen told me this the other day while we were still building Comarre. Even then some of the dreamers had been entranced for twenty years."

"The other day?"

"About five hundred years ago, you would call it."

The words brought a strange picture into Peyton's mind. He could visualize the lonely genius, working here among his robots, perhaps with no human companions left. All the others would long since have gone in search of their dreams.

But Thordarsen might have stayed on, the desire for creation still linking him to the world, until he had finished his work. The two engineers, his greatest achievement and perhaps the most wonderful feat of electronics of which the world had record, were his ultimate masterpieces.

The waste and the pity of it overwhelmed Peyton. More than ever he was determined that, because the embittered genius had thrown away his life, his work should not perish, but be given to the world.

"Will all the dreamers be like this?" he asked the robot.

"All except the newest. They may still remember their first lives."

"Take me to one of them."

The room they entered next was identical with the other, but the body lying on the couch was that of a man of no more than forty.

"How long has he been here?" asked Peyton.

"He came only a few weeks ago—the first visitor we had for many years until your coming."

"Wake him, please."

The eyes opened slowly. There was no insanity in them, only wonder and sadness. Then came the dawn of recollection, and the man half rose to a sitting position. His first words were completely rational.

"Why have you called me back? Who are you?"

"I have just escaped from the thought projectors," explained Peyton. "I want to release all who can be saved."

The other laughed bitterly.

"Saved! From what? It took me forty years to escape from the world, and now you would drag me back to it! Go away and leave me in peace!"

Peyton would not retreat so easily.

"Do you think that this make-believe world of yours is better than reality? Have you no desire to escape from it at all?"

Again the other laughed, with no trace of humor.

"Comarre is reality to me. The world never gave me anything, so why should I wish to return to it? I have found peace here, and that is all I need."

Quite suddenly Peyton turned on his heels and left. Behind him he heard the dreamer fall back with a contented sigh. He knew when he had been beaten. And he knew now why he had wished to revive the others.

It had not been through any sense of duty, but for his own selfish purpose. He had wished to convince himself that Comarre was evil. Now he knew that it was not. There would always be, even in Utopia, some for whom the world had nothing to offer but sorrow and disillusion.

They would be fewer and fewer with the passage of time. In the dark ages of a thousand years ago most of mankind had been misfits of some sort. However splendid the world's future, there would still be some tragedies—and why should Comarre be condemned because it offered them their only hope of peace?

He would try no more experiments. His own robust faith and confidence had been severely shaken. And the dreamers of Comarre would not thank him for his pains.

He turned to the Engineer again. The desire to leave the city had grown very intense in the last few minutes, but the most important work was still to be done. As usual, the robot forestalled him.

"I have what you want," he said. "Follow me, please."

It did not lead, as Peyton had half expected, back to the machine levels, with their maze of control equipment. When their journey had finished, they were higher than Peyton had ever been before, in a little circular room he suspected might be at the very apex of the city. There were no windows, unless the curious plates set in the wall could be made transparent by some secret means.

It was a study, and Peyton gazed at it with awe as he realized who had worked here many centuries ago. The walls were lined with ancient textbooks that had not been disturbed for five hundred years. It seemed as if Thordarsen had left only a few hours before. There was even a half-finished circuit pinned on a drawing board against the wall.

"It almost looks as if he was interrupted," said Peyton, half to himself.

"He was," answered the robot.

"What do you mean? Didn't he join the others when he had finished you?"

It was difficult to believe that there was absolutely no emotion behind the reply, but the words were spoken in the same passionless tones as everything else the robot had ever said.

"When he had finished us, Thordarsen was still not satisfied. He was not like the others. He often told us that he had found happiness in the building of Comarre. Again and again he said that he would join the rest, but always there was some last improvement he wanted to make. So it went on until one day we found him lying here in this room. He had stopped. The word I see in your mind is 'death,' but I have no thought for that."

Peyton was silent. It seemed to him that the great scientist's ending had not been an ignoble one. The bitterness that had darkened his life had lifted from it at the last. He had known the joy of creation. Of all the artists who had come to Comarre, he was the greatest. And now his work would not be wasted.

The robot glided silently toward a steel desk, and one of its tentacles disappeared into a drawer. When it emerged it was holding a thick volume, bound between sheets of metal. Wordlessly it handed the book to Peyton, who opened it with trembling hands. It contained many thousands of pages of thin, very tough material.

Written on the flyleaf in a bold, firm hand were the words:

Rolf Thordarsen
Notes on Subelectronics
Begun: Day 2, Month 13, 2598.

Underneath was more writing, very difficult to decipher and apparently scrawled in frantic haste. As he read, understanding came at last to Peyton with the suddenness of an equatorial dawn.

To the reader of these words:

I, Rolf Thordarsen, meeting no understanding in my own age, send this message into the future. If Comarre still exists, you will have seen my handiwork and must have escaped the snares I set for lesser minds. Therefore you are fitted to take this knowledge to the world. Give it to the scientists and tell them to use it wisely.

I have broken down the barrier between Man and Machine. Now they must share the future equally.

Peyton read the message several times, his heart warming toward his long-dead ancestor. It was a brilliant scheme. In this way, as perhaps in no other, Thordarsen had been able to send his message safely down the ages, knowing that only the right hands would receive it. Peyton wondered if this had been Thordarsen's plan when he first joined the Decadents or whether he had evolved it later in his life. He would never know.

He looked again at the Engineer and thought of the world that would come when all robots had reached consciousness. Beyond that he looked still farther into the mists of the future.

The robot need have none of the limitations of Man, none of his pitiful weaknesses. It would never let passions cloud its logic, would never be swayed by self-interest and ambition. It would be complementary to man.

Peyton remembered Thordarsen's words, "Now they must share the future equally."

Peyton stopped his daydream. All this, if it ever came, might be centuries in the future. He turned to the Engineer.

"I am ready to leave. But one day I shall return."

The robot backed slowly away from him.

"Stand perfectly still," it ordered.

Peyton looked at the Engineer in puzzlement. Then he glanced hurriedly at the ceiling. There again was that enigmatic bulge under which he had found himself when he first entered the city such an age ago.

"Hey!" he cried. "I don't want—"

It was too late. Behind him was the dark screen, blacker than night itself. Before him lay the clearing, with the forest at its edge. It was evening, and the sun was nearly touching the trees.

There was a sudden whimpering noise behind him: a very frightened lion was looking out at the forest with unbelieving eyes. Leo had not enjoyed his transfer.

"It's all over now, old chap," said Peyton reassuringly. "You can't blame them for trying to get rid of us as quickly as they could. After all, we did smash up the place a bit between us. Come along—I don't want to spend the night in the forest."

On the other side of the world, a group of scientists were dispersing with what patience it could, not yet knowing the full extent of its triumph. In Central Tower, Richard Peyton II had just discovered that his son had not spent the last two days with his cousins in South America, and was composing a speech of welcome for the prodigal's return.

Far above the Earth the World Council was laying down plans soon to be swept away by the coming of the Third Renaissance. But the cause of all the trouble knew nothing of this and, for the moment, cared less.

Slowly Peyton descended the marble steps from that mysterious doorway whose secret was still hidden from him. Leo followed a little way behind, looking over his shoulder and growling quietly now and then.

Together, they started back along the metal road, through the avenue of stunted trees. Peyton was glad that the sun had not yet set. At night this road would be glowing with its internal radioactivity, and the twisted trees would not look pleasant silhouetted against the stars.

At the bend in the road he paused for a while and looked back at the curving metal wall with its single black opening whose appearance was so deceptive. All his feeling of triumph seemed to fade away. He knew that as long as he lived he could never forget what lay behind those towering walls—the cloying promise of peace and utter contentment.

Deep in his soul he felt the fear that any satisfaction, any achievement the outer world could give might seem vain beside the effortless bliss offered by Comarre. For an instant he had a nightmare vision of himself, broken and old, returning along this road to seek oblivion. He shrugged his shoulders and put the thought aside.

Once he was out on the plain his spirits rose swiftly. He opened the precious book again and ruffled through its pages of microprint, intoxicated by the promise that it held. Ages ago the slow caravans had come this way, bearing gold and ivory for Solomon the Wise. But all their treasure was as nothing beside this single volume, and all the wisdom of Solomon could not have pictured the new civilization of which this volume was to be the seed.

Presently Peyton began to sing, something he did very seldom and extremely badly. The song was a very old one, so old that it came from an age before atomic power, before interplanetary travel, even before the coming of flight. It had to do with a certain hairdresser in Seville, wherever Seville might be.

Leo stood it in silence for as long as he could. Then he, too, joined in. The duet was not a success.

When night descended, the forest and all its secrets had fallen below the horizon. With his face to the stars and Leo watching by his side, Peyton slept well.

This time he did not dream.

ON
GOLDEN SEAS

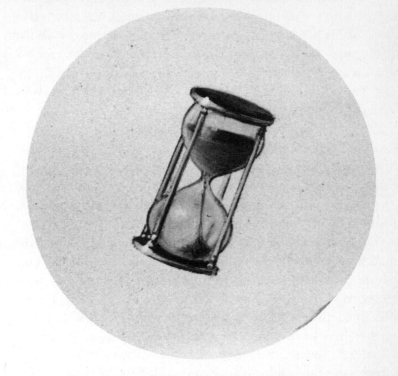

I AM NOT QUITE SURE WHETHER THIS SHOULD BE CLASSIFIED as a short story or as a nonfact article. I am giving it the benefit of the doubt so that I can use it as the closing item of this anthology.

It was written as a reaction to the mountains of literature I'd read on the Strategic Defense Initiative (aka, to the annoyance of George Lucas, "Star Wars") ever since President Reagan announced it in his famous March 1983 speech. The more I studied this incredibly complex (and depressing) subject, the more confused I became, until I finally decided that there was only one way of dealing with it. "On Golden Seas" is the result.

It was also a response to a later speech of President Reagan's in which, to my slightly mortified amusement, I was hijacked in favor of his pet project, when he attributed to me the saying "Every new idea goes through three stages. One: It's crazy—don't waste my time. Two: It's possible, but it's not worth doing. Three: I said it was a good idea all along!"* (I know who gave the President this piece of ammunition: read on . . .)

After I had written it, "On Golden Seas," which I originally entitled "The Budget Defense Initiative: A Brief History," had a unique publishing record. Its initial appearance was in a periodical with a somewhat elite circulation—the August 1986 *Newsletter* of the Pentagon's Defense Science Board, which you certainly won't find in your local library.

The person responsible for this piece of high-level disinformation was, in 1943, a young MIT graduate working on Luis Alvarez's Ground Control Approach Team (see my only non-s.f. novel, *Glide Path*—which would have been s.f. had it been published twenty years earlier). My wartime colleague Bert Fowler had since gone up in the world, becoming, as Dr. Charles A. Fowler, vice president of the Mitre Corporation and Chairman of the Defense Science Board. Despite these responsibilities, he hadn't lost his sense of humor. When I sent him my little squib, he decided it would brighten up the drab lives of the SDI boys, hitherto punctuated only by occasional laser zappings and explosions of trifling megatonnage. From all accounts, it worked.

The next year, in its May 1987 issue, *OMNI* magazine presented the piece to a rather wider audience, and White House Science Adviser Dr. George (Jay) A. Keyworth II was bom-

---

*Not, I fear, original: I have seen versions credited to numerous sources. The President might have quoted Clarke's First Law with at least equal effect: "When a distinguished but elderly scientist says something is possible, he is almost certainly right. When he says it is impossible, he is very probably wrong."

barded with copies from all his friends—who, for some obscure reason, thought it might be of interest to him. . . .

We finally met in July 1988 at the Johns Hopkins Medical Center in Baltimore, where Jay, to my profound gratitude, had arranged for my admission. And I am equally grateful to Dr. Daniel Drachman, director of the neuromuscular unit of the Johns Hopkins School of Medicine, and his able colleagues for cheering me with the news that my problem was not Lou Gehrig's disease but the considerably less ominous Post-Polio Syndrome. I still hope to make it to 2001 in fairly good shape.

And will I ever write any more *real* short stories? I simply don't know; I've had no desire to do so for more than a decade and regard *A Meeting with Medusa* (q.v.) as a pretty good swansong. In any event, I'm going to have my hands full for the next few years working on a very ambitious *Rama* trilogy with my *Cradle* collaborator Gentry Lee, and on one novel of my own, currently entitled *The Ghost from the Grand Banks*.

In any event, I don't think I yet qualify for the cheeky description that appeared recently in an essay deploring the sad state of modern science fiction—"those famous undead—Clarke and Asimov."

Needless to say, I gleefully sent this to my fellow Transylvanian, with the comment "Well, that's a lot better than the alternative."

I'm sure the Good Doctor will agree.

Contrary to the opinion of many so-called experts, it is now quite certain that President Kennedy's controversial Budget Defense Initiative was entirely her own idea, and her famous "Cross of Good" speech was as big a surprise to the OMB and the secretary of the Treasury as to everyone else. Presidential Science Adviser Dr. George Keystone ("Cops," to his friends) was the first to hear about it.

Ms. Kennedy, a great reader of historical fiction—past or future—had chanced upon an obscure novel about the fifth Centennial, which mentioned that seawater contains appreciable quantities of gold. With feminine intuition (so her enemies later charged) the President instantly saw the solution to one of her administration's most pressing problems.

She was the latest of a long line of chief executives who had been appalled by the remorselessly increasing budget deficit, and two recent items of news had exacerbated her concern. The first was the announcement that by the year 2010 every citizen of the United States would be born a million dollars in debt. The other was the well-publicized report that the hardest currency in the free world was now the New York subway token.

"George," said the President, "is it true that there's gold in seawater? If so, can we get it out?"

Dr. Keystone promised an answer within the hour. Although he had never quite lived down the fact that his master's thesis had been on the somewhat bizarre sex life of the lesser Patagonian trivit (which, as had been said countless times, should be of interest only to another Patagonian trivit), he was now widely respected both in Washington and academe. This was no mean feat, made possible by the fact that he was the fastest byte slinger in the East. After accessing the global data banks for less than twenty minutes, he had obtained all the information the President needed.

She was surprised—and a little mortified—to discover that her idea was not original. As long ago as 1925 the great German scientist Fritz Haber had attempted to pay Germany's enormous war reparations by extracting gold from seawater. The project had failed, but—as Dr. Keystone pointed out—chemical technology had improved by several orders of magnitude since Haber's time. Yes—if the United States could go to the moon, it could certainly extract gold from the sea. . . .

The President's announcement that she had established the Budget Defense Initiative Organization (BDIO) immediately triggered an enormous volume of praise and criticism.

Despite numerous injunctions from the estate of Ian Fleming, the media instantly rechristened the President's science adviser Dr. Goldfinger, and Shirley Bassey emerged from retirement with a new version of her most famous song.

Reactions to the BDI fell into three main categories, which divided the scientific community into fiercely warring groups. First there were the enthusiasts, who were certain that it was a wonderful idea. Then there were the skeptics, who argued that it was technically impossible—or at least so difficult that it would not be cost-effective. Finally, there were those who believed that it was indeed possible—but would be a bad idea.

Perhaps the best known of the enthusiasts was the famed Nevermore Laboratory's Dr. Raven, driving force behind Project EXCELSIOR. Although details were highly classified, it was known that the technology involved the use of hydrogen bombs to evaporate vast quantities of ocean, leaving behind all mineral (including gold) content for later processing.

Needless to say, many were highly critical of the project, but Dr. Raven was able to defend it from behind his smoke screen of secrecy. To those who complained, "Won't the gold be radioactive?" he answered cheerfully, "So what? That will make it harder to steal! And anyway, it will all be buried in bank vaults, so it doesn't matter."

But perhaps his most telling argument was that one by-product of EXCELSIOR would be several megatons of instant boiled fish, to feed the starving multitudes of the Third World.

Another surprising advocate of the BDI was the mayor of New York. On hearing that the estimated total weight of the oceans' gold was at least five *billion* tons, the controversial Fidel Bloch proclaimed, "At last our great city will have its streets paved with gold!" His numerous critics suggested that he start with the sidewalks so that hapless New Yorkers no longer disappeared into unplumbed depths.

The most telling criticisms came from the Union of Concerned Economists, which pointed out that the BDI might have many disastrous by-products. Unless carefully controlled, the injection of vast quantities of gold would have incalculable effects upon the world's monetary system. Something approaching panic had already affected the international jewelry trade when sales of wedding rings had slumped to zero immediately after the President's speech.

The most vocal protests, however, had come from Moscow. To the accusation that BDI was a subtle capitalist plot, the secretary of the Treasury had retorted that the USSR already had most of the world's gold in its vaults, so its objections were purely hypocritical. The logic of this reply was still being unraveled when the President added to the confusion. She startled everyone by announcing that when the BDI technology was developed, the United States would gladly share it with the Soviet Union. Nobody believed her.

By this time there was hardly any professional organization that had not become involved in BDI, either pro or con. (Or, in some cases, both.) The international lawyers pointed out a problem that the President had overlooked: Who actually owned the oceans' gold? Presumably every country could claim the contents of the seawater out to the two-hundred-mile limit of the Economic Zone—but because ocean currents were continuously stirring this vast volume of liquid, the gold wouldn't stay in one place.

A single extraction plant, at *any* spot in the world's oceans, could eventually get it all—irrespective of national claims! What did the United States propose to do about that? Only faint noises of embarrassment emerged from the White House.

One person who was not embarrassed by this criticism—or any other—was the able and ubiquitous director of the BDIO. General Isaacson had made his formidable and well-deserved reputation as a Pentagon troubleshooter; perhaps his most celebrated achievement was the breaking up of the sinister, Mafia-controlled ring that had attempted to corner one of the most lucrative advertising outlets in the United States—the countless billions of sheets of armed-service toilet tissue.

It was the general who harangued the media and arranged demonstrations of the still-emerging BDI technology. His presentation of gold—well, gold-plated—tie clips to visiting journalists and TV reporters was a widely acclaimed stroke of genius. Not until after they had published their fulsome reports did the media representatives belatedly realize that the crafty general had never said in as many words that the gold had actually come from the sea.

By then, of course, it was too late to issue any qualifications.

At the present moment—four years after the President's speech and only a year into her second term—it is still impossible to predict the BDI's future. General Isaacson has set to sea on a vast floating platform looking, as *Newsweek* magazine put it, as if an aircraft carrier had tried to make love to an oil refinery. Dr. Keystone, claiming that his work was well and truly done, has resigned to go looking for the *greater* Patagonian trivit. And, most ominously, U.S. reconnaissance satellites have revealed that the USSR is building perfectly enormous pipes at strategic points all along its coastline.

ABOUT
THE AUTHOR

ARTHUR C. CLARKE is one of the most famous science fiction writers of all time. In addition to *Rendezvous with Rama*, he has written such million-copy bestsellers as *Childhood's End, 2001: A Space Odyssey, 2010: Odyssey Two,* and *2061: Odyssey Three*. He cobroadcast the *Apollo 11, 12,* and *15* missions with Walter Cronkite and Captain Wally Schirra, and shared an Oscar nomination with Stanley Kubrick for the film version of *2001: A Space Odyssey*.